A Twisted Fate

A Twisted Fate

Kaylyn Marie Dunn

A Twisted Fate Copyright © 2018 by Kaylyn Marie Dunn. All Rights Reserved.

All rights reserved. No part of this book may be reproduced in any form or by any electronic or mechanical means including information storage and retrieval systems, without permission in writing from the author. The only exception is by a reviewer, who may quote short excerpts in a review.

Cover designed by Cover Designer

This book is a work of fiction. Names, characters, places, and incidents either are products of the author's imagination or are used fictitiously. Any resemblance to actual persons, living or dead, events, or locales is entirely coincidental.

Kaylyn Marie Dunn

Twitter @KaylynMarieDun1

Printed in the United States of America

First Printing: May 2017
Amazon Kindle

ISBN 9781980555285

For my mother,
who always believed in me

A Twisted Fate

Prologue

The world around them had changed drastically. Salem had changed. The people had changed. Evangeline was once proud to call this place her home. Sure, she was nearly blind and was growing worse with every day but at the very least she had a community. She could once call them that. Before the trials began. So many people were accused. Everyone turned on one another. But it was easy to accuse her. With her affections and being the color that she was it was easy to say that she conspired with the devil. But after John's death, no one really cared if the accusations were true. Everyone just wanted them to end. But many more died. Those whose names weren't even remembered. Trials and deaths, just forgotten. Because of Danforth. Because he had so much to prove. That he was a man of God. That he was doing what was righteous. Righteous? Was it righteous that a blind girl sat in jail for crimes she never committed? Witchcraft? She never held such magic. However, she did hold something inhuman. When her vision had completely failed, she began seeing other sights.

Things that hadn't yet occurred. And she found that if she didn't like what she saw she could change it, inevitably changing the future.

The young woman sat in her cell, the night before her execution, and worried over the fate of her young daughter. How would the young girl fare with her mother dead and her father nowhere to be found? Would they come after the girl too? Just then someone pulled open Evangeline's cell door and sat on the floor in front of her. She sniffed the air searching for a familiar scent. She found the apple cinnamon of her sister.

"Carrey? Why are you here?" she panicked.

"Don't worry," Carrey said, patting her sister's knee. "I'm just here to visit."

"You shouldn't be here."

"No one knows that I'm here," she paused. "I can break you out."

"What! No! I'm not going to put you, mother, and Margret in danger too. Do you understand the severity of this situation?"

"But –"

"No! Promise you'll protect Margret."

"Of course."

"And that when you leave here, you'll get mother and Margret and leave this place. Get as far away from here as possible and don't ever come back."

"I can't just –"

"Promise me you'll be gone by morning!"

"… Okay."

Evangeline sighed with relief. Carrey kissed her sister's hand and stood. She made her way back to the door when Evangeline called her again. "And Carrey? Never let anyone see what you can do."

Carrey left then, and once again, Evangeline was alone in the cell. She sat wondering if Carrey would do as she asked. Carrey was always reckless and stubborn. Carrey always thought she knew best. But at seventeen, what could she know? She was still a child, although, the inmate reflected, she had borne a child of her own at seventeen. Our poor inmate. I would have never suspected it would be her I'd come to claim so early. I watched as she contemplated the events of her life, completely unaware of my presence. They never see me until the end, anyway.

We sat quietly until morning, when they came to collect her. They bound her hands behind her back and dropped a bag over her head. As if she could see without it. They led her across the street into the public square where most of the town had gathered. At first, most people had shown up to witness the justice being served, but then it got to a point where they just needed to know who was next. They led her up onto the gallows and draped the noose around her neck. Then they pulled the bag from her head and before her, seated up high on his horse, was Mr. Danforth himself.

"You should've confessed your sins," he spat. Her attention shot up in his direction.

"I have no sin to confess," she spat back. "I have committed no crime. You have mistaken me for someone in your past."

"Witchcraft is your crime!"

"Witchcraft!" She shook with rage. "Do I look like one that could do Witchcraft?"

She did look like she was incapable of such a thing. The woman was small in frame and was so sparse in muscle that her skin basically stuck to her bones. She had hardly been able to give birth.

There would be no way that she could muster the strength to summon power from the supernatural world.

"Appearances are flawed."

"You are flawed!"

"I am wise. I know that the devil is passed through blood. And his magic does the same. And I know that you have a daughter and your magic is mostly likely within her as well."

"You very obviously don't know that my daughter is far from here by now. You'll never, not ever, in your lifetime, find her."

"Who has said that only I would be looking for her?"

"I will tell you this Danforth. My bloodline is something to be reckoned with. I warn you not to interfere in their lives." Suddenly an image flashed across her vision. A young girl, no older than Evangeline's sister. Her appearance was hardly different than Evangeline's. She was lying on the floor in a throne room. Barely breathing. Her dark skin ripped open and spilling blood out on the floor. Evangeline did not like what she saw. Instead, she pictured another girl, still not older than her seventeen-year-old sister. This girl had deep black hair and glowing red eyes, and she snarled in the face of her enemies. "I will have a daughter," Evangeline said. "She be born with blue eyes to set her apart so than you may know that she is of power. When she comes of age her eyes will brighter than the sun. She will wield so much power that even Satan himself will quake in fear of what she might do. She will be the Gifted One!"

"And I will tell you something in return." Danforth said. "I will not rest and neither will my kin until you are all eradicated from this earth!"

"I do not doubt you! But let be it clear that if provoked, she will use her power to demolish this world. Hell may raise by her hand and the blood will fall on you!"

"Then let me also be clear! Your descendant daughter will face my own daughters' hand. And if you chose to give your daughter a prophetic name I will too give mine one. She will be the Chosen One, pure in heart and mind and she will bring the Witch to her knees!"

With fire in her blind eyes she looked away from him. Her blank view was suddenly filled with the sight of me. I nodded once, and Evangeline Morris fell.

Part 1:
Blood

One

He hated me. That I was sure of, if nothing else, surely that. But why? Had I spoken to him before Monday, his first day here? No, I would've remembered those perfect features. Why though, why did he hate me? I had to know.

I sat in Ms. Yang's sixth period history class thinking about everything except what I was supposed to be thinking about. And I loved Ms. Yang's class. She'd been my history teacher since, well, since I had a history class. Every year when I moved up a grade, so did she. I never bothered to ask why because I liked to think I was her favorite student. But, teachers aren't supposed to have favorites. So, I never sought confirmation in fear that I might be wrong.

Nevertheless, I spent the last twenty, almost thirty, minutes of class staring at that guy. His features were sharp. Any and every angle in his face was clear and defined. His chest was big, and his shoulders were broad. His light brown hair was short in a buzz cut like style. And then, there were his eyes. They were brown. Not a light brown, not a dark brown. Just brown, an ugly, muddy brown color that was somehow unpredictably attractive. He was a gorgeous person. One who inexplicably hated me.

It was, or had started off as, a regular week in Zanesville, Ohio. Quaint, happy and peaceful. As a kid, I would play in the grass in front of my house and soak up the soft sun. My mom would call me inside to remind me for the umpteenth time not to go into the street, then let me right back out. My best friend Benjamin Carter and I would play every Saturday until I was twelve. Then we found more dangerous things to do, like climb trees in my back yard.

I had lived in Zanesville my entire life and I had never felt so…evil as this guy made me feel with just his eyes. He realized I was watching him and his gaze met mine. His stare was cold and unforgiving. With such pain registered in them, anyone who saw him hated me too. After a moment he went back to his book, disregarding anything Ms. Yang was saying.

As soon as the bell rang, he dashed out of class into the hallway. I raced after him as fast as my feet would carry me. He must have known I was following him, because his first move was for the boys' room and everyone knew the restrooms are off limits in passing period. They were too short, passing periods. Wait around for any reason and you'd be late for your next class. Still, knowing the consequences of my actions, I waited for him. I waited for a while, too. To the point that I had to hide in the girls' room when the monitor came by. I contemplated going in after him but then I realized that would be the worst possible thing I could do in my life. Follow a boy into the restroom because I wanted to know what he thought of me? No.

When the bell rang suggesting the school day was over, a boy came out. But not the brunette I had chased in there. This boy had blond hair and green eyes. I stood in the hallway distraught. I knew only one boy went into that bathroom. I watched. If one went in, the same should come out later. I looked up and down the hallway for any evidence that the boy actually existed, but he was nowhere to be found. I stood in the middle of the hallway spinning in circles like a goof while this mysterious blond guy watched me. I turned away from his overbearing gaze and began my way out of the school. The boy followed far behind but followed nonetheless.

I sprinted for the double doors at the end of the hallway and burst through them. A gust of the cool evening breeze swept through me, blowing my curling hair into my face. I brushed it away and raced to my truck and yanked at the door. *It's locked.* I rolled my eyes, feeling stupid for forgetting I locked my own truck. Then I saw the boy, the blond that had left the restroom. He was walking straight toward me. What was he following me for? I frantically searched my bag for my keys, but it was too late, he was already coming around the side of my car towards me. He held out his finger... with my keys hanging from it!

"Dropped your keys," his voice took me by surprise. It was deeper than I had guessed. "And my friend said I should probably return them to you."

I looked around him to a dark-haired boy standing under the thick shade of an Oak Tree. He was beautiful standing in the distance like a model or some Greek God. For a second, I thought he knew about my swooning because an amused smirk stretched across his face. Then I found myself wondering how I had suddenly become surrounded by all these pretty guys.

I looked back at the boy in front of me. His eyes too, registered hate. Then I began to wonder why all these pretty guys hated me. It was almost like this guy had to force himself not to be disgusted by my presence.

"Well," the blond said.

I took the keys and attempted to thank him as the boy began his quick stride back to his friend. "Hey!" I called after him. He stopped, just turning his head so slightly, just enough to see me in the corner of his eye. "Do – Are," I stumbled. "... Did I do something to offend you?"

Both boys seemed shocked by the question. The blond turned completely around to look at me. I'm not sure what my face was revealing, or what he was thinking, or what he thought I was thinking. But something in him was breaking. I could feel it in my chest. I looked at him for another couple of seconds until the pain made me want to cry out. Then he turned from me and the pain escaped my lungs. I blew a chunk of curly dark hair out of my face and hopped into my dad's old truck. I rolled down the window almost by instinct. After almost a year of driving that truck I knew never to turn on the engine without first rolling down the window. Thick smoke erupts from the air vents as soon as the engine bursts to life, and I had made that mistake many times before. Maybe I should've gotten that checked out.

I pulled down the sun visor and looked my face over in the mirror. I always thought it was funny t look at myself and see stark blue eyes starting back at me. They almost seemed out of place. Like someone else had put them there. Still it was me. I wiped my hair from my face and looked out my window just in time to hear the last of the two-boy's conversation.

"Angel, you're being ridiculous!" the dark-haired boy yelled.

"Eddie –" the blond yelled back.

I took a moment. So, the blond was Angel and the dark-haired one was Eddie.

Angel went on to say, "she doesn't even know!"

"Yes, she does!"

"She doesn't!"

"Okay so she doesn't know, she'll find out and then we'll have let her go." Eddie huffed. "We will have to come back and find her when she's already right here."

"But she can't be one of them!"

"Then why were we assigned to her?"

I didn't like the sound of that, I hoped so desperately that they weren't talking about me.

"Maybe it's the wrong girl." Angel suggested.

"Is her name Evangeline Welt?" Okay, maybe they were talking about me. "Listen to me." Eddie said. "This is our life. This is our job! You can't just forget that every time a pretty girl is involved."

"What!" Angel gasped, offended. "How she looks doesn't matter and what do you mean *every time*?"

"I don't always want to be the professional one –"

"What are you talking about?" Angel shrieked in irritation. "I am way more professional than you!"

"No, you're not!"

"Eddie, you tried to make out with our last objective."

Eddie laughed. "Tried? I succeeded. And we still completed our mission."

"Never mind, she doesn't know who –"

"Doesn't matter! She will find out!"

Then suddenly they both stopped. It was strange. They were even more gorgeous than the boy in my history class, if that was even possible. Those two. Angel's blond hair was tapered on the sides and back but fell loose on the top, long enough to be pulled into a bun. His eyes were different than any I'd ever seen before. A green so bright and so vibrant, it was like a shade of green created just for him. His face was round, but his jawline was so defined it didn't matter. Then there was Eddie, who so different from Angel but still so beautiful. His eyes were a heavy brown with splashes of blue and hazel and his right eyebrow had a small gash in it. His jet-black hair was long and loose and fell around his face with no specific pattern. His face was thinner than Angel's and his chin had a dimple in it. The way they stood there and looked at me, the way they stared. Like angels, which was ironic. Like they came down and some great artist captured them in stone. Because they were like stone. They didn't move a muscle, and I realized how awkward I looked just watching them.

They knew I was listening. I pretended I wasn't, that I was paying them no mind, but they didn't buy it. I pulled my hair into a ponytail and started my engine. But their eyes were piercing my skin. I left as quickly as possible. I was glad there was no traffic because my mind was everywhere but on the road.

What have I done to them to make me their objective? I thought frustrated. *Who do they think they are that they can just pick on me? And the other kid - the one I chased into the restroom - what happened to him?* I had so many questions. Ones I had no idea how to get answers to. I wasn't going to ask them! There was no way I was going anywhere near them, ever again. *But who are they?*

Then, a loud burst of repeated echoes broke my train of thought. My phone rang. It was Benjamin. I've known him since I was about seven. He was like the brother I never had. He sounded frantic and panicked on the phone. He said that he had something important to tell me. He hoped it would change my life. What did that mean?

It took him another hour to get to my house where I was sitting impatiently on my couch in the living room. It was a plush brown sofa that sunk in the middle, where my dad used to sit. It sat directly in front of the television, facing away from the stairs and front door. I sat working on my English homework while my mom was making dinner in the kitchen. Ben arrived, with a loud knock at the door. I almost didn't think it was him, but his signature *Clank, Clank, Clank* of the knocker gave it away.

As soon as I opened the door he ran inside. "What took you so long? Who's here? Are you okay?" He rushed. His long curly brown hair was a mess, his face was red, and his brown eyes had turned black. He didn't wait for my response, rushing around me into the kitchen and I hurried behind him. "Ms. Welt?"

My mom looked up at him seriously. "Yes Ben?" They looked at each other and an understanding passed between them.

"They are here," was all Ben had to say next.

My mom's eyes shifted and locked with mine. They were suddenly red, and something told me, whoever was here was taking her from me.

"Why are you guys being so dramatic?" I demanded.

But I got no answer. Instead, Ben grabbed my arm and dragged me up the stairs. He burst through my deep red painted door into my room of historic times. Soft, peach shaded walls were covered by poster upon poster of ancient heroes and mythical creatures. A bookshelf filled with books and books of wives' tales, forgotten stories, lost fictions, and prehistoric myths. A bed with a blanket as black as night and a pillow as white as snow. A window that hadn't been opened in years and a closet full of brightly colored clothes.

Ben began riffling through my drawers, demanding that I pack a bag. I didn't make sense to me? What was happening? Where were we going?

He stared at me for a moment blankly. "... If I tell you, will you come with me?"

"Scout's honor." I made an X over my heart.

Ben sat down on my bed with a sigh. "Do you remember those stories your mother told us when we were kids? Do you remember her favorite one?"

"It was about magic or something but –"

"Do you remember what the story was talking about? About the Witches? A vow of revenge?" I shook my head baffled by his nonsense. "A lineage of magic?"

I stopped for a moment thinking, trying to remember. Suddenly, a wave of memories crashed over me. I remembered being seven, maybe eight, and sitting on my bed with Ben as my mom told us stories. Her hair was a lot shorter then, cut into a short afro. Ben also looked a lot different. He skin was more of a fleshy pink color, less like the tan he wore. My mother had told us one specific story frequently, about a woman who died when she shouldn't have. And she vowed that her descendants would avenge her with the death of the world. Done all by the hand of a single girl. Someone they called The Gifted One. Of course, if she wasn't first hunted down by The Chosen One. Her seventeenth year would mark what some people call the apocalypse, what others call the rapture. A girl born with blue eyes.

I shrugged.

"So, you remember then?" Ben exclaimed. "Great! Now pack a bag."

"What! That doesn't explain anything."

He rolled his eyes, "It's not just a story. You're not just a person."

"You're not making any sense."

"Think about it. You have blue eyes! Just like the prophecy said. And Evangeline, just in case you didn't know, you're very, very black. Does that actually –"

24

"Are you honestly expecting me to believe that?" I ask irritated.

"No." Then he began packing himself. "I knew you wouldn't believe me. I don't expect you to, not yet. But it's true."

"What is true? That I'm a descendant of a woman who died a couple hundred years ago? Sure, I can buy that. But a Witch? Is that what you're telling me?"

He ran his hands over his face with a sigh. "I'll explain why we're leaving later but please can you just trust me?"

Ben had always been a little strange, but he had also been my bodyguard, my shoulder to lean on, and my best friend. Even during that brief moment when I thought I could fly. I jumped out of a tree, breaking my arm and his rib when I fell on him. So why would now be any different? On top of that, he seemed genuinely terrified of something. I shook my head and began packing the bag. Just as I got on board he goes and says:

"We're not coming back." *What!* "Just pack, we've lost a lot of time."

With a sigh, I threw some stuff into the bag and we hurried down the stairs. I stopped at the bottom step and stared. My mom was guarding the door?

She was. I almost didn't know it was her. She had her hair tied back in too tight of a bun and her once black hair was now streaked with different shades of grey; her brown eyes faded. She wore black, a color I'd never seen her in. It was an old-fashioned dress, with a corset that tied in the back. That was not the only thing unusual though, her sleeves were short. She never showed her arms, not even to me. But the sleeves weren't cut that way. No, it looked more like she got into a fight with a pair of scissors and lost. All along her arms were small cuts that were faded and healed. They weren't just random markings, they were words. Something ancient, not English. Her wrists were cluttered with bracelets of dry spices and herbs. And she was barefoot.

"What are you doing?" I asked.

When she turned to look at us, she looked cold. After seeing us her expression softened and her age receded. Her hair completely blonde, her eyes fully colored, but the scars remained.

"Evangeline," my mother said. "Go with Benjamin. He's gonna take you to New York and then Quebec."

"Do you know how crazy you sound?"

"He'll explain."

"Wait," I rubbed my temples. "You believe him?"

"I told him." I rubbed my head again. "Just go with him." I stared at her moment. "There is no time, Evangeline."

Ben ushered me toward the door but when my mother didn't move, I halted. "Wait, I'm not gonna leave you."

"Evangeline –"

"Mom!"

She looked at Benjamin and he stood up straighter. Like she was his commanding officer in the military or something. She nodded once, and Ben turned to me and hurled me over his shoulder. Until this moment, I'd had no idea how strong he was. I was up and over in seconds, I hardly even had time to blink. I had screamed and kicked but she looked away and aged again as she shut the door shut behind us. I kicked and squirmed, but Benjamin continued to his car, and threw me in the back seat of his station-wagon. I tried pushing the door back open, but the child lock was on. I kicked the window. Ben just looked at me, and his eyes seemed to say that if I didn't calm down, he was going to make me.

"I'm trying to do right by you!" He yelled.

"I didn't ask you to!"

He shook his head, turned, got in the car, and sped out of the driveway.

Within minutes, I saw the sign:

You're Now Leaving

Zanesville Ohio

Two hours later, I was still steaming mad. But two hours of utter silence is torture. Ben turned on the radio to drown out the silence. But it only made it more awkward. I reminded myself that this was probably just one of Ben's stupid games and that I'd be home tomorrow.

So, with that in mind, I gritted my teeth and said, "Can I at least sit in the front?"

He stifled a laugh. "Sure... But I'm not stopping the car."

"No need." I climbed up over the seat, kicking Ben in the back of the head. He glared at me rubbing the back of his head. I smiled smugly at him. A couple of minutes passed, and one of my favorite songs came on. The mood lightened as I began humming.

"So…" He forced. "How was your day?" He finally asked.

"I chased a guy into the bathroom," I rubbed my hand over my face. "And two other really hot guys decided they hate me. I'm not sure what I did to them?"

"You don't know what you did to annoy two hot guys. I can always count on you to be a little strange."

"Me? Right, cause I'm the one making the least amount of sense. Anyway, that Angel guy was, like, boring into my soul with his eyes. I'm sure it was laser vision or something."

"Angel? The hot guy with laser vision?"

"Oh, Witches are real, but laser vision isn't?"

"Yes... Hold on. Was he with a dark-haired guy?"

"Yeah, how did you know?"

"Oh crap! They saw your face! This is bad." He slammed on the gas pushing us another fifty miles above the speed limit. I stared at the speedometer panicked. "They're Hunters. That's why they hated you and that's why you dropped your keys." I looked up at him confused at how he had that bit of information. "They're tracking you now. We have to get to –"

"Wait a minute, just wait. This is still about this stupid magic stuff, isn't it?"

"Eva. This is real. Okay? This is happening and you're going to have to get with the program."

"What is wrong with you?"

"Eva, it's not going to make any sense because this is happening way too fast for you to comprehend. I know you need time to absorb this but please believe me. You weren't always in the human world."

"Prove it. Prove to me all this is real. Do some magic."

He put his hand on my shoulder, and suddenly I was back at my father's funeral.

Everyone was around me, asking if they could do anything. Like they could possibly make me feel better. I receded into the kitchen and hid in the cabinets. Back then I could still fit in them. I sat there for a while, not crying, not pouting, just thinking. A couple minutes later Ben crawled in beside me. He pulled his hand off my shoulder and the light of the moon on the street was all around me again.

"Would you believe me if I said that was magic?"

"...Ok, so you are a Witch?"

"No. You're a Witch, I'm a Warlock."

"Right… Wait, wait, and wait. I'm a Witch too?"

"Yes" he laughed.

"Ok, ok. So, for the last sixteen, nearly seventeen, years I've been living secretly as a Witch and didn't know it? Why haven't I accidentally done some magic and exposed myself?"

"Because it takes concentration. It's not like in the movies where you accidently freeze time by sneezing too hard, or just walk into a room and turn on the light subconsciously just because you have to ability to do it. Well, I guess stronger and more experienced Warlocks could do that, but they would have to at least have to think about it."

"Let's say I believe you. Okay. Let's say, after living as a human my whole life, suddenly things have changed. Why?"

"You're not just some regular Witch and you're almost seventeen, and they're going to start looking for. You've never use your magic, so most Hunters wouldn't even know you exist but since you are not just a normal Witch. They're going to try to find you anyway and they're going to do everything they can to. Remember you're the Gifted One."

I looked at him stunned but understood. I remembered my mother told me that story so many times. "Right... Who's chasing us again?"

"Hunters. From the Leadership." Ben went on to explain about The Leadership, an organization built to hunt down and destroy Witches and Warlocks. They had force and agility, and those who hunted the Witches called themselves the Hunters of the Leadership, or simply, the Hunters. They were one end of the spectrum. The

Council of Witches, run by a king and queen as their head, was the other. They were mortal enemies.

I decided to give my tentative acceptance to this information, as a means of gaining more. "Okay, so what in New York?" I asked.

"We're going to see my birth father." Ben was adopted after he was left in a park as a young child. He seemed to act like this was a regular occurrence. As if I wasn't about to meet my best friend's father for the first time since he was left in a field.

"He's the one who warned me you were in danger."

"And how would he know?"

"He's a Warlock."

"Okay, this is totally normal."

"And he's not in New York. He's in Bakersfield, California. I'm hoping to be in Kansas by morning, so we can... take a break."

"But my mom said we need –"

"I know what your mom said," he sighed. "Just trust me."

"Okay, because this isn't completely weird." Then suddenly I had a horrific realization. "Oh man," I said. "Being 'The Gifted One' means I destroy humanity doesn't it?"

"Oh relax. There's more to it than that. Everyone wants to believe that we're evil but we're not. My father will explain, just go to sleep. We have a long day tomorrow."

Realizing I really was exhausted, I curled into a ball next to the window and fell asleep within seconds.

I was standing in the middle of a throne room. The room was made entirely out of marble: the floor, the thrones, the four pillars holding up the large dome ceiling. I was wearing a dress similar to the one my mother had been wearing earlier, although mine was white and in terrible condition, ripped and almost shredded. It looked like I was fighting in a war and losing epically.

At the far end the room, Ben was holding Angel by his hair. Three more men behind him were holding Eddie hostage, wrapping his arms up behind him at an odd angle. Ben was cold and angry. I hated that look on his face. And I'm not sure why, seeing that they were trying to kill me, but my first instinct was to save Angel and Eddie. Strange, but something made me do it, even if I had to hurt Ben in the process. That wasn't like me, to put someone I love after someone I didn't even know.

Then the scene changed, and I was no longer in a throne room, but a wide, woodsy forest. It was cut down the middle to pave a road. A highway. And I wasn't wearing white, instead a red silk dress that flowed down to my feet. But it was dirty and worn away, kind of like I had rolled down a mountain. I was also wearing an old, withered, thorny necklace. Something that should've split my skin wide open, but it didn't. Then, I noticed I was leaning back at an angle.

Eddie was dipping me back. His right hand was firm and strong, holding me up at the base of my spine, and his left pressed the small broken branch to my chest where my heart was. He looked at it like he couldn't believe it was just flesh and tissue separating that stick from my heart. Slowly his eyes shifted to mine and our gazes locked. He was suddenly pained. Whatever it was he wanted to say would be a sin to let slip from his tongue. Then he stepped back, removing his hand from my spine and I fell backwards into the dirt.

"You know, I could have killed you," he said.

"Isn't that the point?" I retorted, standing up. "Okay, so, I'm not as great a fighter as a Hunter," I confessed. "But still I took half a class of karate!"

"Did your karate help you here?" He demanded. Then everything was gone.

I pried my eyes open to the morning sun. I looked out the window to find we were zipping across the road in the dewy, open lands of Kansas. I turned to look at Ben, who was still wide-awake. A low hum of classical music was playing on the radio. I had no idea why he liked the stuff.

"So, two premonitions, huh? In one night? I've never met someone who can have two in one night. Then again I've only ever met one you." He looks over at me, recognizing the confusion on my face. "I know they were premonitions because of the way you were breathing. When you have a premonition, your breathing slows almost to a halt. Mainly because your body is operating without its brain. Considering that your mind is in another time, you're basically dead. And the best part is you can't wake up from a premonition. Not until it's over anyway; you're completely defenseless."

"And that great because… you know, never mind. So, whatever I saw, it's going to happen?"

"Indeed. It will feel almost like déjà vu. But, don't tell me though! I like to be surprised. What's going to happen is going to happen and knowing about it beforehand could only mess things up."

I thought back to Ben's angry look. I got a chill. Then thought about how close Eddie had been to killing me and wondering why he didn't. I also wondered which would come first.

"You hungry?" He said pulling over to Mark Arnold's, one of the biggest food chains in the world. "I think they're still selling breakfast."

I shrugged. We went to the drive thru in two minutes at the most. I just got some pancakes, but Ben ate more than double that. He was always a big eater. But that didn't stop him from speeding down the Kansas interstate.

After about another five hours, it was officially 2:30 in the afternoon. And after five hours of mindless conversation, I was bored.

"I wanna go home," I whined.

"Good." He began slowing down. Then I realized the truck behind us had matched our speed of 145. When we pulled to a complete stop, the truck pulled ahead of us, speeding past. Ben gestured for me to get out of the car.

"Why?" I looked out at the grassy plains stretching out endlessly on the other side of my door. Acres and acres of green grassland, spotted with a few trees here and there.

"You're bored. There's nothing else for it to think about so your mind will be focused on training. You can't actually believe I'd take you into the belly of the beast with no training, right?"

Belly of the beast? I thought.

He jumped out of the car and ran over to my side. He pulled open my door. I climbed out of the car and followed him into the field. "I know this is your first time." He said as he led us further into the field. "So, I don't expect much of you." *Ouch.* "I don't expect you to do anything, actually, but your pride will kick in and keep you from asking for help, so we might be here for a while." *Hey!* "Stay here. Don't move." I stopped in place as Ben walked another three feet.

"Ok," he said. "Blow me away, literally." I scoffed at him, slightly annoyed. Very annoyed. What were we even doing out here? Why aren't I at home pretending to get ready school as I watched TV? "Try to summon the wind to do your bidding," he continued. "Push me back past that stump." He pointed behind himself to a tree stump that wasn't even a foot away.

"That's not very far," I said.

"True, but that's just the starting point. It might seem like a mile to a beginner like yourself." I sighed. "Okay. Now focus. Take a deep breath in like you're sucking all of the world's oxygen. Like it's all of yours to claim."

I did so. As if taking that breath was taking everything. It was, mine to own and I had to share with no one. As I did, I felt a low glow in the middle of my chest. A small hum, like something was warming up.

"Okay, you might not feel it yet, normally you won't. But you should have a funny feeling somewhere in your chest or stomach. Once you do, put your hands together and focus that feeling into your palms." I mimicked his instructions. "Then let it —"

Before he could even finish his sentence, everything had changed. What I knew and what I thought I knew was forever altered. I would never be able to see myself the same way. I'd never be able to see anything the same way. Because I was rushing hot air out of the palms of my hands toward him. I'm not sure what I expected, but it wasn't hot air flooding out of my hands with so much force. *This is real. Is it? Were those more than just stories? Was I really supposed to be in those stories? Was it possible?* Well obvious so because Ben flew across the field and smashed into one of the very few trees.

"Ben!" I raced over to him, hoping he wasn't seriously hurt. When I got to him, he pulled himself off the ground and look at me with amazement. His eyes glittered with fascination.

"You truly are the Gifted One," he laughed. "That, my friend, is your magic."

I stared at him moment. "You were telling the truth?"

"Well, yeah."

I fell back on my butt. *I'm a witch.* I thought. *Ben's a warlock. How is that even real? This is the stuff for novels. How could this be true? How could be happening to me? A random nobody from Ohio who's failing algebra. The Gifted One? What did that even mean?* Then I shot a look at Ben. "You said you'd hardly even move a foot!"

"Yeah. But you're so much powerful that I could have guess. You're going to need to learn how to control your magic. Quickly."

"Or I could just not use it."

"I'm afraid you won't have that option."

"Why?" I asked but I wasn't concerned with the answer. There was ruffling in the tree above us. Not like a squirrel or a bird. But something much bigger. It was moving slowly and quietly. And I was surprised to hear it. I shushed Ben looking up the tree. The thick leaves made it hard to see what was up there, but I looked and listened to the voices.

"Didn't I say she was a Witch? *The* Witch?" The first voice asked.

"Didn't I say she didn't know?" The second voice retorted. "Shush, I think they're listening us."

"Hunters." Ben whispered. "Pretend you don't know they're there." He stood up and put his arm around my shoulder like he used to when we were kids. As we began walking, two boys jumped down in front of us. They stood up and instantly I recognized them.

Angel and Eddie.

The sight of them made me want to run. They wore all black. Eddie had a leather whip tied around his waist like a belt, and from his pockets hung little bags of random ingredients. Angel's attire was similar. He wore a bracelet that looked like it could pop out a knife at any moment. And it probably could. He also had that thorny necklace hanging tightly around his neck. The same necklace that I had seen in my premonition last night. His eyes had changed, too. They were filled with, instead of hate, curiosity.

Ben leaned over and told me to run as soon as I got the chance. I looked up at Eddie. He had a wild smile on his face. His canine teeth seemed so much sharper than anyone else's. It made his smile terrifying. Just as Eddie was about to begin talking, Ben pushed me to start running.

I took off toward the car, but there were two of them and two of us, and Ben couldn't take them both, especially with such little sleep he had and that last fall. Although, he would still try. I knew I should've finished karate.

As I started running, Angel grabbed my arm and spun me around, so his arms locked around my waist. I realized what happened just a little too late. Then, I looked up to see Ben smacked in the face with a little gray sphere that dissolved on contact. A mist exploded in his face and wrapped itself around his head. I watched Ben's eyes roll to the back of his head and he crumpled to the ground.

Two

My heart sank. *Not Ben,* **I thought.** *Not Ben.*

I thrashed and kicked at Angel's embrace. I yelled. Angel then picked me up and carried me back towards the road.

"Your boyfriend's fine." Eddie mocked.

I stopped screaming but that didn't stop me from kicking, thrashing, and making a failed attempt at biting. We came upon the truck I had seen flying by when Ben and I first got out of the car. They had always been following us.

Angel stuffed me in the back seat and climbed in behind me. Eddie got in the driver's seat. Angel let go of me after we were in motion. We picked up speed ridiculously fast. We were going 150 in nearly three seconds flat. Only a crazy person would try to escape then.

We sat silently as Angel sharpened the knife in his bracelet. He glared at me from the side of his eyes and Eddie fumbled through the glove compartment with one hand as he wiggled the wheel mindlessly.

"You're not scaring me." I said. "Think you're scaring me? You're driving recklessly so I that I won't jump out of the car. And you," I turned to Angel. "You're sharpening that knife so that I won't try anything funny. But I know you're not going to hurt me because if you were I wouldn't be sitting here. So, you're not scaring me."

Suddenly Eddie slammed on the brakes. I flew forward and hit my face on the back of his seat. He got out of the car, yanked open my door, and pulled me from the car. Upon feeling my feet on the ground, I tried to run, but Eddie grabbed my hair and threw me against the side of the car. My head hit the metal and blood started running from my nose.

He leaned in close to my face and said, "If I was trying to scare you, trust me, you'd be scared." His eyes were cold and cutting into me like a steel blade. "I can make you –"

"You can't *make* me do anything. No one can *make* me do anything."

"Sure," Angel said. "Because that Ben kid didn't *make* you come with him. And I didn't *make* you get in the car with me."

"You're right, you didn't make me. You physically forced me. There is a huge difference."

"Do you want to die?" Eddie snapped.

"What sweet relief that would be."

Angel studied me as if I were an algebra problem he had to redo time and time again. I looked back at Eddie, who still had my hair knotted in his hands and a deadly stare in his eyes. I didn't like it.

"What's your problem?" I demanded. His gaze softened into more of confusion but still held its cruel intentions. "Seriously. What have I ever done to make you hate me?" They both seemed shocked, again, by the question. "Well?"

Eddie started, "Your people –"

"Excuse me! My *people,* you racist fuck."

"Witches," he quickly corrected himself. "You witches are problem."

"Me. What did *I* do? Seriously. What have I ever done to make you hate me personally?" They stared at each other for a moment. "Well?"

"Nothing, I guess." Angel said.

"Nothing *yet*," Eddie corrected. "After finding out what you could do, you might –"

"What I can do? Because I have a little bit of power doesn't change my belief of right and wrong! You all are so thick-headed." I was yelling at him. But I pretend that rush of power wasn't exhilarating.

"You think insulting me is the best course of action?" Eddie grabbed my throat cutting off my air supply.

"Eddie," Angel said, panicked.

"What, Angel?" Eddie snapped.

"Get her in the car."

Suddenly, Eddie was alerted to Angel's panic. But it was too late. Within seconds, a sheriff walked around the side of the car. I realized how incriminating it must have looked. Eddie was literally choking me, and Angel stood there doing nothing about it like his crazed sidekick. It looked like I was being held hostage by two murderers. Which, I reflected, was exactly what was happening.

"What's going on here?" The man asked in a deep, suspicious voice as he examined the scene.

"Nothing, sir" Eddie said, his eyes locking with mine. They were warning me. If I said anything I was dead meat.

But the man took note of that. "I wasn't asking you. Let go of her, that young lady is bleeding." The sheriff pushed Eddie off me, and air rushed back into my lungs. He pulled a handkerchief from his pocket and handed it to me. I wiped my nose with it, leaving a big red stain. "Are you alright?" He said making sure to make eye contact with me.

I considered my options. If I told him they were Witch Hunters and I was a Witch, he'd probably think that this was some role-playing game and he'd leave, and they would kill me. If I told him that these two boys kidnapped me, there's no doubt in my mind that they would probably kill him. The option with the least bloodshed just so happened to be the option of least resistance: to play dumb.

"Yes sir. This probably looks really bad, doesn't it? It does, I know. You see, um…my friends and I," I looked at Eddie. "have... really stupid senses of humor." I didn't know what else to say. Was I gonna say he was my brother? Domestic violence. My boyfriend? Domestic violence.

"So, he's beating you up?" The sheriff looked at Eddie.

"No. That makes it seem like he's alone in all of this. If you were here earlier, you would have seen me kick him in the ribs..." Eddie set his jaw. "We're both prone to having bad tempers." Then the sheriff turned his attention to Angel. He stared back at him defiantly. "He is... the younger brother," I scrambled. "He doesn't approve of our rivalry but he's so introverted and afraid of conflict, so he doesn't get involved," I said lightly.

The man looked between the three of us, then back at Eddie. "You be nicer," he said. "Remember that she is a lady."

"Yes sir," Eddie replied, through his teeth.

The sheriff watched as Eddie climbed back into the driver's seat and continued his stare as Angel took my hand and pulled me into the backseat. Once Eddie had started the truck again, the man made his way back to his car.

After about a mile or two Eddie finally asked, "Are you stupid or something? You could have told him everything."

"Like you wouldn't have killed him immediately. And me right after."

"Do you mean to tell me that knowing that even knowing you could die on this trip, you chose not to try to save yourself because it could risk his life?" Angel asked.

Eddie laughed to himself and Angel sat in disbelief. Then suddenly I was dizzy, I couldn't see straight, and my head was pounding against my skull like an electric hammer. All I knew what I was about to throw up.

Eddie's voice echoed through my head. I could hardly make out what he was saying. He slammed on the brakes. I jumped out of the car and ran to the other side of the road. I threw myself over tree stump and puked. I fell backwards away from the tree onto my back. I couldn't see well enough to recognize my own hand before my face. I was surprised the sheriff didn't pull back up and rescue me. This didn't look too great either.

But instead it was Angel. He was standing over me processing what had just happened. his voice echoed in my head as he called back to Eddie. Letting him know that I had just thrown up blood. I remember him scooping me up like a baby. His arms were so strong and his chest too. It was like his whole body was chiseled from stone and marble.

He put me down in the car and wrapped me in a blanket. I realized then I was freezing. Angel put his hand on my forehead. Still echoing, he told me that some fever had started and that my temperature had dropped ten below. And that at all cost, I should try to stay awake.

Then I was out.

I definitely had a fever dream. I dreamt that I was dancing in meadow and singing folk songs, wearing a dress made from flowers that barely cover everything that it was supposed to. The sky was mixed in everchanging hues of purple, blue, and orange. As if a rainbow had melted across the sky. With finger guns, I would shoot sparks of lightning into the sky, painting it a dark red color. Soon it looked like blood had filled the atmosphere. Plus, to make it worse, a crowd of people I didn't know watched me spin in circles, flowers falling away ever so often.

I woke to the sign:

Welcome to

Denver, Colorado

I could see clearly, I could hear but I was still as cold as a Popsicle. My throat burned, and my chest was on fire. I was leaning over on something. It was Angel. He had shifted his body so that was I curled up under his arm. It was nightfall now and Angel was asleep too. He was outrageously cold. My leaning against him cooled him off...a lot. I might as well have been a portable freezer. I pulled the blanket off me and wrapped it around him before the entire left side of his body turned to ice. Sure, I was cold too, but I was going through some fever. I'd be fine... Eventually. Right?

Eddie watched me from the rearview mirror.

"I don't want h-him to freeze to d-d-death," my teeth shattered.

"Whatever, just make sure you don't."

"S-so now you're sud-suddenly being nice?

"You just can't die on my watch. Our current mission is to get you to Mathrel. Alive. It's just a job." I looked out of the window trying to hide my sudden anger. Eddie yelled to Angel. Instantly he woke up, swinging his arm around, pinning me to the seat. He looked me over and pulled away from me, turning his attention to Eddie. Eddie told him he was about to pull off to a hotel now.

Okay, I thought. *Let's ignore that fact that you just hit me in the chest with your big ass arms.*

We got off on the next exit and immediately came upon a Hinton Hotel. Angel and Eddie got out first. It took me another minute to remember that just four hours before, these two boys had taken me hostage. One choked me. The other hit me in the chest, just a moment ago. Why did I trust them?

I jumped out of the car and began walking in the opposite direction they were headed. I strolled casually and thought I would get away with it. But I was wrong.

Angel grabbed my arm. I stared at him a moment before turning and trying to pull away from him. But spun me around so that he had both of my arms in his grasp. I wasn't getting away. I kicked myself for not just taking off in a run immediately. I kicked myself harder for being so embarrassingly weak.

He looked me over for a second, his green eyes were so much darker under the moonlight and his eyelashes casted long shadows over his face. I wasn't sure what he was looking for, but his stare made me uncomfortable. Then pulled off his jacket. He put it over my shoulders and draped his arm around me. I thought he did it to steady me, unsure if I was still dizzy. But then he grabbed my hand and locked his fingers with mine. Together, we walked into the hotel.

Eddie was having a conversation with the receptionist. When he spotted us, he waved, calling Angel his brother. Apparently, his story was that Angel was his brother and I was his fiancé. We had gotten turned around on our way to their mother's house. It was meant to be a one-day drive and we didn't plan to stop. He was expecting Paul, his new friend, to give him a free room for this story.

"Come on Paul," Eddie persisted. "It's just one night. Plus, look at me. Do I really look like the kind of guy who would ask twice for a hotel room? You have got to know this is important." Paul just looked at him. Then Eddie grabbed the guy's tie and pulled it down so that Paul slammed his face on the counter. Then Eddie leaned in real close and said, "don't make me ask a third time." Paul quickly grabbed the key to Room 217. "We'll be gone before morning," Eddie laughed.

I stare over my shoulder at the man as we walked over to the elevator and pressed the button for floor two. As the doors closed, Angel stepped away taking his embrace with him.

"We could have easily paid," Angel said.

"Sure," Eddie agreed. "But this way is a whole lot more fun."

When the doors clicked open we walked down the hallway quickly. Eddie slid the keycard into the slot and we all went in. The room smelled like lemons. There were two beds, both a light brown color, while the room itself was different shades and blends of brown. It was earthy, and very cozy.

"I'm going to take a shower," I announced.

They ignored me turning on the TV. I went to the restroom and locked the door. It was just something I did. The little, and only, bit of security I could control, was the lock on the door. I took a quick five-minute shower and reflected over what I had learned in the last two days.

    A. I'm a Witch
    B. My best friend is a Warlock.
    C. Said best friend is lying in a field
    D. I am "The Gifted One." Whatever that means.
    E. Two boys may or may not be taking me to someone named Mathrel to be killed.

F. I am now trapped in a hotel with these same boys.

I got out of the shower and changed back into the clothes I'd been wearing for the last two days. When I stepped back into the room, Angel and Eddie were engulfed in a serious conversation. They stopped as soon as I came in. I looked at them for a moment and they stared back.

. "What is the full description of your job?" I asked crossing over to the bed they sat on.

"We are paid to track down Witches," Eddie said. "And kill them in the least conspicuous way possible. If we can get them to do it themselves, it's a lot easier." I gaped at him. "You asked."

"Didn't even bother to sugar coat it, did you?"

"Why would I?" He glared.

"You barely even know me, yet you've already decided to hate me. Don't say it's because I'm a Witch because I just found all that out today. You're thinking that you understand the book when you haven't even opened the cover. I am a person capable of standing outside of a crowd I never even knew I was a part of." I was on my feet then. "So, treat me like a person. A single soul, separate from a colony of stereotypes. Magic or no magic, I still have a mind and have the capability to think beyond my environment. Do you?"

"There you go insulting me again." Eddie stepped into my face and glared. "Listen, demon. You prove that you deserve a treatment separate from your magic buddies and then, and only then, will I give it to you."

"You are real son of a —"

Eddie swung at me but suddenly I was nowhere near the line of fire. Instead I was on the other side of Angel with his arm around my waist, swinging slightly off the ground. I looked around to see Angel had caught Eddie's fist.

"Okay," Angel said. "You're a person. I think we can remember that."

Eddie gritted his teeth. "You're always gonna be a Witch."

"You should go to sleep," Angel said. "Tomorrow you're going to get another wave of anxiety as your immune system changes." He looked me over realizing that I didn't know what he was talking about.

"Today being the first time using magic, that means today and tomorrow your immune system will start changing to adapt to the new blood running through your veins."

"But tomorrow," Eddie interjected. "You're gonna become a walking furnace."

This is my twisted life now? I thought.

Angel put me down, claiming first watch. He turned off the light and TV and sat in front of the door. I fell asleep after Eddie's snores became tolerable. But it wasn't peaceful. I had three premonitions.

In the first, Ben was there. He was pulling my face, so I looked in the mirror. My face was riddled with tiny scars.

In the second, Angel was rushing me out of the same throne room I had seen before. Eddie led the way, screaming for us to hurry. My white dress was stained red. Blood. Angel had it all over his stomach and chest. Eddie also had it running down the side of his face and most of his arm. A girl with an unstained pink dress ran beside him. She kept looking back to make sure we were with them.

Then, the third one. A fat man sat in a velvet chair in, what looked to be, the middle of a library. He had a long grey beard and silver eyes. His voice echoed through my mind as he said, "final decisions!"

Then I was awake. I looked at the clock to find it was 11:38. Barely an hour had gone by. Angel still sat by the door. I crawled out of bed over to Angel and sat in front of him in the doorway. "What's this prophecy about?"

"...Well, I'll presume you know the stories. The wars and vowing of revenge. But the Leadership vowed to never let the Witches get their revenge. The vows were simultaneous and with them, the prophecies. I can guess you know the Gifted One."

But I didn't. Not really. Not as well as I should have. "The second was of the Chosen One, she would be the one who saved the all of humanity from Witches. The children would be born together. Upon their seventeenth birthday, an epic duel would commence, and the world would either live on or perish."

"When you say 'save' and 'perish,' you don't mean that Witches plan on destroying the world. Do you?" He nodded. "But Ben said there was more to it than that. That the world wouldn't just die."

"Maybe he knew you weren't a murderer and had to lie to you."

"He wouldn't do that!" I yelled, suddenly filled rage from the slander presented by my kidnapper.

Angel grabbed my arm, pulled me toward him, and covered my mouth. "Never wake Eddie while he's getting a good rest." He looked over my shoulder. "That guy's already crazy enough." I was so close to him I could smell the slight scent of the soap he had used that morning. Slowly he let go of me staring at my hand. "I didn't mean to offend you," he said. "Your seventeenth birthday is in two weeks, yes?"

I nodded, suddenly remembering that I had a birthday. I didn't normally celebrate anyway. After my father died on my seventh birthday, it became the anniversary of his death. For a little while, I was terrified of waking and hearing 'Someone you love so dearly is dead but here, have this present and forget about it.' Or something like it. When I could even bear to her his name again, the day became just like any other, and I hadn't celebrated since. "I usually don't do anything," I said.

"You're birthday's two weeks after mine." He said nonchalantly.

It took me a second to realize what he was saying but when I did, "Happy birthday!" he nodded. "Hey, if I survive this thing, I'm going to have to get you a present for not being a total jerk. I hear kidnappers these days are complete assholes."

He laughed softly. That was the first time I saw him smile, and I could barely see it in the darkness. "…Go to bed now."

I nodded and crawled back into bed and this time I slept. No premonitions, no dreams. I just slept.

Three

When I awoke again, the sun still wasn't up, but it was obvious that it was morning. Angel and Eddie were heavy in conversation.

"What do you think Mathrel wants with her?" Angel asked.

"Well, it's clear he won't kill her. He would've asked us to do it already," Eddie said.

"Do you really think –?"

"All I know is we keep her safe and get her to Mathrel."

"Eddie, what if it's not *on* her seventeenth birthday. But *of* her seventeenth birthday. As in, anywhere in the year that she is seventeen."

"I thought about that too. Should we wake Evangeline, now?"

I sat up then. I rubbed my eyes and pretended they were still droopy from sleep. When I looked at Angel and Eddie I squinted. They both looked at me, moving nothing but their necks. Eddie glared at me a moment before suggesting that we get moving. I crawled out of the bed and followed the two boys from the room. Once we were in the elevator, Angel's fingers locked with mine. For some reason, with his hand around mine, I became really anxious.

When the door clicked open, Eddie went over to the front desk. Angel and I continued out to the car. He walked over to the passenger's seat and looked at me intently. His stare stayed locked with mine as he opened the door. I realized that our hands were still locked together when his grip tightened and began hurting my hand.

"I need to tell you something," he said. "And listen carefully." I stared at him. "We're taking you to see Mathrel." I nodded. "You should also know Mathrel *always* gets his way. He makes *every* final decision. *All* that pertain to the Leadership. So, don't get on his bad side. I don't know what he might do about that. And I can't help you if he decides he doesn't like the fact that so much power lives inside a teenager. I'm not saying he's power hungry, but I'm not saying he's eaten yet, either."

"I understand." I nodded. But I didn't really. Mathrel is a Hunter. How could he benefit from my power? It's magical.

Then Eddie banged into the car. I jumped, as Angel dropped my hand. I climbed into the passenger's seat and Angel made his way around to the driver's.

I stared out the window at the ever-changing landscapes of Colorado. The mountains, the rivers, and the forests. It was very beautiful. But after two hours of intolerable silence I was bored. Again. The bad part was Eddie was too. He put his feet up on my armrest and asked, "So Eva? Tell me a little about yourself."

"Um... I'd like to say I'm good at art. And I pride myself on my exemplary I-Spy skills."

Angel laughed to himself as Eddie broke out in a loud cackle. "Funny! But seriously. Is there a thing about you we don't already know?" The mood was suddenly really intense. Even Angel had his eyebrows knit.

I thought hard about what I could say next when my eyes started to blur, and I got dizzy.

"I. I am...I feel sick." Angel quickly pulled over and I jumped out of the car. I hurled myself over a lump of rock and spewed blood. When it had all come up, I sat back on the ground. I couldn't see, I had a massive headache, and my throat and lungs were on fire. Angel scooped me up and put me in the backseat. Eddie was driving now.

"At least it happened early so we got it over with." Eddie said. "It's already feels like an oven in here." He rolled down the windows and I realized how hot I was. Like a pig wrapped in a blanket on the 4th of July. Angel was trying to grab my attention. He pulled at the collar of my plaid shirt trying to find out if I had t-shirt underneath it. I nodded. As he began unbuttoning my top shirt, his hands shook. I would have almost thought I was scaring him. When he had finished he pulled my arms out to reveal my baby blue tank top. He pulled off my shoes and socks and, man, was I happy to be wearing shorts. But, even with all that, I was ablaze. I almost couldn't breathe. I panicked as my body strained to accept oxygen. I wondered if I could've died right then. If my body had rejected the magic and I just burned to death from inside out. Then I shut myself up, stopping and making myself concentrate on breathing. Angel was staring at me intently. I tried to avoid his stare, but he continued watching me for the next hour and a half.

When I could breathe, and it felt like my head wasn't trying to kill me anymore, I sat up. My throat wasn't so hot, but I was. I leaned against the window as my hair flew wildly. I was cooling off gradually.

I turned to Angel. "I don't understand you," I said. "I mean, I feel like there is more to than you just trying to act like the cool guy." His eyes were locked on my hands.

"Because," Eddie said, "things that you're taught like, compassion, kindness," he looked in the rearview mirror at me. "Mercy. It doesn't fit in my world. As children, when something made us laugh or smile it was taken away or destroyed, and it was never found again. To keep us focused on the mission. It was our earliest form of training."

I was stunned. "You were deprived of a childhood, you're not mad? Not even a little bit?"

"Oh, Gifted One! Oh, Gifted One! Tell us about your childhood!" Eddie yelled.

"Don't do that. This isn't about me. I didn't always get what I wanted either. But I liked going outside and falling and scraping my knees. I also like being able to sit and watch TV. So, excuse me for loving my life and appreciating it so much. I'm just trying to understand you."

"Oh, you love life so much?" Angel said. "But you don't even celebrate your birthdays."

"I don't celebrate my birthdays…" I wondered if telling them would even matter. That truth was so soul crushing for me that for years I couldn't even look at his pictures. That truth rocked my world so devastatingly that for eleven years I didn't celebrate once. My face was dripping with tears before I realized I was crying. "Because my father died on my seventh." I think that was the first time I verbally acknowledged what happened since that day.

But I wasn't grateful to them. Eddie and Angel's insensitivity had gone too far. I threw open my door and Eddie slammed on the brakes. I jumped out of the truck and sprinted across the road and into the grass. I hadn't realized how far I had made it in two seconds. I tripped over a rock and fell to the ground. My stomach slammed into the ground, knocking the air out of me. I curled up into a ball. Grass was sticking to my skin where tears had wet my face. I had never really cried for my father. Not even the day I found out. That day I never shed a tear. Not at the funeral either. I never said a word, that day. I never looked at anyone at all, that day. Now, it all flowed out. Like a dam had burst. Out of my eyes into the dirt. I hugged my chest because the pain was unbearable, unreal, and unfathomable.

Someone came up behind me and stood over me. I turned to push whomever it was away, but they were stronger than me. They hardly moved, if at all. I realized who it was as he sighed, squatting down behind me. "I'm sorry," Angel said. "I really am." I turned around and pushed him away. He jumped back and hugged me. I attempted pushing him away, but he held me still. I stopped and cried into his shirt. "I know what you're feeling. Or maybe I don't." He stammered. His clumsiness made me hug him tighter. "My mom died when I was seven. I can't relate my experience to yours, but I can say that I'm sorry."

I looked at him, tears still streaming from my eyes. "What's your problem," I demanded, feeling so stupid. So vulnerable. "You're kidnappers! Quit being nice." These people might be trying to kill me. And I let them see me cry.

He helped me to my feet and led me back to the truck. It took longer than a couple seconds that time. Eddie was waiting with the passenger's door open. When I reached the road, I realized my shoes weren't on and my feet started to fry on the concrete. Eddie helped me into the car. When the door snapped shut, Angel turned to him. I could barely hear what they were saying through the glass, but I could make out some of it.

"I can't do this." Angel said. "We can't do this."

"What do you mean?" Eddie asked.

"She's different. Different than any other Witch or *girl* we have or will ever meet. This constant bickering back and forth we have going. It's got to stop. We can't... In the last two days, she's gotten on this serious emotional roller coaster and hasn't got off and won't anytime soon. And we are not helping in any way."

"Why does it matter?" Eddie questioned. "Mathrel might have her killed."

Angel looked at me through the window and said something so low that I couldn't hear. Whatever he said made Eddie uneasy. *Who was this guy? How is this nice a person? Especially if I am who they think I am. Or if they're childhood was really that desensitized. Who was his?*

Still, Eddie climbed in the backseat and Angel rounded the car to the driver's. He shut the door and looked at me. I wondered how long this would last before he said what he was thinking.

I didn't know why. I had no idea why, but I felt strange. I can't explain it. Like it was hard to breathe but not like I was choking. Like, I found Angel's presence ...nerve-racking. I couldn't figure out why I felt that way. As we entered Salt Lake City, that feeling just got worse.

Three hours probably went by and I went from hungry to starving. It was around 12:30 when we exited Elko, Nevada.

All the way up to this moment, there was silence. Then Eddie broke it, complaining about his hunger. Angel suggested we stopped at the internationally renowned drive-in diner, Phonic.

It took us a minute to find it. A literal minute. We turned the corner around the first exit and it there was. We rolled in and parked. Angel ordered our meals and as we waited Eddie reminded me of someone. He demanded to know what my relationship was to Ben. Probably wanting to know if he'd follow us. Of course, he would. He's my best friend. He's definitely coming to rescue me from these Witch Hunters. Eddie told me that he'd wake up after 24 hours. I began to panic realizing that he'd be laying out, vulnerable, in the middle of a field for an entire day, with Witch Hunters running amok.

Immediately after the interrogation, a woman rolled out on roller blades. As soon as Angel paid we flew out of the lot and back onto the highway. Angel drove with one hand on the wheel and the other stuffing a burger in his mouth.

After ten minutes of silence and the echo of munching ringing in my ears, I was once again bored. I then realized that normally, whenever I went on the road, I would have to have something to do. I was easily bored.

I tried remembering the last time I was in California. With my dad. I remembered going to the beach and playing in the water, barely able to swim. I was probably six. It seemed so far back, faded and hard to keep a hold of in my mind. The faint memory was held together by flashes of scenes and faces. Especially of my dad's long curly beard. I remembered the abundance of sand that had collected in it. Him pulling the towel through it to dry it off.

"Santa Rosa is right next to the beach, right?" I asked, a wild idea coming to mind.

"...So?" Eddie demanded. I turned back to face him. "No," he said quickly. "We have to go see Mathrel."

"Does he know what time we're going to be there? Just don't tell him."

"Of course, you want us to lie to our Commanding Officer."

"I haven't been to the beach in ten. I can hardly remember what it's like and I could very well die with Mathrel. And the last thing I would see would be your face." He rolled his eyes. "Please."

He watched me for a moment before gritting his teeth. "Fine." He finally said. "But just an hour."

Four

By 4:30 we were just entering California. I loved California. My family and I used to go every summer. But after my father died, we fell out of the tradition.

Two more hours went by and the sky started turning a mango orange and a fluorescent purple color. Within those hours we saw the sign:

Now Entering

Santa Rosa, California

I was so excited to get got of that truck. Seriously, my butt was numb. In the next thirty minutes, we arrived at a two-story cream-colored house. It had tinted windows and a yellow painted roof. As we climbed out of the car, I pulled on my plaid shirt and shoes. I assumed the house was Eddie's as he rearranged his keys to unlock the door. I followed the two boys inside. The interior of the house was dark and morbid contrary to its bright exterior. Shades of dark brown and black took control of the living room. A grey carpet led up the stairs that Angel and Eddie were taking. They turned a corner into a bedroom splashed with reds and blues. Eddie went through a black dresser and threw a pair of swimming trunks at Angel. When Eddie looked at me he realized I couldn't wear a pair of his trunks. He led me across the hall into a room laced with purples and light blues. He pointed to a white dresser and told that should be able to find something in there.

"I didn't know you had a sister," I said.

"You didn't ask." He sighed. "Her name is Loyce." The way he said it sounded sad.

"Is…she okay?" I asked.

"Oh, yeah. She just doesn't come around as much as she used to." I nodded a little. "She didn't go rogue or anything! She's actually Mathrel's finest Huntress. That's why she doesn't come around." I nodded again. He rolled his eyes and closed the door as he left. I went over to the pure white dresser and began rummaging through the drawers. I felt like a burglar looking for goods. In the bottom, right drawer was a bathing suit. It was a pink and green bikini, it reminded me of something Patrick Star would wear if he were a girl. I didn't normally wear bikinis. I didn't like the attention they brought. But I changed into it.

When I had it on, I realized it was a little too tight on me. So, I pulled my baby blue tank top and jean shorts on over it. Then tied my plaid shirt around my waist. As Loyce obviously wouldn't be back anytime soon, I also borrowed a pair of flip-flops.

When I trotted down the stairs I found Eddie lounging on the couch. A picture of a girl hung on the wall behind him. She was probably in middle school at the time. She had thick black hair, cut into a bob around her face. She held a knife whittled from wood in one hand, and a steel one in the other. Her deep brown eyes stared at the camera menacingly. I looked away quickly.

"Come on Angel!" Eddie called. "Even the girl beat you!" He stood up and charged towards the stairs, revealing his red and black trunks, his black sandals, and his bare chest. He called for Angel again.

I thought I'd seen enough movies and been to enough pool parties to know what sexy was. But I was wrong. Sexy was standing in front of me, screaming up the stairs. Sexy was a boy, who hated my very existence, scowling at his best friend. Sexy was the guy with thick black hair and the scar in his eyebrow that was probably not as bad as it looked. Sexy was his intimidating glare and apparent irritation. Sexy was not at what I thought it was. Sexy was Eddie and I was speechless.

Eventually Angel flew down stairs. He wore black and grey trunks, black sandals and a grey t-shirt.

We all climbed back into the car and set towards the beach. The sun was closing behind the water as we came up on the turf. It was beautiful, the orange in the sunset turned deep purple. The water rocking ever so slightly and waves crashing onto the shore then rolling back slowly.

Eddie handed his towel to Angel and bound down the beach toward the ocean. Angel and I made our way down slowly behind him and set out the towels. I sat down promptly after a wave of salty air hit me in the face. I took a deep breath, taking in all the nature of the scenery. I lay back in the sand feeling comfortable, but Angel didn't share my enthusiasm.

"I despise the beach," he said darkly.

"What!" I exclaimed. "Why?"

"Because the sand is everywhere and it's itchy. Plus, the smell of hot dogs pollutes the air, and somehow the sand always finds its way into my shorts. And did mention I don't like sand?"

"HA!" I laughed. "Did you just say something funny?" He looked at me confused. "Did you just say that? Because that made me laugh." He pulled a corner of his mouth as if he understood what I was saying and was now amused. It was silent for a moment and I searched my brain for something to say. "Did, um," I stammered. "Angel... What's your last name?"

His face curled into a full fledge smile. "Adams. Angel Adams."

"Whoa! Don't the guys with the same letter in their first and last name end up being crazy ... or serial killers?"

"Yeah. In the movies."

"Movies are based on real life. I mean, look at Peter Pan. He kidnapped children. Ring any bells?" He didn't say anything, and I thought I had made him feel uncomfortable. "You know, I don't understand you guys. I don't understand how you could be so committed to... murder."

"It's just a job."

"You don't really believe that. You wouldn't be so broken if you if you did." He stared at me blankly. "You think I can't see it?"

"It's just complicated," he rolled his eyes. "There's too much to explain right now."

"I've got plenty of time."

I stared at him. "Fine," he sighed. "Do you remember what I told you before about how being happy wasn't part of our childhood? Don't forget that. And don't tell Eddie I'm telling you this..." He blinked slowly. "Okay, two years ago, Eddie had a girlfriend. Mia. She was nice. Really nice. And smiled way too much, if that's possible. But because of her, Eddie smiled. Not those fake smiles he'll give you every now and again. No, actual smiles, actual laughs. She made him *happy*. But she was human, and therefore also expendable. And easy to make an example of.

59

"Eddie and Mia dated for close to 3 months. Then suddenly she was gone. The house she lived in was being rented by a new family. Her neighbors didn't remember her. Her friends didn't even know a Mia went to their school. It was like Mia Jones never existed. The only reason Eddie didn't drive himself insane was because I remembered her too. But that didn't keep him from shutting down. Or from putting up walls so thick, a wrecking ball couldn't save him."

I gaped at him, completely perplexed. "Why did you tell me that?"

"Because. I'd rather put a little lock on my tongue and see you and talk to you tomorrow, than tell you everything and have you suddenly disappear. Because you're a Witch and far more expendable."

I looked down at my hands and frowned. What a sad life. A sad, twisted life. "Do you know if…" I began.

"If she's alive?" Angel finished. "We have no idea."

I looked over to Eddie. He was sitting at the edge of the shore, letting the water crash into him. Angel stared at me as I stared at Eddie. "So, what you're saying is," I laughed. "I make you happy?"

"You make me…confused, to say the least." I forced myself to look at him and locked my eyes with his. "You bring up all these emotions I don't understand." He clenched and unclenched his jaw. "You're so…different. From everyone else in this *universe*. You…you're strong, and independent, and stubborn. From the moment I met you, you've consumed my thoughts. And for me, for the person I created myself to be, that's terrifying."

My heart was running wild. Beating faster than a drummer on Speed. I could've sworn a person could hear it over the screaming of a rock star. I curled my mouth and bit my lower lip. He studied my face. I let my mouth fall open. "I'm sorry about what happened to Eddie. But…"

"But what?"

"But I'm not Mia. Things don't just happen to me." *What did I just say? I thought. What was I doing? Was that some sort of twisted form of flirting? Just two days before I hated this guy! And now I was implying... what? That he should embark on some risky romance with me? Weren't these the guys that kidnapped. Weren't trying to kill me? Aren't they still? What the hell! This a trap. Right? Isn't it? I'm not doing this.* "I shouldn't have said that."

His eyes dropped from mine to my hands. I watched as his blonde hair ruffled through the salty wind. He put his hand on mine. "Eva," he said. "I think –"

"If Mathrel doesn't kill me and you are who I think you are, let's be friends. But only then."

He pulled his hand away as Eddie was running up from the surf. "What are you guys talking about?" Eddie asked shaking out his wet hair.

I pulled my gaze away from Angel and the awkwardness I had created. "We were talking about you, actually." I said. He glared at me a moment. "Yeah. I really had no idea how much of a wuss you were."

"Excuse me!"

"Really! Who goes to the beach doesn't swim out? You just sat at the edge of the shore."

"You didn't get wet all!" I shrugged. "Oh no." He grabbed my arm and ripped me to my feet. Then began pulling me down to the ocean. "You too, Mr. I Do Nothing at All," he yelled back at Angel.

Eventually all three of us were in the water up to our necks, competing to see who could swim out the farthest. I was out first. I never really liked deep waters. But Angel and Eddie kept going and going. And going. When they returned, I was laying on the shore like a whale. They grabbed me by my arms and feet and threw me back into the water.

It was almost strange. Three teenagers playing mindlessly like children in the water. Although, it hilariously fun. But what made it so strange was the fact that I was so comfortable with them. I had to keep reminding myself that those two boys who wanted to kill me just days before. How were they the same boys I frolicked in the ocean with?

Maybe twenty minutes later, Eddie was pulling us from our fun, back to the world of murders and orders. Angel and I followed Eddie back to the truck. I climbed into the backseat and Eddie stood next to the door as Angel went off to change. Then Eddie went when Angel returned. I suppose they couldn't give any opportunity to escape. They probably also couldn't give any clues to Mathrel that we had gone to the beach, even though I would be dripping wet. When he returned, Eddie clambered into the driver's seat and Angel into the passenger's. From the beach, we drove ten minutes to an apartment building. I was seriously surprised by two things:

1. I was completely dry by the time I got out of the car.
2. These boys, so rough and tough, had a headquarters disguised as an apartment building.

I guess they were just surprising boys.

As I followed them into the building I realized it was just a regular apartment building. People were checking their mail and children were running up the stairs. I continued to follow them down into the storage room where things got really creepy. I continued, and I could swear I felt something reach out of the darkness to touch my leg. Suddenly we stopped, and I ran into Angel's back.

We stood in front of a concrete wall. Eddie put his hand on it and a green light glowed from the wall in the shape of his hand. Then with a click, a door popped open. We went down several flights of stairs and finally we made ground. The air was a little humid and it was almost hard to breathe.

"We're under the basement." Angel said.

"At least thirty feet under." Eddie said. I started breathing hard, like I couldn't afford to lose a single breath. "Come on," Eddie said. "Don't get all claustrophobic on me."

"I feel like I'm a mouse in a box," I said.

"You get used to it."

As we continued to walk, the boys rearranged themselves. Angel was behind me and Eddie was in front of me. We walked in a line, on guard, like they were protecting me from some unknown threat that could come from either side. Or maybe preparing themselves for an attack I might make. That seemed more likely.

We turned a corner toward two large wooden doors. I almost couldn't believe this was all under a basement. Through the double doors was a large, velvet-lined library.

As we proceeded into the library, I saw there was no check-in counter. Just rows and rows of books. I could've gotten lost in all these walkways. So many ups and downs, and lefts and rights. Then I realized it was a maze. If you didn't work here, you couldn't know how to get through. I won't lie, it was cool.

Eventually, we came upon the center of the maze where three velvet armchairs surrounded a black coffee table. In the center chair sat a large man. He had a long beard and messy hair, all of which was grey. His eyes were dull and silver. He wore a white shirt and brown pants held up by suspenders. He had a book in his hand, but I couldn't recognize the title. The language was ancient. It looked just like the writing carved into my mom's arms. He had a smile painted across his face. It looked forced, like he just smiled to establish a tone. It wasn't real. He probably didn't have a real smile.

He didn't look up when he said, "Angel! Eddie! You've returned!" When he did glance up, he only moved his eyes. "Oh! Who's your friend?" He stared at me.

"This is Evangeline Welt." Eddie said.

"Evangeline," he sang. "Come here."

I took a single step forward, obeying the command, but not its intent. That might have been rude, in fact it was, but I didn't trust this guy. Every alarm in my head was going off. *Bad news! Bad news! This guy's bad news!*

"Oh, I don't bite," he said. Maybe he didn't but I did. Why didn't he get off his butt and come to me?

I walked until I was about two feet away from him. He reached out, dropping his book. He grabbed my hand and yanked me toward him. He studied me with his strange smile, but his eyes showed eagerness and impatience.

"Well," he laughed. "Aren't you full of surprises?" He stared into my eyes, laughing. "That's a shade of blue I don't ever seen before. Magnificent!" I threw him a fake smile, pretended to laugh, and ripped my hand away. He tilted his head to the side. "Please. Sit." He gestured to the seat beside him. I made my way to the seat, not taking my eyes away from him for a second. "I can feel your energy," he said.

"Excuse me?" I wasn't quite sure what that meant.

"It's fresh. Did you just start using your magic?" I nodded. "How long ago?"

"Two days."

"Wow... Two days and you're already stronger than Warlocks with lifetimes of experience."

The way he said it unsettled me. Like he was accusing me of something. My gaze darted from him to Angel and Eddie. There was something really weird about this guy that I didn't like. I couldn't pin point it. Like it was on the tip of my tongue, but I just kept spitting it out. Who was he? "Well …yeah." I said.

"Yeah? Yes, well I suppose that will happen to a girl of your bloodline."

"My bloodline?"

"Never mind that. My name is Mathrel. I'm the man in charge here. I sent my son to keep tabs on you for the last week. Who would've thought that our undoing would be in one tiny little *Witch*." He gritted his teeth behind his smile. "But Evangeline –"

"You sent your son to follow me?" I cut in, glaring. "You provided you son as my personal stalker?"

"I tried but he failed me as he often does. I would've sent Loyce Markus, but she was unavailable." The smile jumped back. "Alright. Tell me, Eva, when is your birthday?"

"April 25th."

"Wow! With just two weeks to go, we should probably make a decision now."

"…A decision? What kind of decision?"

"If we should kill you now or later!" I panicked and stood up. Angel and Eddie shifted but didn't move from their positions. "No, I'm joking! I joke, I joke." Mathrel laughed hysterically. "But seriously," his smile fled. "We need to make a decision. What are your thoughts about the prophecies?"

I sighed. Slowly, I sat back down. "Well, there's not much to think about. The world could be saved or something else. It doesn't really matter what it is, I've already made up my mind."

"Something else?" He studied me. "Do you know what that something else is?"

"Um, well I've heard world demolition. I've also heard that it might be something else. But if it's anything other than saving a world I don't think it matters."

"You're a Witch –" he turned to Angel and Eddie. "You brought me a Witch, didn't you?" Angel said nodding slightly. He turned back to me. "And you don't know your own prophecy?"

Eddie stifled a laugh. "Edmund! Please, compose yourself." Mathrel demanded. Then he turned back to me. "Let me sum it up for you then." His voice dropped as he said, "the Witches want to bring magic back so that it becomes part of everyday life. And then execute all of humanity to live in it openly. The only people to walk the face of this earth will be Witches and Warlocks." His voice brightened, "crazy, right?"

"W-what?" I stammered. "That's genocide!"

"I know," he smiled his great, big smile.

"No, that can't possibly – that's not true." He nodded. "It can't be! Ben –"

"Who's Ben?"

"Benjamin Carter." Angel said. "A Warlock. The boy who was training her when we intercepted them."

"Ben would never ask me to do that!" I yelled.

"Why not?" Mathrel stared.

"Because...we were both raised in the human world. He knows all about this stuff and he said that's there's more to it than that..." He continued to stare at me. "And we both studied World War II. We know how devastating that was."

"Hmm." He nodded.

"And, my mother was his trainer, I guess. She –"

"She wasn't his parental figure. How well could she guide him? Who are his parents?"

"Mr. and Mrs. Blanch. They adopted him."

"You're sure? That's what he told you?"

"…Are you suggesting he lied to me for almost ten years?"

"Your mother trusted him?" I nodded. "And you trust your mother?"

"With everything I am."

"How do you know –?"

"If there is only one thing in this world I know, even better than I know how to breathe, it's my mother. She would *never* lie to me."

"Ok…Back to Ben. Do you trust him, too? As much as you trust the oxygen in your lungs?"

I had to bite my tongue. I trusted Ben, I really did, but he wasn't always truthful with me. My mom always told me the truth. She often said, "Honesty is a sad road, but the kindest one to take." She always said it was safer to know the hard truth than be sheltered from pain. My mother *is* honesty. She even told me about my prophecy. Not right out. But in bedtime story. She told me even still.

"Uh Eva," Eddie said, exchanging a look with Angel. "I have to tell you we know some bad things about this kid."

Slowly I stood up. "You all don't know him. I do."

"We know more about him than you do. His birthday is June 20th in Las Vegas, Nevada." I nodded. "His father is Tannin Carter the 11th." The sound of his name made Angel twitch. "The king of the

Council." Oh, that's why. "His mother, Eris Carter. She was the queen but was murdered by Kytra Carter, who is now queen."

I was stunned. I couldn't believe it. "You're lying."

"We're not." I knew they had to be telling the truth. It made too much sense. He had said he was taking me to see his father. The Warlock King. Of course! They were going to talk me into burning the world! All of humanity! Could he really look me in the eye and lie to my face? Could I have been played for ten years?

"With who his parents are," Eddie continued. "We believe his very existence was devoted to making sure you fulfilled your prophecy."

It made sense. *You weren't always in the human world,* Ben had said to me. His parents could have told him that. My mother didn't want evil in my life. Slowly, as all of it sank in and my throat started to close, I looked at Angel. "I want to go home," I said. Eddie shifted uneasily, and Angel looked pained as he clenched and unclenched his jaw. My face fell. "What is it?"

"There's uh," Angel stammered rubbing his knuckles together. "There isn't much to go home to …When um, when we got to your house the other day…your um, your mother –"

"You killed her!"

"No! When we got there your house was already destroyed and your mother…"

I turned away from them. I couldn't believe it. I wouldn't believe it. My mother wasn't dead. I refused to believe it. I would know if my mother died. I would feel it, literally. When my father died, I knew before my mother woke me. I had felt it in my chest, like my ribs were breaking or my lungs were collapsing. Like a mental link was cut. Like a chunk of my heart was ripped away. If my mother died I would know.

I pulled my plaid shirt from around my waist and put it back on. I turned to face them and said, "I want to leave."

Mathrel's long creepy smile was stretched across his face. "You can't," he said. My gaze trailed over to him slowing. "The Witches will be looking for you. If they find you, they'll persuade you to join them." I stared in disbelief for a moment. "You're one of them. It's —"

"Are you stupid?" I demanded. "It doesn't change my belief of right and wrong. Why are you all so ignorant?"

He was taken back by the outburst. "You're right." He frowned, peeling himself from his chair. "I understand you're hurt. But," he put his hand on my shoulder. "If you do what you're told, we can help you make your *final decisions*." Those last two words rang in my ears like a gunshot and a feeling of Deja Vu ran up my spine.

I looked down at his fat fingers encasing my shoulder and brushed his hand away. "I don't need any help from you," I said. "Or anyone else like you."

Mathrel's eyes narrowed. Suddenly, three men sprang out from the maze of books. One of them grabbed my arms and the others crossed to Eddie and Angel and stood behind them.

"Take her to room 33," Mathrel said.

"Father," The man holding me said. "Let me do it here, now?"

Father? I turned to look at him. It wasn't some random goon Mathrel sprung on me. No, it was the beautiful boy from my history class. Mathrel's son.

"Excuse me?" Mathrel glared at him so menacing, even I wanted to pull away. "You've done enough. Take her to room 33." The Boy began to pull on me.

"Wait!" Angel yelled, freezing everyone in place. "Mathrel, what are you doing?"

"She's already made up her mind." Eddie interjected.

"If she's not with us, she's against us." Mathrel declared.

"No!" Angel cried. "That's not true! She just found out her mother is dead. Can you blame her if she's a little bit angry?"

"I can blame her," Mathrel said, that smile stuck to his face like glue. "And I will blame her. A witch is a witch, boy. We're just doing —"

"She could help!"

The smile melted off Mathrel's face like liquid. "Angel, learn your place." The guard behind kicked him in the back of the knee and Angel fell. "You're defending a *Witch*. If I didn't know any better, I'd think…" then the smile was back. "But of course, I know better."

I didn't know what he was about to say. But whatever it was put both Angel and Eddie back in check.

He turned his attention back to me. "Room 33."

The boy picked me up. I kicked and thrashed and my attempts at biting proved effective. He let go of me, leaving me second to run. But he recomposed in a second and grabbed my arm, coming toward me with a syringe he had pulled from his pocket. It was filled with orange liquid. Angel's eyes popped out of his head and Eddie lurched forward like he was going to help, but his feet stayed planted. The boy grabbed my face and pushed my head to the left. He shoved the syringe into my neck and squeezed the orange liquid in. Within seconds, my vision blurred, and I was out cold.

Five

When I woke up I was in a box room. Four walls, a floor, and ceiling. There was no apparent entrance, so I wasn't completely sure how I had gotten there.

As I regained my consciousness, I realized there was a girl looming over me. She had big, bright, urgent brown eyes. They weren't big by nature, she was clearly just in a serious panic. Pencils were holding her red hair back, but it was obvious she had been running or something because the edges and the back strands of her hair were falling down around her face. She wore a black sweater and black jeans with black tennis shoes. I was beginning to think black was the official color of the Leadership. The outfit complimented her well; she had a small waist and long legs.

Something clicked over by my hands. I looked over to see that I had been restrained and she was unlocking the fetters. When she had removed the chains around my feet she helped me up. I suppose I was still a little dizzy because I wasn't sure how to use my feet.

I rubbed at my neck but there was no evidence of an entry wound from the syringe. The girl was adjusting herself so that all my weight fell on her. On the other side of a wall I could hear voices, but I wasn't sure which wall. One man greeted Angel and Eddie. But as the other began to question their presence here he was cut off by a loud bang, bang, plop! Then there was another beep and a quarter of the wall to my left slid open to reveal Angel and Eddie. Angel questioned what the girl was doing. She claimed to be trying to save my life. Angel ran over to us and scooped me up. As we began back to the door, Eddie demanded that the girl come with us. She nodded and took a little black pouch from the cart on the far wall. I hadn't seen it earlier. It blended it into the wall. Literally, the cart was almost invisible next to the white paint. Eddie grabbed her wrist and we – or they, supporting me – ran down the corridors. As we reached the stairs that led to the exit we heard screaming from the tunnels.

"Evangeline Welt is missing!"

"Get Mathrel!"

"Where are Angel and Eddie?"

We scrambled through the basement. When we reached the lobby of the apartment complex, people were jumping out of our way. I supposed it looked like I was dying or something because people basically threw themselves into walls trying to make a path. Eddie threw the girl into the passenger's seat and he jumped into the driver's. Angel put me down the back seat and climbed in behind me.

My drowsiness was wearing off, but it was replaced by a lurching pain in my gut. I felt like throwing up but there was nothing to throw up. Plus, my brain was pounding against my skull, granting me a massive migraine. And on top of all of that, my internal organs were working against me. I then realized whatever they had injected me with was meant to kill me.

"Angel," I whispered. "I'm dying."

The girl turned back to look at me. "Stop the car," she said. "The poison is now in her bloodstream." She said. "Soon her lungs will fail and then so will her heart. And all of this will be for nothing. Now is our only chance."

Eddie stared at her but pulled off onto the beach. Angel grabbed me and carried me to a tent was. Eddie kicked out two teenagers who were on their phones. Who goes to the beach to hang out on their phone, anyway? Angel put me down on a beach towel as Eddie was yanking the curtain shut. I was in so much pain; it felt as if every nerve in my body was fighting against one another.

"Ok," the girl said. "This is going to hurt... a lot." She unpacked her medical bag revealing two syringes of pink liquid and a third of orange, similar to the shot that had started all of this. She also pulled out a scalpel, a pair of pliers, a needle and thread, some gloves and gauze.

"One of you will need to help me. The other will have to stand guard so no one comes in when she starts... screaming." Angel and Eddie exchanged a glance and Angel stepped outside. Eddie grit his teeth, blatantly pissed to be stuck with the task. "Okay," the girl said. "Take off your belt." The look on Eddie's face said, *are you serious?* "Just do it," she ordered. Eddie did so. She also proceeded to take off her belt. "Now tie it around her arm." She demonstrated by tying her belt around my right arm, just above my elbow. Eddie did the same to my left.

Then she cleaned the scalpel and the inside of my elbow, where all the major veins lie. She did that to both arms. She looked at Eddie then to me. They both had the same look on their faces. FEAR. What were they afraid of? I was the one who was dying. Then I remembered what she had said about me screaming.

She cut into my skin ever so slightly, just enough to break the surface. I didn't know what she was doing. I thought, *why not just go in?* Then she pulled open the wedge she had just made and revealed three veins. All of them bulging in and out, and covered in bright red, sticky blood. That's why she didn't cut in all the way. She couldn't risk cutting one, I guessed. My hypothesis was correct. "I had to cut it open," she explained to Eddie, "because Witches' veins move when they feel threatened, unless they are exposed. Then they act like normal human veins."

She picked up one of the syringes filled with pink liquid and flicked it. I had a feeling that this was the thing that was going to make me scream. Eddie looked me over quickly then his eyes met mine. I stared back at him, mainly because I couldn't look at the needle. But, I felt every inch of it as it entered my vein. *Is this the worst of it?* I thought. *When am I supposed to start screaming?*

Within the next second a fiery pain lit up the left side of my body. It was unbearable. It was like someone cut me in half, straight down the middle, and on the left side of that split, they started a fire. But the pain was about 10 times worse than that. Then, while that fire heated hell far past its limits, someone else took a rusty nail and slashed through my internal organs.

Somehow, through all of that, I managed not to scream. Yes, it was the worst agony I had ever felt, but I was capable of keeping my excruciating wailing of inhumanity to more of a muffled yell of despair. The girl then sewed up the wound, took off the belt and proceeded to repeat the process on my right arm. Within the next two minutes, both of my arms were sewn up and my whole body was ablaze.

At one point in time I started to hyperventilate, which somehow brought a strange relief to my hands and feet, although the rest of my body endured that burning pain for another ten minutes. When it was all over and done with, my eyes were closed, and my breathing slowed almost to a complete stop. Eddie had moved back to a corner of the tent and sat crossed legged. The girl to my left had both of her hands around mine, petting me softly.

I flung my eyes open to realize it was now after dark. Maybe the medical treatment had taken a tad longer than ten minutes. A light hung from the top of the tent to illuminate the area. I looked down to realize the girl had also wrapped my stitches in bandages.

"Hey," Eddie said.

The girl looked up quickly. She let out a huge sigh and gave me an enormous hug. "Are you alright?" She asked, sitting back.

Angel stuck his head in through the curtain. "Good. You're not dead," he said pulling himself inside.

"Now, what do we do about you?" Eddie asked looking at the girl. We all turned to look at him.

"Who, me?" She asked.

"Yeah. How do we know we can trust you?"

I looked over at the girl who was staring at Eddie open mouthed. "We can trust her." I said.

"How do you know that?" He was still eyeing her. The way he had once eyed me. I sat up, surprisingly easily, staring at the girl. Eddie was growing impatient. "Well…how do you know you can trust her?"

I continued stared at the girl, who seemed suspicious of my looking at her. "What's your name?" I asked.

"Caieta."

I thought back to when my mother said, so long ago, everyone's name had a meaning. It defines who a person is, or the steps they will take in the life, even if they don't know the meaning. A name is like one's personal prophecy. She had given me a book full of names, their meanings, their origins, and their potential. I wondered why I was just remembering it now. Caieta is helpful one, doctor or nurse. "Caieta," I whispered. "The helpful one."

She stared at me. But that's not why I trusted her, though. The mere fact that she had helped me, no questions asked, at the risk of herself. She still had her hands wrapped around my arm to steady me.

"Hi," I said. "I'm Eva."

Her face lit up. "Wow. I have never met someone who studied the names. I thought I was the only person weird enough."

"So, did I," I laughed.

"But you know what's so ironic?"

"What?"

"Your name. It means new life." Funny, I had never thought about my name. Or my mother's. Or Ben's, for that matter. "And it's ironic," she continued. "Because, well, you're deciding if life as we know it continues or will begin anew."

I gasped at her, stunned by her amazing observation. I knew no one, besides my mother, who studied the names in as much detail as I did. Well, it wasn't really a study. It was more of a hobby, really. Either way, I didn't know I wasn't the only one who did it.

"Whoa, whoa, whoa! What's my name mean?" Eddie asked.

I looked up at him. "Eddie doesn't have a meaning." I said. "It's usually short for Edward or Edmund. Edmund means 'protector' or 'guardian,'" I said, slowly.

His jaw dropped but his expression was neutral. I couldn't tell if he was happy or angry with the meaning.

"Well," Angel said. "What does my name mean?" Angel crossed his legs and Eddie sat down in front of me. I guessed we'd be there a while.

"It means 'messenger,'" Caieta said.

He pierced his lips and knit his eyebrows together. "Messenger?"

"Yes. From the Greek," Caieta supplied, helpfully.

He nodded. "...Alright."

Hours went by and it was soon 1 a.m. It was still very dark outside, but instead of being black, the sky was more a deep purple. No one was really tired though and I was beginning to wonder why we were sitting here. Was it for my benefit? And what happened to those teenagers? Wouldn't they want their tent back? Either way, we all just sat and talked about different little things. Stuff from funny topics, like Jim Carrey's best movies, to less interesting things, like better ice cream flavors.

In fact, Eddie and Caieta dwelled on the subject of ice cream. So, as Eddie tried to prove chocolate was superior to strawberry and Caieta tried to prove strawberry was superior to chocolate, Angel and I began our own conversation.

"The other day you said something about Ben being like your brother." Angel said. "Well... What are you going to do the next time you see him?"

I thought about it. I remembered everything I had learned about Ben recently. My stomach began to hurt. He had lied to me. Everything I thought I knew about him was a lie. "I don't know," I said. "I just pray it's nothing stupid."

An awkward silence passed between us before something occurred to Angel. "What does Evangeline mean?"

I thought hard, trying to remember if my mother had ever told me, or if I had glanced at it in my book. "Um... I don't think I ever looked at it. But I think my mother said I was her good news. I think that's what she meant."

"Can I ask who gave you the nickname Eva?"

I thought back some more. "Um… Ben. Why?"

He thought to himself for a moment. "I have a theory. What if Eva is the Council's new life and Evangeline is the Leadership's good news? They just don't know it yet. What if Ben gave you that name trying to rewrite your… destiny, let's say?"

I thought for a moment, completely distraught. Turns out Ben knew my entire life, and I knew nothing. "How naïve of me," I said.

Six

Angel and I watched as Caieta and Eddie continued to try to prove their tastes were better. They bickered for a little bit before Eddie suddenly stopped.

"Did you hear that?" He said. Angel nodded, uneasily.

Eddie signaled for Caieta and me to stay put, as he and Angel jumped out of the tent and circled around it. I watched as their shadows made their way around the tent three times.

Angel stuck his head in and said, "Okay. I guess it was –"

He was cut off by the sound Eddie made when he was hit in the head with a rock. Eddie fell to the ground on his knees. Angel spun around and struck the new third figure in his face. The figure wiped his lip and lunged at Angel and tackling him into the sand. They rolled around, each sinking blows into the other, here and there. My heart was racing, pounding in my ears. Caieta sat next to me, gripping her knees and watching the figures intently. Eddie regained his senses and ran over to the boys. The figures were very different. Angel stuck out the most. He had broad shoulders and short hair. Eddie's hair was long and fell around his face in a mess. The others were also messy but shorter and fell in waves. Eddie pulled the boy off Angel and flung him into the sand. Angel sat up quickly, coughing and holding his throat.

"You're going to hit me from behind? Really, coward?" Eddie yelled. "Come on, face me!"

The boy peeled himself from the ground and laughed, "Gladly."

I recognized that voiced. I had listened to it for years. I grew up with that voice in my ear. I knew that voice. I jumped up just as Eddie ran at him.

I flew out of the tent and yelled. Everything came to a screeching halt. Eddie skidded to a stop in the sand, Angel peered up at me, Caieta stuck her head out of the tent, and the boy turned to stare at me. My suspicious were correct. It was Ben.

He dropped his fists and yelled, "Eva!" He ran over to me and hugged me. I didn't want to hug him. I didn't want him to hug me. I didn't stop him, but I also didn't hug him back.

"Are you alright?" He asked, looking over my face.

I didn't want to talk to him. I didn't want to see him. I didn't want to look at him and watch as he pretended to care. I pushed him away.

He stared at me for a moment. Then he grabbed my arm just below my stitches. "What's this?"

I jerked my arm away from him. "It's what saved my life."

"An *injury* that *saved* your life?" I stared him. "…What's wrong with you?" He turned his head slightly away from me but continued to stare. "Eva," he said. "Let's go."

I clenched my jaw. "No," I said through my teeth.

He pierced his lips and glared at me. "What's wrong with you?"

"Tell me the truth." He gawked at me. "Did you know?" He shook his head, confused. "Don't lie. Don't lie to me. Just tell me you knew. Cause you knew, right? Just tell me." He shook his head again. "Ben!"

"I've been losing my mind hoping you're okay and not dead. I've been driving for days with a headache that has seriously impaired my vision. And now you're accusing me of... what? What did I do?" I could feel the pain in his voice. It stretched out and smacked me in the face.

I wanted to say I sorry and give him a hug. But this time I knew. I knew it was fake, his emotions and his words. So slowly I said, "My mom told you to take me to New York. You didn't. Why? Tell me! I'll believe you, just tell me now!" He stared at me for a while and I started to think, *maybe he's telling the truth. Of course, he is. These people are master liars. Not Ben.*

Then it was gone. Like with a flip of a switch, Ben's face went stone cold. Suddenly he looked like someone else. Like instead he was someone who was ready to punch me in the throat. "Fine," he finally said. "You're right. I lied. I've been lying. I was actually going to use you as a weapon. That's all you are, you know. Now let's go." He grabbed my wrist and started tugging me through the sand.

Angel jumped to his feet, Eddie charged at him, but Caieta beat them both. She jumped up and punched Ben in his face. He stumbled back, and his lips started bleeding again, but he kept hold of my wrist. She grabbed his hand and beat his wrist until he let go of me. Then Ben looked at her, grabbed her forearm and flung her. She spun through the air twice then hit the ground. I wasn't sure if it was magic or brute strength or a combination of both. But I did know I was surprised by how much strength he suddenly had.

Eddie then had a grip on him and forced him to his knees. Angel helped Caieta whose forehead was bleeding. We all stared at Ben. I was on the verge of slamming him in the face. He glared at me and pursed his lips.

"Who are you?" I demanded through gritted teeth.

"Benjamin?" he glared up at me. "Is that who you want me to be? That's not who I am!"

I grabbed by his shirt, shaking Eddie's grip on him. "Who are you, huh? What happened to you?"

"Bradwer. That's who I am. That's who I've been." Pain wrenched through my body. I could feel tears pooling in my eyes. "You were so blindly –"

I pushed him so hard, so full of rage. I didn't realize how angry I was until I saw lightning jump from my palms at him. Ben went crashing into the sand fifteen feet away, his shirt smoking. Eddie studied me before putting his arm around my should and beginning back to the truck.

"Eva!" Ben called after me. "Did you feel that power? It was exciting, huh? To hurt me? It was fun wasn't it, you monster! Come with me, I could show just how much fun you could have." I continued to the truck. "I won't tell you again!"

I stopped then and looked at him over my shoulder. "Is that a threat?"

He didn't reply, so I continued to the truck. After a few minutes, we were cruising through the busy streets of California. Caieta was bleeding profusely through the little gash on her forehead. When it stopped, Eddie did his best to stitch it shut but it was obvious that it would be a scar she would wear for the rest of her life. She told us, we can go Billings, Montana. Her godmother lives out there. She could help us. And more than that she would.

Three hours rolled by and the sky was a slightly darker shade of blue. I hadn't said a word since we had confirmed where we were going. I kept thinking about Benjamin or Bradwer. I wanted to cry. No. I wanted to scream. Actually, I wanted to punch someone. No, I wanted to cry. I was so confused. Only because he was right. It was it exciting. And I took all the pleasure in hurting him. And that terrified me.

After I saw the sign:

Now Entering

Reno, Nevada

I finally decided to push him Benjamin to the very back of my mind. Doing so, I finally realized how tired I was. I looked back at Eddie and Caieta. Eddie's head was flung backwards over the headrest. Somehow, instead of a snore, he made the opposite sound. Something like the sucking of a vacuum. Caieta was curled next to the window. I looked at Angel. He had his hands tightly stuck to the wheel and his eyes were locked on the road. I wondered why I trusted him. He had kidnapped me, but in the same right he had saved my life. knew hardly anything about him. And what I did know gave me no insight to who he is. But I remembered he had told me something about his mom. That she dead. I wondered if it was true.

"Hey Angel," I said. "Can I ask how your mom died?"

He looked at me, then back out at the road. "My dad killed her." My mouth dropped open. That was true. I could tell. "He thought she was working against the Leadership… but I knew better."

"What happened to him?"

"He died in combat with a Warlock." I struggled to find something to say. But found nothing. "Her name was Aaheli," he continued. "His was… August."

"Were you afraid of him?" Was what I finally thought to say.

He looked at me. "Absolutely." He looked back out at the road.

"…So, you mean to tell me your entire family's first and last name start with A?" I said in an effort to lighten the mood. Why did I even bring up the subject?

He laughed. "Yeah." His smile faded. "I guess that explains my father's insanity, huh?"

I watched him, but he continued to stare at the road. "If you saw your father again, what would you say?"

"…I don't know. I don't think I want to see him again."

Silence filled the air and although I was very tired, I didn't want to sleep. Not because I was afraid to dream or anything like that. I just simply didn't desire to. Although I had almost died, it was my mind that was drained. I decided to lie back anyway. As I did, I realized something.

"Angel." I said. "What's going to keep Ben- Bradwer from following us?"

"I immobilized him with the gas."

"When?"

"That brief moment when you were kicking the car wheels, demanding that God tell you why he was treating you like this." I laughed awkwardly. "We have at least 21 more hours before he wakes up and three more after that before he can retrace your steps."

On that note, I decided to sleep. Six hours went by and I woke to morning. It was around 10:30 a.m., and a conversation had commenced between Eddie and Angel.

Eddie leaned forward on the back of my seat and said, "Okay. She saved her life. But she means helpful one. Who is she helpful to, exactly?"

"... I don't know, but if she was working against us, why didn't she just let Evangeline die?" Angel shook his head. "Or help Benjamin escape with her?"

"I don't know, Angel. But I do know that you're being an idiot. We're enemies of the Leadership now! Hunters, along with Witches and Warlocks, are trying to kill us! You'd better know what you're doing. She'd better be worth it." I suddenly realized he was talking about me now.

"You know that she is!"

"I know this girl could change everything."

I sat up then. I pretended my eyes were still heavy with sleep and looked at Angel. "Where are we?"

"Elko, Nevada." Eddie said leaning back. "Hey Angel. We should pull off when we get into Twin Falls." Angel nodded, smiling.

I looked at Eddie then back at Angel. Ten seconds after Eddie put his feet on my armrest he put them down, leaned forward, and turned on the radio. From the stereo, out blared the loud blast of a bass guitar. This woke Caieta. The surprise, though, made her punch Eddie in the throat as he turned to look at her.

"Oh, my gracious!" She yelled. "I am so sorry!"

"What was that?" Eddie coughed. "You're a nurse!"

Caieta froze and looked at him like she might punch him again. "Every Hunter learns a variety of fighting skills."

"Not girls!"

"Yes, they do."

"They don't *have* to."

"I'm huntress, I felt almost obligated to." She stopped for a moment. "Even your sister did." Eddie froze. "Loyce Markus learned an abundance of fighting skills."

"How did you know Loyce was my sister? How did you know I *had* a sister?"

She looked away from him out of the window. "If you don't remember, you don't need to know."

Seven

An awkward moment passed, and I decided someone had to break the tension. Or really, it just lingered on.

Finally, after half an hour of annoying songs and silence between the four of us, Black & White came on. They were a musical duo made of sisters, or half-sisters. They've been singing since they were 12 after they found out they were related. Just recently they were found dead on an accident. The song was "Big Fat Liar." Just the base dropped, and Eddie and Angel started screaming and singing along.

I couldn't understand most of what they were saying. It was much louder than words could be interpreted. That's heavy metal rock, I guess. But it and the boys' singing along lightened the mood, that's for sure. Two hours later, we were pulling off on an exit into Twin Falls, Idaho. Caieta questioned why we were stopping and Eddie greeted her with the most dangerous smile. He questioned how it is that she'd never been to Ricky's Rodeo. According to him, they served the best burgers in the USA.

"How long until we get there?" Caieta asked, clearly sold on the idea.

"We're here!" Eddie announced, nearly throwing himself out of the truck.

I turned to look out my window and all I saw was a dirt lot that held a shack house with a sign reading, 'Ricky's Rookie Rodeo.' It didn't seem like much to me. Especially since we were in the middle of nowhere. I would've thought we were in the wrong place had it not been for the sign. However, I couldn't be sure if we were even in Twin Falls.

We all climbed out and made our way toward the oversized shed. More cars lined the entrance, but it was still a surprise when we saw that the place was packed. It was also a surprise when the interior of the restaurant wasn't ugly. It was very Western. Leather booths, game heads on the wall, a bar, waitresses dressed up as milk maids, waiters as cowboys, and customers everywhere.

Across the room we caught someone's attention. He had long dark grey beard and a thick mustache to match. I noticed he too wore a cowboy's uniform as he made his way towards us. As he got closer I saw he resembled someone. He came over to greet us, hugging Eddie and Angel. Angel turned to me and Caieta to introduced us. Caieta smiled, shaking his hand. I stared at him blankly. When he saw me, he looked just as shocked as I did and stepped back a bit.

After regaining his stability, he cleared his throat and introduced himself. I stopped staring at him and shook his hand. I had to apologize for that as my surprise was blatant on my face. I let him know that he very much like I used to know.

He stared at me for a moment and smiled weakly. He looked back at Eddie and put his hand on Angel's shoulder. He led us to a booth with less of a crowd. We got seated and Ricky said he'd be back with menus.

As soon as he left Caieta turned to me, ready to question me on what just happened. "Do you know him?"

"Nope, I said."

"Does he know you?" Eddie asked.

"Nope."

"Something happened back there." Angel said.

"Well, he looked like my dad. I mean like, they could be twins."

"So, we found your papa's doppelganger." Eddie said sarcastically, shrugging. "Amazing!"

"Her father is dead." Angel said. "If that was her father's doppelganger he'd be dead too." He looks up at me. "It's just how fate works."

"So..." Caieta said. "Who is he then?" She said it like a case just opened in a Sherlock Holmes book.

"It doesn't matter right now," I said.

"She's right," Angel agreed. "We just need to worry about getting to Caieta's godmother's. Then we're going to figure out what to do from there."

"Well," I said. "That would be easier if I knew the whole prophecy."

"I told you the whole prophecy."

"No, you and Benjamin both told me just the end of it. The fight to the death part. I need to know the whole thing."

"The whole thing!" Eddie exclaimed. "There's not much more to it."

89

"Okay. Well we need to pick apart what little there is to know until we find something. Just enough to keep us prepared for the next week or two."

Ricky returned with the menus. As soon as he left, Eddie finish his sentence. "Well, your birthday is in eleven days. After that we might not even see each other again."

"You see," Angel said. "We're still unsure if the battle lasts her whole seventeenth year or just as long as her birthday."

"What if it lasts the entire year?"

Ricky was back and asked what we would like to order. Without hesitation Eddie ordered four Rookie Burgers. We spent the time waiting for burgers and debating if yearlong war would really have meant anything significant to them. I'd be fighting the war either way. Against this mysterious Chosen One from the Leadership. Funny that none of them knew who she was. Even so, Angel had somehow convinced himself that he had some sort of duty to me, therefore either way he had to be at my side. Caieta figured she'd tag along just in case someone needed some stitches and Eddie was up for any kind of fight.

Then Ricky brought out our burgers with the assistance of a 40 to 45-year-old woman with sea blue hair and mocha colored skin. Ricky also put down four glasses of root beer and some hot sauce. I watched as Angel and Eddie's faces lit up and their mouths started watering. I guess they hadn't had these burgers in a while. The burger did look delicious. It had a grilled patty under fresh lettuce, thick tomato slices, a juicy beef patty, grilled onions, baked sauerkraut, mustard, and homemade mayonnaise and topped off with a sesame seed bun, alongside a potato waffle and ketchup. Looking at it made my mouth water as well.

I looked over at Caieta. It seemed to be having the same effect on her. Eddie and Angel were already stuffing their faces full of the dish. I quickly began to do the same. As we ate, we continued to talk about the random pieces of this... mission. But every time Ricky walked by, I lost focus. I explained to them just how much this guy looked like my dad. All the way down to the scar in his right eyebrow. Just as I said that, I realized that Ricky carried the scar in his left eyebrow.

"So…what?" Eddie questioned. "You think your father is back from the dead?"

"No!" I said quickly. "He just… I don't know, forget it." I pulled a fake smile and said, "It's just weird."

We finished eating and we paid our bill. As we were leaving, Eddie told the woman at the front desk to tell Ricky how much we loved the burgers and they'd see him again next time. But, before we walked out Ricky raced over to us.

"Hello!" He said. "Are you honestly going to leave without saying goodbye?"

"It was good seeing you, Ricky." Angel said.

"Yeah," Eddie said. "And your burgers."

He laughed and turned to Caieta and I. "Nice to meet you Caieta." He shook her hand. "And you too, Evangeline." He stared at me a moment before shaking mine. I stared back studying him. "By the way, your eyes are beautiful."

Caieta cut into the strange goodbye. "Wait a second, how did you know her name? They introduced her as Eva."

He continued to stare. "Just a guess. Looked like it might be in her blood."

"My blood? Yeah, well, it was nice to meet you too… Richard." The name Ricky is usually an abbreviation of Richard or Ricardo. I wasn't sure, but I decided to take a guess.

He tilted his head slightly and smiled saying, "touché."

Even with the joke still up in the air, it was awkward and Caieta was glaring at Richard vigorously. Eddie clapped his hands ripping through the tension. He ushered us out of the door and into the car. Caieta and I were seated in the back. Then he glares and asks me again how I know Rickie. But I didn't know him. I didn't think so. He just looked like my dad. How so identically? I didn't know. And no. He didn't come back from the dead. He wasn't Jesus.

Then we began on our journey. But it truly wasn't a journey to remember. It was long and boring, and we couldn't find a radio station other than 80's blues. I was horribly bored. Truly, truly, horribly bored.

But eight hours later we were in Billings, Montana searching for Caieta's godmother's house. She lived in something of an old neighborhood. The streets were wet, and the air was thick. And every time I looked out my window I felt the urge to whistle. I'm not sure why.

The woman's house was older than Moses. It had three old, large, and cracked wooden steps that led to the wooden porch. The whole foundation all on its own, *without* the weight of a house, was unstable. The front door was a light crimson color. As we made our way up, Caieta pulled a key from under the mat. Upon entering the house, she pushed a blue button on the wall next to the door.

The inside of the house was old-fashioned and smelled like old-person perfume and oatmeal. The furniture was something you would find in a 1950s black and white movie. The coffee table and the nightstands surrounding the couch were white wood with polished wooden stands. The couch and the two armchairs were crème with buttons making a pattern down the middle. Then there was a piano at the edge of the room facing the center. Hanging all along the walls were different instruments. Trumpets, guitars, flutes, clarinets. I could see all of that through the kitchen door where I stood. Just to my right was an island with a grey top. To my far left were the stove, oven, and cabinets. Above me were knives. Hanging, from what used to be a chandelier, with hooks where the knives were attached. It hung just above my head. We hurried into the living room.

Once inside, we saw a staircase behind the couch. Down those stairs stepped an elderly woman. Her pinky, blood-flushed skin matched Caieta's, though her hair was grey and thinning. She was wrapped in scarves in a variety of colors. She had an orange and green scarf tied around her waist, a blue and red one tight around her right arm, and a yellow one tied around her body and left arm. She wore brown slippers too big even for a giant.

She came running down the stairs and hugged her. "Oh baby, how did you get so big? Oh, it's been so long. I haven't seen you in ages. You've gotten to be so much taller." Caieta attempted to cut in. "And you're so pretty." Caieta attempted again. "Your hair has grown out." She tried again. "Oh, and you have –"

"Bibi!" Caieta yelled grabbing her face in her hands.

"Is there something you want to say? Oh girl, did you forget I was deaf?" The woman went to sit in the armchair. When she was seated she said, "Oh you got friends. My, it's been years since you bought a friend. Introduce me." Caieta introduced us all one by one. She repeated after Caieta as she said our names, mocking Eddie a little. "Oh, it's good to meet you Evangeline, Angel, and Denny."

"Eddie," he over enunciated.

"Teddy? Freddy?"

"Eddie."

"Oh! Edmund. Haven't we met before?" Eddie just kind of looked at her. "When you were seven or eight?"

"Well, I wouldn't be able to remember anyway."

"Bibi we're here because –" Caieta began.

"Who wants tea?" Bibi cut in. Caieta rolled her eyes. "I'll take that as everyone."

One cup of tea later, we were all sitting on the couch with the exclusion of Bibi who was sitting in the armchair on the other side of the coffee table. Caieta tried to communicate once more. "Okay, Bibi, here's the thing. We are in a bit of... trouble and your land is untraceable. Literally it's not even on the map. So, could we...Stay here...For a little while? Just until we've figured out what to do."

"How about I tell you what to do and you leave?"

"No Bibi, it's not that kind of trouble. It's complicated and I don't think you'd understand. We're in a mess and –"

"You need to leave."

"No, you're not hearing me."

"I'm hearing you loud and clear. As loud and as clear as a deaf woman can. Your friend, Eva, is a Witch, her best friend, Ben, is a traitor, and on top of that you're being hunted by both the Leadership and the Council." Caieta stared at her for a moment. "Honey, I'm deaf. Not dumb."

"How did you know exactly what was going on?" Eddie asked.

"Because I heard it." She said as if it were obvious. We all stared at her a moment.

The woman pierced her lips. "Oh, I was hoping to never have to tell you, because the more people that know, more identifiable I am." Caieta stared at her for a moment confused. "You see… I am a Sense."

"What?" We all asked in unison.

"One of the five."

"Like sight, sound, touch?" I asked.

She nodded.

"But, wait how – so – that means –" Caieta fumbled.

"Okay. A long, *long,* time ago the five senses were not just something you learned about in school. They were the blind, the deaf, the mutilated. But only one for each of these group will be chosen to represent their kind the only way they could. By doing everything they couldn't. The blind will see everything, well everything of importance. The deaf would hear, the mute would speak. And so on. And not the way they were meant to be used.

"For instance, I am deaf. So, if a car were to come a hurtling down the street toward a baby, instead of hearing the crying of a mother for her dead child after the fact. I would hear the ending of that child's life before the driver even got in the car. But only if there was something that I could do about it. So, this is what I'm going to tell you. Go to Evangeline's home. Tell her mother –"

"Ma'am," Angel cut in. "Evangeline's mother is... dead."

"No, she's not," she said nonchalantly. I know you think you saw her. But hear her. I hear her heartbeat and the blood pumping through her veins. It's kind of creepy."

"Sorry," Eddie said. "I don't mean to be rude but...we did see her!"

"And I hear her! I hear her worried sick about her daughter. I hear her trying to sleep at night but failing. I hear her chewing her nails instead of eating."

I knew she wasn't dead. I thought. Now, I didn't want to say I didn't believe, but an old woman thinking she has magical abilities is no surprise in the loony section. But her knowing our situation, Eddie's real name, and my mom's nervous habits only made me believe her more.

She leaned forward and said, "Edmund, take a leap of faith. Go to Evangeline's home and tell her mother everything you've learned." And with that Bibi stood up and ushered us into the kitchen. Then she turned to Caieta and she said, "There's a roast in the fridge for you." She laughed. "Travel safely."

"Ms. Bibi?" Eddie said as she was about to leave the room. She turned, and a smile stretched across her face. "I know you hear everything, but I have the slightest feeling that you're knowing my full name has nothing to do with that. Can I ask you how you know me?"

The smile didn't fade as she walked back and rubbed his cheek. "If you don't remember," she said. "Then you don't need to know."

Eight

In the following hour, we had all climbed back into Eddie's truck. But just before we left, Bibi ran out and whispered to me, "You need to know, great power brings even greater sadness." She left, and we began on our way. I wondered if she was trying to be cryptic. If she was, it was working.

It was going to be a 24-hour drive before we got back to my mother. But I was so ready to see her. After all that had happened, I was fine with the painful ride.

We spent seven hours going over different details of the prophecy. I knew the whole thing with my eyes glowing brighter than the hottest sun when I turned 17. Well, not in detail like that but I knew I was meant to be born with blue eyes. And I was. But there was something missing.

At about 4am I sat back to go to sleep. I got comfortable, but it took me a while to fall asleep, even with the exhaustion I was feeling.

Lately I was always feeling exhausted. But when I did fall asleep, I had the worst dream. Or at least I hoped it was a dream.

We ran across the street, through a few parking lots, and then collapsed in the middle of the park in a beautiful neighborhood. The grass was a deep green and smelled like it was freshly mowed. There was a blue and yellow colored jungle gym and swing set to the right of us. To the left was a basketball court and baseball field.

Angel fell first and fell hard. The entire front side of his shirt was stained with blood. Caieta lifted his shirt to reveal a gash that ran just below his belly button to right hip. "Holy..." Eddie whispered.

"What?" Angel asked. "How bad is it?"

"You knew?" I demanded. "Why didn't you say anything?"

"It wasn't important."

"It wasn't import– Yes it was!"

"It didn't cut anything vital," Caieta said examining him. "But if we can't stop the bleeding soon, he'll die anyway."

"Well... do something!" Eddie yelled.

"With what? I have nothing with me!"

Angel was beginning to lose consciousness. "No, no, no. Stay awake. You have you stay awake." I begged. *But his eyes got smaller and smaller until they eventually closed.*

Then I woke with a scream.

"Whoa!" Eddie said. "It's just me." My door was open, and he was leaning over me, smiling. I hadn't realized it at the time, but I loved his smile.

"What is wrong with you guys?" I yelled.

"Look, I'm sorry." He raised his hands and stepped back. "I just thought you might be hungry."

"No that's not what I meant." I said, rubbing my hands over my face.

He glared at me confused. "Then what?" He stepped closer.

"I just don't get you and Angel. It's like you have to act so strong and brave but you're just human." He shook his head, stepping closer. "Yeah, yeah. I know you're Hunters with divine abilities to kill Witches but you're just human. You get cut, you bleed, and then you die. So, do I. That's how it works." He stared me a moment with his lips pierced. "Just," I rubbed my eyes. "Just promise me, you won't try to be a hero." He nodded.

I rolled my eyes and laughed. Then I realized just how close he was to me. He still glared at me as he looked over my face. I could hear the sound of his breathing, he was so close. I could the details in his eyes, the different shades of brown and the flakes of green. They were like marbles. He licked his lips, pulling my attention.

Then suddenly he stepped back. "We're in Minneapolis. Minnesota," he said, smirking. "We stopped for breakfast."

He and went back to Caieta and Angel, who were eating burritos. I laughed at myself and followed him. We had stopped at a rest stop. One of the few that served food. They sat at a small green, wooden picnic table in the grass. They were even having a civil conversation, which I didn't think was possible. We were all happy and laughing, all together as friends. For a moment in time, nothing was wrong. For a single second in our timeline, there was nothing to tangle or pull it. We were just there, and that was okay.

After breakfast we finished the rest of our trip. Not stopping unless to eat or for the one-time Eddie had to use the restroom. We arrived at my mother's house just before 9 o'clock. The tan paint on the house looked grey in the night. The lights in the living room glowed through the windows. We all looked at each other, not sure what to do. I told them I'd go first, and everyone nodded at me. I climbed out of Eddie's truck. Slowly, I made my way to the front door. My heart raced faster with every step I took. I was so terrified that I might find the truth wasn't what I thought it was for the one hundred and first time that week.

I pulled my key from beneath the ceramic frog on the porch and unlocked the door. I pushed it open and stepped through with my eyes closed. I opened them to find a skillet swinging toward my face.

I screeched as I narrowly avoided falling on the floor while blood ran down my face. I looked up to find my mother holding a frying pan in batting position. Her hair was still slightly grey and ancient writing sill invaded her skin. She wore blue jeans and a grey t-shirt. Looked up, I jumped to hug her. She dropped the pan behind her and hugged me back. I probably hugged her tight enough to pop her eyes out of her head.

Then I pulled back and gawked at her. "You hit me in the face with a frying pan."

"Well," she knit her eyebrows. "I wanted to injure the person in the case it was an intruder. But didn't want to *really* hurt them in the case it was you."

"Mom," I gaped. "You hit me in the *face* with a *frying pan*."

"Well, I think it's better to burst your cheek open instead of your chest."

"But what if it wasn't me?"

"Then I would keep hitting them," she said confused that I didn't know that. "Or drop it and blown their chest open."

Yep, that was my crazy, candid mother. Well and alive. I missed her.

"But...I was told that you were dead. That you were seen dead."

"Well," she shrugged. "Technically, I was. I stopped my heart for ten minutes. Simple magic trick."

"Oh, as long as it was simple." She laughed and hugged me again. "Oh! There are some people I want you to meet." I ran out to the car and knocked on Angel's window. After seeing my smile, they followed me into the living room. I turned to them and said, "She's made friends with a frying pan so be careful."

"Is that what happened to your face?" Eddie questioned.

I led them into the kitchen. My mother was making sandwiches. But as soon as she turned and saw Angel and Eddie she dropped the bread to the ground and plucked the frying pan from the sink. She then proceeded to hit Eddie in the face, Angel in the stomach, then Eddie again, in the face.

I struggled to with her to drop the pan. But she screamed, telling that these were the boys that showed up after Tannin's men. Caieta seemed baffled by that discovery.

"Tannin's men were here?"

"Yes!" My mom spun to face her. "They were here looking for Evangeline! Who are *you*?"

"I'm Caieta. Why would they come if Ben was taking her?"

"What are you talking about? After they left these two appeared. You need to stay away from my daughter!" She charged at Angel and Eddie and they turned ran into the living room.

I tugged on her arm a final time, she froze and turned to look at me, confused. I sat her down and explained everything that had happened in the last four days as Caieta stitched up my cheek and Eddie's left eyebrow and chin. I started with the morning in Kansas, leaving out the parts when Eddie pulled me out of the car and Angel on the beach. I stopped with my uneasiness to come inside and see her.

She sat quietly for a moment looking at us, studying. Then she got up and hugged Angel. Then crossed to Eddie and Caieta and hugged them too. She thanked them for helping me and turned back to hug me. She seemed unusually emotional. With good reason of course, she just found her daughter was more dangerous then she realized and aided only by three strangers. I understood. I had just never seen that from her before.

Eddie cleared his throat and said, "You're welcome. But we don't know what to do next. We were kind of hoping we could stay here and wait thing through."

Tears welled up in my mother's eyes. She pulled back from me and smiled. "No, you need to go to New York. After you father died, I sent you to your grandmother's. Do you remember that?" I nodded. It was the only summer I didn't spend with Ben. "During that time, I went on a series of trips. I went to New York and met a woman with screaming red hair." She paused looking off. "There are things that she knew, that I can't explain how she knew them. She'll know how to help you and what you should do next. She also told me to go Quebec. But I didn't. Go there after meeting with her."

"Okay. We'll go tomorrow –" I tried.

"Go now." I nodded quickly. "Evangeline," she stared at me intensely. "Go now."

I stared back at her. "Is there something you're not telling me?" I questioned.

She whispered something I could hardly hear. She whispered again but I still couldn't hear her. Again, she whispered but I couldn't hear her.

She swallowed hard. "I can't leave Zanesville." I stared for a moment. "I was cursed. I don't know why or who did it. But after I returned from New York, these markings showed up on my arms. They basically say I can't leave Zanesville without turning into a pile of ash. That's why I never went to Quebec."

My heart ran wild in my chest and my brain pounded against my skull. My hands were shaking, and I could feel my tongue swelling in my mouth. I blinked hard and managed, "I can fix this. I can figure out –"

"Evangeline," she said softly. "I love you. You're the sweetest girl to walk to face of this earth. But if you don't leave this house, I swear to you, you'll be a dead girl." I shook my head. "I can't help you with this!" She yelled. "This is your prophecy! You need to go and figure out how to beat this! I will be of no use to you." I shook my head. "You can go. And you will." She looked over at Eddie and some strange understanding passed between them. She had done the same thing with Ben. It made me wonder if it was magic.

Either way, Eddie crossed over to me, wrapped his arms around my waist and carried me out to the car, ignoring my screams of protest. Angel and Caieta followed behind and helped stuff me into the car. I promised if one more person picked me up, I would be breaking someone's ribs. Angel jumped into the driver's seat and Caieta ran around to the passenger's.

"I hate you all," I screamed when Angel floored the gas.

"No, you don't," Eddie said.

I shook with rage and anxiety. Suddenly breathless, I breathe and think.

"Your mom was right," Caieta said. "She can't help you with this."

I glared back up at her and she spun around to face forward. "Evangeline," Eddie said. He was staring at me intensely. Not moving, not blinking, just staring. It made me nervous. I felt like he was seeing something I didn't want him to see. Like he was peeling away layer after layer of the thick wall I was failing to keep up. He had broken it away and was staring at the terrifying truth behind it.

"She's going to be fine," Angel said. "I know it."

He was calm. So steady. I stared at him through the rearview mirror. The streetlights occasionally broke through the windows, illuminating his blond hair and green eyes. I believed he did know, and that was what I needed.

"I suppose," I said. "Either way, I just went home but I'm still wearing these shorts." I sighed and threw my head back over the headrest and went to sleep.

I awoke to an epic scream. Only I realized then that I wasn't awake. I was in a premonition.

I was in the throne room. It was destroyed. One of the four pillars holding up the ceiling had collapsed. The thrones at the top of the stairs were reduced to rubble. The floor was stained with blood and my dress, well, it wasn't really a dress anymore.

I was charging someone. Ben. I was charging Ben. My right hand was clenched around a broken wooden pole. Ben braced himself for impact. He was crouched down, with his knees bent and his arms out. He expected me to tackle him or lunge. So, I jumped up over his head. He was surprised but he had quick reflexes. He ripped a spear from the hands of the guard standing behind him. He raised it up over his head and slammed it into mine.

Then I woke, with a jolt.

Angel looked at me from the scene he was watching through the window. Eddie and Caieta were on the side of the road, fighting, yelling. He looked back saying, "we're in New York. But we're lost. Eddie blamed Caieta, Caieta blamed Eddie. Then he insulted her...roughly. He demanded to know whatever it was she was hiding from him. She got out of the car saying she'd rather be lost alone than be treated like a criminal. He got out telling her not to be stupid. And now they're fighting over who's going to drive." He looked back at me and shrugged.

I leaned over him and looked out the window. The street was lined with huge old building after huge old building. The ground was cluttered with discarded papers and the street was crowded with cars. I got out, walked around to the driver's seat and got in. I locked the door, honked, and waved them over. Angel laughed to himself behind me. Stunned, both Eddie and Caieta walked slowly over to the truck and climbed in. Eddie in the back and Caieta beside me.

"Where are we going?" Angel asked.

"What is the most popular place in New York?"

"Times Square." Eddie said.

"That's where we're going, my friend."

"It's also the most crowded." Caieta said.

"More people, more answers. In a crowd there's more likely of a chance to find someone who knows something."

"Or nothing," Eddie said bitterly.

We drove through the streets for an hour. Then we decided to park the truck and walk. After all, people walked everywhere in New York, right? Although fifteen minutes later we called a cab. 50 minutes after that we were walking through Times Square. Skyscraper after skyscraper, hanging posters and billboards, flashing lights and glowing signs filled the square. It was still kind of early, maybe 9:30, but it was still so crowded, far beyond comprehension. Far more crowded than every street I've been on combined. Okay…maybe not that crowded. But there were a lot of people. I was pushed and shoved like a soccer ball at a kids' game.

Suddenly, a man carrying two suitcases shoved me aside. I would've fallen on my face if Eddie wasn't so quick on his feet. He grabbed my arm and pulled me back.

I smiled awkwardly at him. He shrugged and looked around. "So, we're here. Now what?"

I looked around me. Nearly spinning as I turned to survey my surroundings. I kept looking for something, anything that was any kind of clue. A sign that had misspelling. A poster with red eyes. Anything. The more I searched, the more I felt like someone was watching me. I stopped looking at the signs and started searching through the people. I rushed through the crowd, looking over the people beside me and those who weren't so close. The farther I went the stronger the sensation got. Then I broke through the crowd, nearly falling into the street. I felt it. Directly in front of me someone was staring. I scanned the crowd of hustling people desperately.

Then I stopped. A woman, dressed in scarves, was standing in the middle of the crowd. She made people walk around her as she stared at me. Her skin was as white as snow, like a walking corpse. Her lips were painted the deep red of blood. But worst of all, her eyes were hollow. No pupil, or color at all, resided in her eyes.

She was blind.

Nine

We stared for a moment, and then she turned and ran. Instantly, I jumped into traffic and raced after her, ignoring the screaming and honking of people and cars around me. I was on a mission. She would've disappeared into the crowd of dark suits if it weren't for the loud colors she was wearing. I chased her three blocks, closing in on her slowly, when suddenly she disappeared into a small door on the side of a building.

It was an old door, so swollen and cracked, it no longer fit perfectly into the whole cut for it. I stood there for two minutes before Angel, Eddie, and Caieta ran up behind me, huffing and puffing.

"Thanks for the warning!" Eddie huffed.

"She disappeared behind that door." I said. "The blind woman." I said.

"You chased a blind woman down the street?" Eddie questioned.

"But she saw me."

When I first stepped in, I saw white. I thought my vision was failing me. Then I realized everything was white. It was a small house, painted completely snow white. The furniture in the living room was a white as well. The couch, the armchairs surrounding it, the marble coffee table, the lampshade, and the candles that stood like torches, all white and held up by ivory wooden legs. It was beautiful. Like winter had run through headfirst and left a gorgeous room in its wake.

The woman sat on the floor in front of the coffee table facing the couch, staring at the marble. She had changed. She was wearing a plain, white nightgown and her hair was down. It was a bright fiery orange color that fell across her chest and into her a lap. She stared at the table, not seeing a thing.

It was sad, how beautiful her home was and she unable to see it. I thought back to Bibi. How her house was decorated with musical instruments that she couldn't hear. The woman sitting in front me was pretty, too. She was probably in her early 30's. Her nose was small and round. Her eyes were vacant, like whatever color had been there was sucked away, leaving only a pale grey color behind. But they were big and surrounded by long orange eyelashes. Her lips were full and pink, and her cheeks high. She reminded me of a doll.

She probably didn't even know it.

I wondered if this woman once had sight or if Bibi could once hear. I thought back to what Bibi said. "Great power brings even greater sadness."

I opened my mouth to speak but she raised her hand and gestured toward the couch. We crowded into her living room and divided ourselves between the armchair and the couch. I sat directly in front of her and she stared blankly at me.

"I know who you are," she said. "I know why you're here. After all, I did see you coming." She smiled faintly, then returned to her frown. "But I can't tell you." Her eyes moved frantically around the coffee table.

"Why are we here if you can't tell us anything?" Eddie demanded.

"Because, Edmund, if you give a man the tuna he'll never learn to fish."

"Are you talking in riddles?" I could see Eddie growing more and more irritated at this woman's vagueness.

She shook her head. "You're an imbecile." He glared at her and could see a match being light in his eyes, but he didn't say anything.

"Miss...?" I asked.

"You may call me Ms. Jenova."

"Ms. Jenova, what can't you tell me?" She leaned back slowly staring at the coffee table. "Why can't you tell me?"

"Because if you give a man the tuna he'll never learner to fish on his own. But I can teach you how." Then, she blinked three times. "Tonight, a party for two fallen stars will dance in the streets." Then, she blinked three more times.

"You're sending us to a party?" Eddie questioned.

"You stupid boy!" She barked. "There are so many other things going on you just don't understand! Haven't you learned not to mess with forces greater than your own?" Then a smile ripped across her face. "Oh, wait. You have, and you don't even remember it."

"What is that supposed to mean?" He demanded.

She threw her head back and laughed, a loud creepy cackle. She dropped her head, her hair falling around her face like she was possessed. "If you don't remember, you don't need to know."

It was quiet and awkward for a moment. She stared back at the coffee table. "The festivities began at eight o'clock. Times Square. Now," She glanced at Eddie. "Get out."

We all stood and began filing from her home. I waited a moment and stared as she ran her hands over the marble coffee table. When everyone had left before me, she looked up at me.

"Evangeline," she said. Her face longing and sad. Bibi hadn't been sad. Or maybe she was and just good at hiding it. "I can't tell you what to do. You must decide for yourself. But I send you this party tonight because there you will learn something about your companions. With the knowledge you must decide whether you trust them and hold fast to that decision. Wavering may have… world shattering consequences" Then, I saw it, just behind her head, burnt into the white wall in black:

Great power brings even greater sadness.

I gasped looked back at Jenova. My suspicions were confirmed. She wasn't always blind. That's where the sadness came from.

Then I turned and raced from the house. I slammed the door shut to find myself amid an argument.

"Tell me!" Eddie demanded. "I need to know!"

"Eddie," Angel said. "Maybe you don't."

"Yes, I do!"

I grew intensely angry with him in that moment. "No, you don't Eddie!" I pushed him. "What you *need* to do is get over yourself!"

"Excuse me?"

"What the hell was that back there? We went to magical being, who has the power to see the future, to ask for help and guidance and you have the nerve to say anything other than yes ma'am?" He rolled his eyes, so I pushed him again. "I get it! You'd rather kill me because I'm an evil cold-blooded Witch! So why don't you just leave?"

Eddie stepped at me and grabbed my arms. He stared at me for a minute, glaring. "If I wanted to kill you, I wouldn't be in fucking New York. I assure you, if I wanted you dead, you would be dead." Then he let me go. "But I was wrong. About Witches. And about you. I don't want to kill you."

Eddie and I stared at each other for a moment before we came down from our rages. Then Caieta cut the silence. "So, I'm going take this as a good time to tell you that I'm also a Witch."

"What?" Eddie barked.

Caieta began a story. Back in The Council of Witches Caieta's father realized Tannin's plans for the world's destruction and wanted nothing to do with it. He was content with his current life and the way the world was working. So, he packed up his wife, who was also a Witch, and his daughter, Caieta, and retreated into the Leadership. He was sure they would be safe, that they would lead normal lives in the Leadership. Especially after he stripped Caieta of her magic. But after his death, her powers were gone all together. She was a witch without magic. Effectively, she was human.

But that didn't matter at that moment. We have a party we needed to get ready for. We brainstormed on what kind of party it could be like and how we should dress. We thought it may be a casual party for we would be dancing in the street. But then it may be formal for it was a party for stars. But isn't overdressing always better than underdressing? We agreed and began our next trek through the city. We walked from street to street debating on what the fallen star party could be or mean. But first, we had to figure out where we'd find the outfits.

Finally, we reached a store we thought was perfect for the occasion. Caieta and I broke off from the boys and tried on dresses while they tried on suits. About an hour later we met back up with four outfits worth $254 in total. I was glad they still had the credit card from the Leadership.

Right across the street we saw a really crappy hotel, but we just needed somewhere to change, and a gas station was completely out of the question. We checked into two rooms. One for Caieta and me, and one for the boys. We agreed that at 7 o'clock we would meet back up. Fine by me. That gave me plenty of time to decide how I was going to do my hair and makeup. Six hours to get completely ready.

Caieta pulled her hair up in a bun with little wisps left down, free to do as they wished. She wore a deep shade of purple lipstick to compliment her dress. It was black silk with thick tangled straps that made a web-like design down her back. The dark dress was a gorgeous contrast to her fair skin. She looked like a million bucks. I did my hair in braid that fell down my back.

I had bright red lipstick to go with my blood red dress. The dress was also cut deeper in the front, a long thin slit down to my stomach. All the revealed skin was covered by a red lace that came up over my neck. We both painted our nails black to save time. It was truly needed considering how much time we spent on everything else.

We met back up with the boys a little after seven. We had to be sure our nails dried. The boys didn't look too bad either. Eddie wore a baby blue button up shirt and a bow tie under his black suit. He also applied plenty of product to his hair, so his thick locks stayed slicked back. Angel wore a white button up shirt and a tie as well as a black suit. They looked like proper gentlemen. Like sponsors, or businessmen here to save the world from poverty, and a bunch of other things they would say to make themselves look good.

Eddie and Caieta took the lead downstairs. Angel and I hung back, standing in the hallway for minute. He handed me the thorn necklace from one of my earlier premonitions. The one that looked too outrageously dangerous to hang around one's neck. He told me he wanted me to wear it. I took it, examining the jewelry carefully before draping it over my chest. He also told me that it was his mother's and he thought it would look better on me than him.

When we were all downstairs we saw that Eddie had found his truck. We rode around in circles for a while, feeling completely lost. But strangely, we weren't. Eddie was driving, Caieta sat up front, and Angel sat in the back with me.

We arrived and found we were dressed perfectly for the occasion. Everyone was in formal attire. Button up shirts and ties and long gowns. We blended in easily. But we kind of wandered around, wondering if it had started already. Angel looked down at his watch to find it was ten before 8 o'clock.

We to a building with two shooting stars painted on it. It was a glass building. The walls were literally windows. Every story a new one and on the very top floor were white shooting stars painted across the window. We went inside and got on the elevator to the roof where the party was. Just in time too. Angel's watch turned 8 o'clock just as the elevator doors clicked opened. It was packed full of people. We were so high above the city, its lights didn't affect us, so there were four lights sitting on the ground in the corners facing inward, leaving large gaps of darkness. And there was a steel stage that was illuminated perfectly. It was set up in the middle for anyone to walk up and...say goodbye? There were two caskets on the stage. One black and one ivory. I looked around and saw that some people were crying and others wiping tears away. Almost all at once we realized this wasn't a party.

It was a funeral.

There were two women sitting on the edge of the stage that everyone kept hugging and patting on the back. One with her hair pulled up, and makeup smearing down her face, was wearing pure white. It fell against her dark skin making her dress look so much purer. But because it was so white, I might've thought she was getting married instead of mourning. The other woman also had runny makeup, but her hair fell down her face, as if she was trying to hide the tears. She wore a black dress that made her skin look sickly pale. Like she was dead or dying.

They must be the mothers, I thought.

"We're at a funeral?" Eddie asked. "Why did it have to be a funeral? Of all the places to be invited to, it had to be a funeral." He went over to the food display. It was sitting on a table at the very edge of the roof. One wrong step and the whole thing would go over. He leaned over and started packing his face with cocktail shrimp.

"Why are we at a funeral?" Angel asked me.

"I have no idea, but Jenova sent us here, so it must be for some reason. Right?" I asked. Caieta and Angel nodded in agreement. "Let's go talk to the mothers."

"Being one that made a lot of moms cry. I don't want to talk to more grieving mothers, no thanks." Angel said awkwardly.

"Oh, as a Witch Hunter," I said, spitefully. He stared at me a moment. "Ok, go make sure Eddie remembers to chew before he swallows." Then Caieta and I made our way over to the women sitting on the edge to the stage crying. I approached the woman in black.

"I'm so sorry for your loss," I said.

"No," she said through tears. "It's alright, they had a good life. Right?"

"Of course," I said softly.

The woman seemed so sad. Her long brown hair stuck randomly to her face where tears used to be. Her eyes were so red I'd be surprised if she wasn't seeing things in a shade of pink. She kept rubbing her hands. Like she was trying to apply a useless lotion onto leather. She rubbed so roughly, so forcefully, she probably wore away a layer of skin. I grabbed them from her and looked into her eyes.

"What happened, if you don't mind my asking?"

"You don't know? Good. You shouldn't be wondering who dies and who lives. It's a very sad way to live – it's NO way to live. You're young, be happy." She pulled her hands away and patted the stage next to her. "Sit." I sat down next to her. "My daughter," she said. "She and her half-sister they, they were in a terrible accident. They both died."

"What was your daughter's name?"

"Isabel Black."

I gasped. I was shocked. I was stunned. "Isabel Black? As in Isabel Black and Jessica White, from the musical duo *Black & White?*"

"Yes. Yes! They're dead!" She began to cry again.

I patted the woman's lap, gave her a hug and my condolences. Then, I stood up and walked over to Angel who was now also stuffing his face full of food. I joined them, packing strawberries into my mouth. "*Black & White,*" I said. "The musicians. We're at their funeral."

Eddie swallowed hard as I jammed more strawberries into my mouth. "We killed them," he said.

"What?" I gasped, nearly choking.

"They were targets. Their father is Warlock." He looked out into the city for a moment. "I was just doing my job."

"Why are you telling me this?"

"Because I don't hate you." He turned to look at me, but I stared down at the plate of fruit. "I was bred to. And I want to. But… there's no reason to. Absolutely no reason." He spun me around to look at him. "I'm telling you this because you made me realize that I was wrong. I'd have never admitted that if it wasn't so drastically true. But now two innocent girls are dead because I couldn't figure that out on my own." I pulled out of his grasp. "I'm sorry."

"Sorry? They're dead." I said spitefully. I knew that they were Witch Hunters. And I knew that they killed people. But seeing it with my own eyes changed everything. Two innocents were dead, and they did that. "What? Did you think that they'd wake back up the next morning like nothing happened? Well, let me tell you now that they're not going to. Or maybe it was just because they died as Witches, so it was fine?"

We all stared at each other for a concentrated moment. "I didn't think that we had a choice." He finally said. He stared at me for a second, trying to tell me what he meant without using the tongue that constantly failed him. It was the job they were raised to do, to hunt and kill Witches. They were to find them and then they were to exterminate them, and that would be it. No if, ands, or buts about it. Witches are evil, Hunters are good, and they had to rid the world of them. Of course, it wasn't true. However, for Angel and Eddie, it would still have been the case if it hadn't been for me. Now they had a choice. Now they had a past. A conscience. Guilt.

"I'm sorry," Eddie said again, gritting his teeth. I had shamed him for his ignorance. But now he knew. Somehow that made me feel awful.

"It's ok," I said. "It's done." He looked at me, a little bit confused. "Eddie, it's okay. You can never undo what you did. But you can move one. You can be forgiven."

He glared at me and shook his head. "No, I can't. You don't get it. I thought you *all* were evil. I actually thought you needed to be exterminated. Like termites or something." He grimaced. "How could I think that about you. You, you are… perfect. You are… No, I deserve to go to hell."

He was so ashamed. I wanted to hug him. To make him feel better. To tell him that I needed him. Waited, needed? No, I wanted to tell him he was good. I realized why we were here then. What I was to learn about my companions. About Eddie. And I did trust him. Even more now. Unbelievably so.

Then Angel came running up. "We have to move fast," he said, gesturing to a guy who just got off the elevator with a group of men.

It was the guy from my history class. The one who hated me. Mathrel's son. He still looked so bitter. He was wearing a nice suit with a black button up shirt, and black sunglasses. The rest of the men were dressed the same. Like cryptic Men in Black. "What's he doing here?" I asked.

"Mathrel must've sent Benzi to retrieve you," Caieta said quickly.

"Benzi? Who names their kid Benzi?"

"It means good son."

"It sounds like a gerbil's name."

"Mathrel only sends him out on missions he thinks no one else can handle. Only if Loyce is unavailable, of course."

"And…I'm that mission?"

"It seems so," Eddie said.

"Well, I guess it's time to leave." I turned in the direction opposite Benzi's gaze, hoping he never saw me. As soon as I did, I was grabbed and pulled into the shadows.

Ten

I was standing just outside of the light. Inches away from where I had been just seconds ago, but it was like I was gone. Like I had been ripped from existence into a void. A little black bubble. I could see everyone around me, everyone in the light. Encased in darkness as I was, they could not see me. Like I was invisible.

Eddie was looking around frantically, his hair bouncing stiffly around on his head. Panic spiraled them. *Where did she? I was just looking at her.*

They explored the roof, anxiously skirting around the dark shadows, avoiding them like the plague. It was almost subconscious. Since we were kids, we've all been cautious of the dark. By nature, we know that the dark is associated with evil. They looked for me, making sure not to be seen by Benzi and his men. They looked, trying not to alarm anyone. They looked, weaving through the unsuspecting people to find me. They looked and looked and looked, but not in the only place I was hiding.

I was going to scream, to say something, anything so they knew I wasn't dead. But I couldn't. Whoever it was that had pulled me away was behind me. One hand plastered over my mouth and the other around my torso, pinning my arms to my body so I couldn't move. He was stronger than I was. Far stronger, more than all the training in the world could ever get me.

He leaned in. "Alright," he whispered. "I know you're probably seriously scared. But listen carefully. I am not going to hurt you. You *need* to trust me because the things I say you will need to hear, you need to know, to do what you need to do. I'm –"

He was cut off by a woman stumbling by. "Sorry." She said. But it was not just a random woman, it was Caieta, still eagerly searching.

"I'm going to let you go." He continued. "Go get your friends and meet me in the elevator. Be discrete."

Slowly he let go. I didn't move. Stuck stiff in the darkness. "You know," I whispered. "There was a better way of going about this."

"True. But with the Hunter showing up it wouldn't have been effective."

"…Who are you?"

"You're about to find out." He stepped out into the light and turned back to look at me and the thick mustache above his lip curled into a smile. I wasn't sure I right at first. It seemed so impossible. So unrealistic. But it was true.

"Richard?" I asked as he turned back and headed for the elevator. I jumped into the light scanning for my friends. I spotted Angel first and raced toward him.

"Angel, Angel." I rushed. "Go find Eddie and I'll get Caieta. We need to move now." I turned and found Caieta already standing next to the elevator interrogating Richard. I hurried over to her. She was shouting.

"What are you doing here? You're working for them, aren't you? What are you doing? What are you doing! They trust you! They trusted you so much they didn't even think to suspect you. Even when you were acting all freaky to Evangeline at the diner! What are you doing! And why do you look so much like her father?"

"Caieta." I said. "Not now. Get in the elevator."

"Not with this guy I won't!"

Angel and Eddie ran up behind me. "Ricky, what are you doing here?" Angel asked.

"What *are* you doing here?" Eddie asked. "…And why now? Of all the times to show up! I can't believe this! I'm suspicious of everyone! But not you!"

"And why do you think that is?" Richard antagonized.

"Richard!" I snapped.

"What! What!" Eddie yelled and jumped at him.

I stepped in front of him and yelled. "Enough!" It was loud. A loud terrifying yell that stopped the crowd. For a moment I wasn't sure it was me. It almost sounded… demonic. But it worked. Everyone was looking at us. Everyone, including Benzi. They charged. I looked around at my friends and Richard. They stared down at me, stunned, while Benzi advanced. But I ushered them into the elevator when it opened, and it clicked shut just before Benzi could stick his fingers in.

"There's a lot I have to explain." Richard began. "But there's not enough time. I had no idea why I was here. I got an invitation from the women in white. The Sense. I wasn't going come. Then you came to the diner and even still I didn't want to come. I didn't want to face my actions. But I needed to tell you. I have a twin brother." I sighed, rubbing my temple wondering what this had to do with anything. "He is a Hunter," He continued. "A great Hunter. Or was. He left the Leadership to have a family with a Witch. And I let him. But I stayed in the Leadership. Up until the time he was tracked down and killed. After that, I left. I set up shop and led a human life. Then his daughter showed up at my diner. The daughter I tried to deny I knew about. The daughter I tried to blame for my brother's death that was actually my own fault. 100 percent my fault. The daughter that was suddenly grown up and the only picture I'd seen of her had done her no justice. The daughter who was innocent but fighting a battle she knows nothing about because I was too much of a coward to face her. My niece, Evangeline. And I don't have a lot of time to explain. But that makes you a –"

"Blood." Angel finished.

"A Blood?" I questioned. "What's a Blood?"

"A hybrid of Witch and Hunter."

I thought back to what Ricky had said before. "'Looked like it might be in her blood.' That's what you said at the diner."

"Now there's no time to do a lot of chit chatting." Richard said. "Your mom didn't know he was a Hunter. He didn't know she was a Witch. They thought each other neutral. Human. Now, you need to go to Quebec. Your mother should've. It would have saved you so much time. Still when you get there, there's another Sense that can tell you way more that I know. He'll help you. That is a guarantee. Get there as fast as you can. I'll stay here and –"

"Fine. Fine!" I said. "Whatever!" I huffed, pulling off my shoes preparing to run. "I just don't get why you never said anything! You knew this entire time. You even knew when I was born, but you said nothing! Then, I was running across the country but still nothing! My mom is at home, fending off Hunters! My dad is dead! Except for these three, everyone else in the world is trying to kill me! Then, you! The only person who could truly give me answers, said nothing! I just don't understand!"

"There's something else," Richard said sadly. "Both prophecies are yours." I stared at him. "The Gifted One and the Chosen One. They're both you, a Blood in complete control of the world's fate. That's why Mathrel wanted you to choose his side. To embrace your Huntress. To be the Chosen. Because you can't just decide not to destroy the world, you must decide to save it. That is your job. Your destiny. Or whatever bullshit you need to tell yourself to pull out the warrior in you."

"You could've said something at the diner."

"You're right. But it's too late. We're here now. And... You need to go." He leaned down and ripped the side of my dress. "That'll make it easier to run."

I pouted, "This dress was nearly seventy dollars." Caieta behind me did the same, pulling off the entire bottom half in the process. Angel and Eddie pulled off their jackets and ties and threw them on the floor. When the doors clicked open we'd be ready.

Almost ready.

Richard reached out and hugged me. Then, the doors clicked open. I stepped back, and we began running.

We raced down the street. My feet pounding on the ground step after step after step. The echoes of our footprints rang through my head, even over the loud bustling of New York. We danced through pedestrians and around cars, trying desperately to put as much distance as possible between Benzi and ourselves.

My heartbeat pounded in my head as the new information I had acquired bounced around. I tried to process everything. Richard was my uncle. My father was murdered instead of dying in an accident. I was a Blood.

A Blood.

A hybrid.

A crossbreed.

A mongrel.

A murderer.

And a savior.

The blood of a Witch infusing itself with the blood of a Hunter had created me. An abomination. The product of Romeo and Juliet's twisted romance, designed to rescue or obliterate Verona. My parents might as well have changed their names. A Blood…I am a Blood.

What did that even mean?

When we were safely inside Eddie's truck, we sped onto the highway. It was dark and eerie. Everyone seemed to have the same word plastered to their tongues.

"A Blood," I said. "Why is it called that?"

"No one knows." Angel said.

"Half Witch, half Hunter." Caieta said. "It's fascinating."

I realized then that they were all staring at me. Eddie from the rear view, Angel turned around, and Caieta faced me. They just watched. Waiting for me to do something…wonderful? Magical? What did they want? "Stop staring at me!" I demanded. Instantly they all turned away, as if obeying my commands. "I'm going to sleep." I announced and curled in towards the window.

When I woke up, it was morning. We parked along the side of the road at a slight downhill angle. On one side of the road were tall, thick trees. They were so closely knit, I was surprised they didn't have just one set of roots. On the other side were the same trees with much more spacing between them, and a huge opening alongside the road. It was big enough to fit a soccer field in. Angel was out of the car, standing in the middle of that field, staring up at the sky. Angel and Caieta were leaning over me, watching me closely.

"What are you doing?" I asked.

"Oh, you're awake?" Caieta laughed. "Good. We're almost to Quebec. Maybe forty or fifty minutes." Caieta was staring at me from the seat next to me and Angel was leaning over the passenger's seat.

"Great... Why are we stopping?"

"Well, you're a Huntress," Angel said. "So, you have got to have some sort of fighting ability in your blood."

"My blood." I rolled my eyes. "Yeah, if it wasn't swallowed up by the magic."

"Let's hope it wasn't!" Caieta said quickly.

"What if the magic in you just enhanced the Huntress in you?" Angel asked.

"What if it didn't?"

"Well, let's find out. We're going to start training you for combat!" Caieta laughed.

"*Hand-to-hand* combat?" I demanded.

They nodded in unison and pulled me out of the car. For almost three hours, Angel and Caieta taught me all the basics. How to properly punch and kick. How to stand in an appropriate fighting stance. How shift my weight to make myself lighter and quicker on my feet. It was easy stuff, but I was outrageously tired and exhausted. My muscles ached, and my limbs burned.

I sat in the grass with Caieta trying to cool off. And while doing so, a few things kept bouncing around my head. The first being the question of why Richard was so afraid to talk to me? Did his abandonment to my father really make him feel so guilty? The second, how did Angel and Eddie not know that Benzi was sent to find me? And why didn't Mathrel tell Eddie and Angel that I was the holder of both prophecies? And finally, was the purpose of the funeral only for me to find out about Eddie's remorse? Or speak to Richard? There had to be another reason we were sent there. Right?

I voiced these questions to Caieta. While she wasn't really in the loop with most of the Leadership stuff and she knew hardly anything about Richard, she did have a theory about the funeral.

"Well," she said. "Jenova said that you can't be taught to fish if she gives you the Tuna, right?" I nodded. "Well, I think this was teaching Eddie and Angel how to fish. Especially Eddie. We already knew about their past, we knew what they did, and we knew what they thought they felt about it. But I think that seeing what happens after the fact was a rude awakening. I think now they are very aware of who they are fighting."

That made sense. Of course. This may be a journey that I have to take but it's about more than just me.

I was still sitting in the grass when Eddie finally looked away from the cloudless sky and said, "Okay. My turn." His face was as expressionless as a blank piece of paper and his body was as stiff as a board.

He walked over and pulled me to my feet. "Prepare yourself." He said, putting his fists up and stared me.

"No," I shook my head. "I'm done for the day."

He threw his right fist at me, I leaned back narrowly avoiding his knuckle.

"What the crap!" I yelled.

"Okay," Caieta said, grabbing Angel's arm and running back to the car.

Eddie stared at me, still expressionless. "Ready now?"

"Stop."

He threw his left fist, I ducked. "Good." He nodded.

"Fine. You want to play? Okay. I'll play your stupid game."

He looked down at his feet then back at me. Then, he leaned down and picked up a stick. More of a staff because of how thick it was. He stared at me as he snapped it in half. Both sides were about as long as his arm. He threw me a piece and readied himself for battle.

I looked him over once. That expression was back. Mean. Angry. Emotionless. So, I swung at him. My staff came at him to the right, hit his own stick, and bounced away. I stepped back and swung again. This time my staff hit his and I applied pressure against him. He was stronger than me though, and he pushed me back.

He spun the staff in his hands a couple of times and brought it down on me overhead. I jumped back, and it hit the ground with a clash. I lunged at him and he moved to the right. I lunged again, and he ducked. He moved towards my feet, swinging the staff to trip me. I jumped. He lunged at me and I brought my staff down over his, breaking it into a fraction of its former glory.

I gasped in amazement at the strength I didn't know I had. While still celebrating, Eddie jumped, kicking my staff from my hands. Then, in my state of shock, he lunged at me. I leaned back, throwing my left arm in the air to keep myself balanced. He grabbed me and pulled me closer to him.

Next thing I knew, I was tilted at an angle.

Eddie was dipping me back. My hand gripped his bicep tightly, so I wouldn't fall to the ground. His right hand was firm and strong holding me up at the base of my spine, and his left pressed the small broken branch to my chest where my heart was. He looked at it like he couldn't believe it was just flesh and tissue separating that stick from my heart. Slowly his eyes shifted it to mine, and our gazes locked. He was suddenly pained. He looked like whatever it was he wanted to say would be a sin to let slip from his tongue.

Then he stepped back, removing his hand from my spine, I lost my grip and I fell backwards into the dirt.

"You know, I could have killed you," he said.

"Isn't that the point?" I retorted, standing up. "Okay, so, I'm not as great a fighter as a Hunter," I confessed. "But still I took half of a karate class!"

"Did your karate class help you here?" He demanded.

"No, but I'm half Hunter, I'll –"

"That's right!" He cut in. He turned on me quickly, standing inches away from me. "You're a Hunter! But you can't protect yourself! What kind of Hunter is like that?" He screamed into my face, but I didn't move. "You're a disgrace! A sad, pathetic disgrace! And I've gotten myself into this horrible, wicked disaster with you! You're dragging me down!"

I stared for a moment, completely stunned, and almost hurt. "But somehow you can say you don't hate me," I said slowly. "What is wrong with you?"

He glared at me. He breathed heavily through his nostrils. He looked so angry, so terrifying and I didn't know why. All I could think was, *what did I do?* My imagination ran wild. *Was being a Blood so much worse than I thought it was? Was it such a disgrace? How could I not know? But how could I know?*

Then, suddenly he sighed and looked down at my hands. "I looked right at you. I looked right at you and didn't catch it. I knew it…but I didn't know. I convinced Angel that you had to die. You're a Blood, a Huntress, the savior of our world and, and so much more. I was supposed to kill you." He looked up at me. "And I was going to."

I studied him. "Stop doing that." I said. "Eddie, you can't keep punishing and torturing yourself for your past. You're not the same person. I think. In the last two days you said you were wrong more times than you probably ever said it in your entire life. I can't speak for the dead, but I think you're making up for your mistakes."

He stared for a moment. Deciding what he was going to say, or maybe do, next. His eyes glanced around my face as I studied his. He was so gorgeous. I thought about kissing him and how much of a bad idea that would be. Eddie? Pssh. I couldn't kiss Eddie. No matter how deeply he was looking into my eyes. No matter how inviting his lips looked. No matter how fast my heart was beating in my chest. It was Eddie. Right?

I looked down and stepped back and in same instant, he had leaned in so close to me that I could smell his skin. "I don't hate you," he whispered. He was so close I could swear he could her my heartbeat. "I'll admit... I tried... But I can't." He was so close to me that I could see the faint freckles under his eyes. "And I don't want to."

Eddie pulled my shirt into him, Caieta came running up. "Oh, my gracious!" She yelled. "What have you done to her?" She grabbed my elbow revealing the huge gash and the blood streaming down my arm.

"I was training her," Eddie rolled his eyes.

"You were damaging her." She pointed to another gash in my knee.

"She's a big girl, I think she can handle a couple of scraped knees. And if she can't, we have a bigger problem on our hands, don't we?"

"Don't make assumptions of what she can and cannot handle."

"I'm fine though," I said quickly.

"See? She's fine."

"You tried to kill her," Caieta snapped.

"But I didn't, now, did I, Caieta? No. I didn't."

"Why are you such an ass?"

"Why are you such a bitch?"

Then, whap!

The left side of Eddie's face turned bright red in the shape of Caieta's hand. I waited for Eddie to turn and rip her throat out. But he didn't. He stared at the grass and blood dripped from his nose. I began to wonder how hard she had hit him. I was growing more and more anxious with every growing second. Angel grabbed Caieta's arm and put himself between her and Eddie. Slowly Eddie looked back up at Caieta and wiped his nose with the back of his hand.

Finally, he said, "You slapped me that day."

"What?" Caieta snapped.

"When your dad took my memory. You slapped me for insulting him? You were always a daddy's girl." She stared at him blankly. "Almost three years were snatched from my mind."

"Sorry," Caieta said making her way to stand in front of him.

"We were best friends." She nodded. "Six, seven, eight. I couldn't remember any of it."

I stared at them. Watching this encounter as Eddie's lost memory came flooding back to him. That I understood. What I didn't understand was what that meant. I went over to ask Angel about it.

"Memories create a person's personality," He said. "Such as if you nearly drowned as child, you'll probably have a lot of irrational fears. So, the Eddie without the memories of Caieta, he was mean, scary, a tad temperamental, and very volatile. But the Eddie with memories of Caieta... I don't know who he'll be. We'll all find out, I guess." Angel stared at them, Eddie and Caieta. I knew what he was thinking. *Is this guy still my best friend? Do I even know him?*

But we had no time to ponder that. I could hear the trucks roaring just down the road. "Guys, we gotta go." I turned and saw the three black trucks barreling towards us. "Oh, we need to leave now!" We all filed into the truck, Eddie in the driver's seat, which was a bad an idea with parts of his brain still regenerating. But Angel and I still jumped into the backseat and I pulled on my seat belt.

Eddie pulled off the road into the grass. The trees were thicker and so much closer together than I had anticipated.

"Why are we doing this?" Caieta asked.

"If we started on the road, we would've been surrounded in seconds."

"Well, at least now we have seconds!" She mocked.

Eddie wove through trees and around bushes, then he reached over and grabbed Caieta's hand. For a split second, a mere moment, he looked at her. When he looked back through the windshield, we were running headfirst into a tree.

***

I was fading in and out of consciousness. Short flashes of unforgettable scenes played through my memories. I remembered what the impact of hitting the tree had on my chest. I flew forward but the seatbelt across my chest held me in place giving me whiplash. I remembered the windshield and windows breaking and cutting my face. Ten, twenty, thirty, tiny pieces of glass stuck in my skin. I remembered two large men dragging me out by my limp arms. They were dressed in black suits and made care not to drop me. I remembered Benzi checking my vital signs. He pressed his fingers to my neck and searched my eyes. I remembered coughing and trying to ask about my friends. I remembered Benzi stuffing me into his car. And I remembered screaming.

***

When I woke next, I was airborne. In airplane thousands of feet in the sky. My vision was blurred for a couple minutes. For those minutes I laid still on the cold metal bench. When I could finally see, I was able to identify three pairs of black boots in front of me. I sat up quickly.

It was awkward and quiet. I sat alone on a cold plane across from three men who watched me intently. I stared back, waiting for any excuse to hit any one of them. The plane shifted from turbulence and I was up quicker than even I had realized. The men were up instantly ready to retaliate. We watched each other anticipating the next move. In the next moment Benzi had broken through the curtain separating the plane and was reading the scene.

He turned to his men. "Sit." They followed his command. Then, he turned to me. "Sit." I inspected him quickly. "Sit down," he repeated. I surveyed him closely but didn't move. "Evangeline Welt," he spoke in a harsh tone. I raised my chin and looked at him down my nose but sat back down slowly.

"You're a mess," he said. "And angry."

"Only at you!" I snapped.

"Really?" He questioned. "Not at Bradwer? Benjamin Carter? He didn't betray you? You're not mad at him?" I glared him but didn't deny it. He sat down next to me, examining my face. "You see, angry witches always result in murder. And murder alone." He watched me, waiting for me to react. Maybe punch him.

"Who do you think you are?" I demanded. "Do you speak to everyone like this?"

He stared at me, stunned. I realized then that all of the people I speak to always make that face at one point or another. When I first met Angel, and asked him if I did something wrong, he made that face. When I let the cop walk away, Eddie made that face. When I told them both to stop judging me at the hotel, Eddie and Angel both made that face. When I defended Caieta at the beach, she made that face. Then, as I confronted Benzi, he made the face. I wondered what it meant.

"Seriously, how rude can one person be? You don't even know me, you have no right to speak to me like that!"

He leaned in close to me. "I think, oh wait, I *know* I'm the only reason you're not dead."

"Oh really?" I demanded. "Because when your father ordered my death it was Angel, Eddie, and Caieta who saved my life. Not you."

"Was it Eddie or Angel who pulled you out of that car?"

"I wouldn't have needed to be pulled out if we didn't run into that tree. And we wouldn't have run into the tree if we weren't being chased by you!" He didn't say anything, just leaned away. "Oh, nothing to say have you? You think you're so great because you're some Leadership prince or something, right? That you're better than everyone else?"

"Yes. I am. I have world-class training. I've mastered fighting techniques that a sensei with decades of practice couldn't master. And I rid the world of evil. I am better than every Hunter in The Leadership, every human in the world. And most certainly you Witches! You scum of the earth! I am better than everyone!"

I leaned in, close to his face, and looked into his eyes. "There it is," I whispered. "You think you're better than me because I'm a Witch. You thick-headed, ignorant, Neanderthal. You hate me because

I'm a Witch. You're discriminating against me!" His eyes popped open. I looked away from him to the three men across from us. They looked just as shocked by the statement. "You didn't realize? Just because this isn't the 1940's and I'm not in the back of plane doesn't mean that you're not discriminating against me. I was born this way." I looked back at Benzi. "I'm a black witch, with blue eyes. If you're going to hate me, hate me for what I do with my abilities. So, far, it's just been self-defense, by the way. That's why I hate you. Not because you're a Hunter. But because you're a murderer! Ask any human, any human at all. Ask them who they would side with. The Witch who uses her deadly gifts for self-defense, or the Hunter who uses his defensive training for deadly purposes? I assure you, they wouldn't side with the assassin!"

"Even if they knew what I was fighting for?"

"Murder is murder! You ignorant…" I stared at him completely distraught; unable to believe he was trying to justify such a violent act.

"But Angel, and Eddie, and Caieta. They've all done the same thing."

I scoffed. "First of all, Caieta is a nurse. Second, Eddie and Angel, it never once occurred to them that maybe they got it wrong. When they did, oh the remorse. They recognized the mistakes of their past and never thought twice about ever going back. You obviously thought about this before and then just kept going. Justifying it to yourself whatever you found to make yourself feel good. *They* are better than you." I sat back, crossed my legs, and looked away from him and his three cronies.

Benzi got up and went back to the curtain. But I caught him before he went through. "One question," I said. "Why send Eddie and Angel if you were already going to get me?" He stared at me blankly. "Oh, you didn't know that they were at the school that day," I laughed. "Looks like daddy didn't think you could get the job done."

He huffed and disappeared behind the curtain. I sat back and smiled to myself.

Hours later the plane landed, and I was restrained and ushered off. Then I was pushed into a black car that was waiting for us. I saw Angel, Caieta, and Eddie being shoved into three other black cars. I wondered if the Leadership only bought black cars. We rode through the California streets for a while before pulling into the parking lot of the now-familiar apartment complex.

I was dragged out of the car and would have fallen if Benzi hadn't caught my arm. He whispered something to the man and he immediately walked away. Benzi nodded at me and led me inside.

My friends were behind me, gagged and tied at the wrists. They were each tugged along by two men on either side, pulling them by their arms. Though I was tied up, I wasn't gagged. Benzi led me in on my own. No guards. He knew I'd do as he asked. I knew he wouldn't hurt my friends if I cooperated.

We walked quickly, every step anticipated and calculated. Benzi opened the door for me and led us down to the basement. I wondered what the people in the lobby thought was happening. We waited until the basement door shut behind us before he popped the secret door to the Leadership open. One by one we trailed down the stairs, into the headquarters, and into the library. We moved through the books with ease, with Benzi leading us. I was trying hard to remember the order. First left, third right, second right, first left… But eventually I got confused and quit. To memorize a maze like that, one would need a map to study for hours, and hours, and hours. Finally, we made it to the opening with the armchairs and coffee tables. However, we didn't find what we were expecting to find.

Blood stained the dark wood of the bookshelves and the vibrant carpets. Guards lined up along all exits. But not guards, they wielded no weapons, but they were on guard. They were Warlocks. They wore big, heavy wool cloaks that came all the way down over their feet and hung thick over their faces. Mathrel's guards had either been killed or beaten and thrown to the floor. They made a pile of men in front of the second exit. Mathrel himself was tied to his armchair with socks stuff in his mouth. His big, creepy smile was nowhere to be found. His face was red and looked strange under his grey hair. His nostrils flared, and his eyes showed hatred as he stared at Benjamin, who just so happened to be barefoot.

Ben didn't look the same. He looked insane or…bloodthirsty. The veins in his face exploded out of his head. His hair stood up at random angles from his face. Each strand suspended in the air from static or…absurdity. He was filthy; dirt from the past week caked onto his skin. His eyes, his once soft, kind eyes were bloodshot. He glared at me from across the room. He pulled his teeth back and snarled, "Get them! All of them!"

Part 2:

Sweat

Eleven

The Warlocks surrounding Ben charged at us. Angel, Eddie, and Caieta were still tied up and completely defenseless. We were wildly outnumbered. Even with Benzi's men we weren't even a fraction. I tried my best to pull my hands from the restraints, but I was failing miserably. One of the cloaked men walked over to me slowly. He loomed over me by a whole foot. I stared up at him, trying to see under his hood as I pulled at my restraints. Suddenly they snapped, falling down around my feet. I pushed the man and turned back to my friends.

Angel, Eddie, and Caieta were also fighting with the restraints. I had gotten the gags from their mouths, but their hands were still tied. We all looked at each other and the same thought passed through our minds. They turned, and we ran through the maze. We wove in and out of bookshelves quickly. But we didn't make it very far. Three cloaked men jumped from the shelves and surrounded us. It almost like they literally jumped from the bookshelf, or from the books themselves. They just stretched out of them.

The first man pulled a rope from his sleeve. He tied it around Angel, Eddie, and Caieta's hands. He pulled them along like cattle. The other two came at me. I kicked and punched at them, but they quickly grabbed my arms and dragged me back to the center of the library. Benzi was lying on the ground, out cold and bleeding profusely from God knows where. All of his men were also out. The Warlocks dragged us passed them, beyond Mathrel, before Ben.

Ben's eyes were as red as a volcano, like he had used hot sauce as eye drops. His lips were chapped and caked with dirt. His face was smudged with filth and his hair stood up at every end.

We watched each other for a moment. He glared at me and swayed slightly. If I didn't know any better, I would have thought he was on drugs. I glared back at him, waiting for his next move.

"Kneel." He finally said.

"Excuse me?" I questioned.

"I said, 'kneel.'"

I gaped at him. "No."

"What!"

"*I said,* 'no.'"

Within the next second there was a bright stinging in my face. A hot pink mark burned on the skin of my left cheek. Ben had just reached out and slapped me.

Rage boiled to my voice. "Who the in the hell do you think you are, you little –"

"I'm sure by now you know who I am, and who my father is," Ben cut in.

I huffed. "Tannin Carter. The great Warlock king of the Council. Yeah, I know!"

"Then you should know what that makes me."

"A little shit!"

He slapped me again and stepped towards me, into my face. "That makes me a prince! You should be honored to even be in my presence! And I said kneel!"

"You stupid fool." I mocked. "You and Benzi both think because you were born with a powerful title it makes you something. You are nothing! Nothing but pawns! You are toys used by your parents!"

"You insolent –"

"You're idiot!"

"Kneel before me now!"

I spat in his face. He stumbled away from me, wiped his face, and glowered at me. I glared back at him. He glared at me then turned to the man behind him. "Pack them away and let's go," Ben said slowly.

Another cloaked man appeared. He walked towards me, flicking a syringe of blue liquid. I gasped and attempted to run but the men on either side of my held my arms, keeping me still. He walked over to me, grabbed my face in one hand and stuck the liquid in my neck with the other. I heaved a single cough and fell out cold.

I had a premonition.

We were at a house party. Eddie, Angel, Caieta, and I. Benzi was also there; he was with a girl. She looked remarkably like Eddie. Her dirt brown eyes shared Eddie's constant glare. Her thick black hair fell curly around her face. And she stood like she was always ready for a fight.

I wasn't sure why we were all there. Or whose party it was. I don't think that mattered. I think it was the fact that we were all laughing and happy and I was so desperately craving that.

I wondered how far in the future that was and how long I'd have to wait for it.

When I awakened, I wasn't sure if I was actually awake. It was pitch black and I couldn't tell if I could feel my feet. My hands were tied tightly behind my back and my legs were taped together. I was curled up in a ball, trapped. I had been stuffed into a trunk. It was sealed off, with seven holes stabbed in the top. I began to breathe rapidly. Then I panicked.

I started screaming for Eddie and Angel and Caieta. I screamed for them to answer me, but I was only told to shut up. And it wasn't by Eddie.

I sat quietly for another ten minutes. I realized I was in a car. There were probably three other people in the car with me, not including the driver. Another twenty minutes after that, we parked. Suddenly the trunk was being lifted and carried up some stairs, through a long corridor, and up some more stairs. Then I was dropped on the floor and a loud bang vibrated through the room.

"Be careful with that!" A voice echoed off the walls. "Do you not understand the importance of this chest? Get away! Move!" I heard a shove and two clicks on the side of the trunk. Then in one swift motion the lid swung open and the bright light lanced into my eyes. "Evangeline!" The man standing over me cried. I couldn't see him just yet. My eyes were still adjusting. "So good to have you with us!" He grabbed my arms and ripped me from the trunk.

I stood now, kind of hopping to stay balanced. I could see him then. We stood in the middle of a large concrete room. The ceiling was high overhead and made of glass. At the edges of the room were six large openings. Each one leading down into an identical dark corridor. I wasn't sure which one we had entered from. But I knew it was the one with stairs. I recognized him from somewhere. He wore a nicely fitted black suit, which was a huge contrast to the cloaked men around us. He looked like Ben… and Angel. A mix of them really. He had Ben's thick curly hair, which was a light shade of brown on this guy. He had Angel's green eyes, which were a tad bit wider on Angel. He wore Ben's thin lips and Angel's chin.

"Who are you?" I demanded.

"Oh, my apologies. I am Tannin Carter. King of the Council." I gaped at him. "And you are Evangeline Welt. Princess of the Council." He nodded. "All will be explained to you. But for now, let's get you out of that…tape." He snapped his fingers and out of the air two men wearing the same heavy cloaks appeared. They cut me from my restraints.

They peeled the tape from my legs slowly, one by one. When my hands were free I pushed the man aside. I pulled the chunk of tape off in one quick motion, skinning my legs in the process.

Then the two men disappeared just as quickly as they appeared. Tannin stood in front of me looking me over. I was still wearing the silk dress from the party. But it was ripped to shreds and I was barefoot. My face was scratched, and my hair was a ball of mess. "Beautiful dress," he lied.

"I didn't buy it this way." I declared.

"Oh good! Because you look terrible." He smiled. "Follow me." He turned and began toward the corridor farthest from us. I didn't move. I just watched him. He stopped and looked back at me. "Well, come on."

"Where are my friends?" I asked.

"They're fine. Although, if you'd like it to stay that way you'd better come with me. Now."

I stared at him but began walking behind him as he went into one of the corridors. The cramped hallway was barely lit. A small lantern was posted to the wall every ten feet. It kind of reminded me of an old historical movie. Finally, we came through and stood before a wooden door. Yeah, exactly like a historical movie. He was about to lock me in a tower. He unlocked the door and pushed it open.

He gestured for me to enter and slowly I walked through the cement doorway. Quickly, I surveyed the room. It looked like an old dressing room. On the wall in front of me, on the right, was a steel rod and hanging from it were old 1800's dresses. Directly in front of me was a makeup table with a huge mirror. The wooden desk that was once painted red had faded into a chalky pink color. Sitting on top of it were dusty makeup products. The powder stations. The old curlers. I wondered how long they had been waiting for me. The other half of the room was cluttered with old clothes. Mounds and mounds of clothes that exuded their own awful scents. Then on the same wall as the one I entered through were two other doors. The one to my right was steel, and the one to my left was hidden by the piles of clothes. I turned to look back at Tannin.

He smiled at me and said, "I'll send Brad in to speak with you. Oh wait, Ben. My apologies." Then he pulled the door shut. I stood in front of it, waiting for it to open so I could attack and make my escape. I stood there for three minutes before Ben strolled in through the steel door.

He turned to look at me slowly. "Benjamin." I spat.

"Well, actually it's Bradwer." He pretended to smile.

"Bradwer?" I racked my brain for its definition. "Traitor?" I scoffed. "I should have known."

"Yeah," he mocked. "You should've." I glared at him a moment and he rolled his eyes. "I want you to stop being stubborn."

"Stubborn? I'm stubborn because I don't want to be a murderer?"

"…Think back to when we were friends. For ten years, we were best friends, you and –"

"For ten years you lied to me about everything I know about you."

"For your protection! Evangeline, don't you understand? Your life will never be the same." For a moment I thought I saw my old friend. But just as quickly as he came he was gone.

"So, what? Your lying to me would have made sure things didn't change? Hey, stupid! Reality check! Even if I never met you, my life would have changed at my seventeenth birthday."

"Just, just," he shook his hands at me, searching his brain for something else to say. "How often do you use your magic?"

"I don't."

He stared at me a moment. "Why?"

"…Because I don't need to."

"Have you seen yourself lately?" He grabbed my face and pulled me to the mirror. "You were once pretty. Beautiful even." He stared at me through the mirror and squeezed my face. "Now look."

He squeezed harder. "But you could be prettier if you tried." He turned and whispered in my ear. "It's just a little magic trick." He let go of my face and stepped behind me. "A simple, easy magic trick." Slowly he left the room and I was alone.

I stared at the mirror, barely recognizing myself. I had the stitches in my cheek from my mother. And little scabs forming all around my face from the car crash. Ben was right about one thing. My life would never be the same.

I picked up my hand and held it in front of my face. *One time couldn't hurt, right?* I thought. *After all, it is my magic and I'm not hurting anyone. It's just a magic trick.* Slowly I rubbed one of the little scars on my nose, blue mist exploded off my skin and instantly it was gone. I gasped in disbelief. I had half expected it to backfire and make the wound worse, but it was completely gone. I leaned forward into the mirror and rubbed both hands over my face. Blue mist encased my face and then it just faded. I dropped my hands in my lap and stared at the face that was suddenly mine again. Every mark, scar, or bruise I had acquired was suddenly gone. I stared, baffled.

Then, with a loud bang, Caieta was shoved through the steel door carrying two dresses, a white one and a pink one. They were old. Something you'd see as an under gown for a princess in an eighteenth century English movie. Inside, corsets were sewn in as lining. I recognized the white one, but I couldn't remember from where.

"Evangeline?" She gaped at me. "You're alive!" She dropped the dresses, raced over to me, and hugged me. "Have you seen Eddie or Angel?"

"No," I huffed. "I was hoping you had."

"No. But, they've treated you well," she said examining my face. "Your skin is clear."

"Oh look!" I ran my hands over her face erasing every scar visible. Including the one Ben had gifted her at the beach.

She looked at herself in the mirror. Quickly, she examined her face. She ran her hand over her upper lip. There was once a cut there from the broken glass. It wasn't there anymore. "Are you using your magic?" She stared at me through the mirror.

"Yeah. It's not as hard as I thought it would be."

"Don't you think you shouldn't be using it. Isn't that what they want."

"I'm…I'm just using the abilities I was gifted with."

"Okay."

"Okay." We stared at each other for a moment. She watched me watch her. "Um," she began. "Benj– or, Bradwer. He said we need to change into these dresses," she pointed back at the two dresses on the floor. "And to pull your hair back into a bun. We have seven minutes. I don't know why, but if it gets us out of this room, who cares?"

She went to gather the two dresses from the floor and gave me the white one. She stared at it, like she couldn't understand it. We changed quickly, pealing ourselves from our old, tattered party clothes. We took turns pulling the corset shut in the back of the dress for each other. There was a quiet moment of awkwardness when we realized we were barefoot. Then we proceed to do our hair. Caieta pulled my hair into a loose bun at the top of my head. She used a strip of fabric she tore from an old dress to tie it in place. She pulled it in half and did a few other things I couldn't keep up with. Resulting in a small bow at the top of my head.

Moments later a cloaked man broke through the steel door and stared at us from beneath his hood. "Follow me," he said, then turned and left the room. Quickly we hurried after him into the dark corridor. We walked in silence through the dark for a long while.

Finally, we broke through two large wooden doors into a large opening. *The throne room,* I guessed. The entire room was made of white marble: the walls, the floor, the columns holding up the domed ceiling, the stairs that led up to the two obnoxiously large thrones, and the thrones themselves. Along the walls were two other wooden doors. In front of each were two guards. I looked around to find Tannin sitting in one of the thrones. Bradwer was standing beside him in a cotton button up shirt and dress pants. In the second throne sat a tan woman with long silk black hair falling down around her face. She wore a long, golden silk dress that draped over her like she was a Greek goddess. I almost didn't recognize her, but her bifocals gave her away.

"Ms. Yang?" I demanded.

She laughed and stood. "Great! I was wondering if you'd recognize me." Then she ripped the glasses from her face and threw them. "I guess I won't be needing these anymore." Slowly she walked over towards me, her dress trailing behind. She stood in front of me, looking between Caieta and I. "You look great. Really you do. Thank you for being so cooperative Catta?"

Caieta rolled her eyes.

"Ms. Yang –" I began.

"NO! Not Ms. Yang. Kytra. Call me Kytra. Or mom!" She laughed. I stared her. "Oh. Too soon? Okay. But after the wedding, I want you to call me mom." She laughed.

"Wedding?" Caieta and I asked in unison.

"Oh no!" She laughed. "Did I spell our secret? Sorry."

Bradwer rolled his eyes and began down the stairs towards us.

"Who's getting married?" Caieta asked.

"Evangeline is, of course," Kytra laughed.

"It wasn't supposed to be this way," Bradwer said walking up behind Kytra. He pulled her out of the way stood in front of me.

"Who is she supposed to marry?" Caieta demanded.

"Who other than a prince?" Tannin called from his throne.

"A prince?" I questioned. "Where are you going to find a prince of worthy status?"

"Why would I need to find one when I already have one?" I walked around Brad to see the man sitting nonchalantly in his throne staring at the marble floor. "Well, as a king…" he said and smiled. I gasped, coming to a horrifying realization. "My son would be considered a prince."

"Like I said, 'where are you going to find a prince of worthy status?'"

"What?" Kytra questioned. "It's not like he's unattractive."

"But it's Brad!" I snapped. "Brad! Currently my arch nemesis! And if he wasn't…it's still Brad!" I screeched. "First, eww! Second, he was once my brother. Third, eww! Fourth, we're both under eighteen. It's illegal."

"Actually," Kytra sang. "With your parents' consent it's legal to marry at *sixteen*."

"My mother would never allow it."

"Oh, my apologies but your mother is dead." She tried hard to suppress a smile.

I thought back to what my mother said. *Tannin's men.* Of course. They had planned this from the start. Take my mother out and make me marry Brad. I gaped at the three of them and their unwavering confidence. "And if I refuse?"

"Then you take a blood oath," Tannin declared. "You'll cut your hand, say ritual oath, pledge thing and we'll all drink that blood with wine and cheese."

"What? I thought blood oaths were with a stone tablet."

"Humans maybe. But Witch's blood will just evaporate."

"So, ingesting it was the next best thing?"

"Magic runs through our veins as you know. So…" he searched for a way to explain, getting up and walking toward me. His eyes caught my elbow. It was still purple from the stitches days ago, I should've fixed that. "Those cuts on your elbow pit were injections into your veins, yes? She had to cut them open to get to your veins. Your veins would've moved if she went through the skin. The magic in our blood keeps things constantly moving." He began toward me. "But once you've broken skin they stop. They act just like normal human organs. So, anyway, blood oath or wedding?" He stood before me looking down at me.

"You can't drink my blood," I declared. "But I'm not getting married either."

"Well," he laughed. "You have to pick one."

"I think you're missing the point."

"I think *you're* missing the point," he snapped.

"I am not pledging myself to you or the Council! Not through marriage or blood."

"So, find another alternative? Is that it?"

"No." I gaped at him, confused by his confusion. "I am not, under any circumstances, pledging myself to the Council."

"Oh, you've pledged yourself to the Leadership?" Brad asked.

"No." I turned back to look at him. "You aren't sororities. I can't pledge today and graduate and forget about you tomorrow."

"Yes, you're right. But I'm not understanding your hesitation."

"You're not understanding? I am not pledging my allegiance to a cult!"

They all stared at me. "A cult?" Kytra demanded.

"A cult," I repeated.

Suddenly, two guards ripped me from my feet and carried me into the middle of the room. They dropped me, and everyone slid against the wall. Brad threw his arm in front of Caieta and pressed her against the wall.

"There will be five challenges." Tannin called. "Water, air, earth, fire, and agility."

"Magic?" I questioned.

"Magic. If you win one, we'll let you keep your tongue for saying the 'C' word. Win two and we'll still let you choose your pledge. Win three… and we'll let you walk."

"What?" Brad exclaimed. "What did you say? You can't let her go!"

"I won't," he smiled.

"I never agreed to this." I said.

"You don't agree to anything. Begin!"

A single man stepped from the wall. He walked out before me and pulled back his hood. He had dark greasy hair that fell loosely around his face. His eyes were dark and cold, lifeless, almost. He was at least a foot taller me. I stared up at him, waiting for his first move. Suddenly he raised his hands and pushed them, palms facing out, at me. Gallons and gallons of water shot out of his palms.

I screamed and closed my eyes. I threw my hands up to defend myself against the undefeated demon. I braced myself for impact, but it never came. I opened my eyes to find a wall of ice stood between the man and me. I looked down at my hands, slightly crystalized, then back up at the wall of ice. I told myself to imagine little drops of water forming in my palms. Not even seconds later my hands were dripping wet. I smiled and thought *icicles*. Two ice daggers grew from my hands.

The man kicked the wall, turning it into a pile of snow. I lunged at him, stabbing the cold dagger into his chest. As it barreled towards him it melted away, inch-by-inch, as it proceeded closer to him. When I made contact, it was just my wet fist. He stepped back, jolted by the impact. I swung my other dagger. He jumped back. I barely missed him, cutting a huge gash in his cloak revealing his bare chest. He looked down at his clothes and bared his teeth at me. He lunged at me, grabbing my face in his hands, encasing my head in a bubble of water. I gasped for air, only receiving water. I sucked in gulps of water after gulps of water. Then I came to a shocking realization.

I'm drowning.

In my panic, I remembered seeing Caieta fighting against Brad to help me. But the more she fought, the more guards surrounded. *If I die now,* I thought. *My friends die too.*

I still had the second dagger in my hand. I brought it up and plunged it through the man's right arm. He yelled in agony and jumped back from me. The bubble popped and fell down around me. He stared at his arm and the huge dagger forced through it. He melted the ice away, but the hole remained. He yelled again and looked back me.

I could hardly breathe; I could feel the water in my lungs. Using that feeling as motivation I formed an ice glove around my fist and punched the man in his face. He fell down onto his back with a thud. I broke my hand out of the glove. He fidgeted on his back, yelling in another language. I pointed at him and slowly, thick pieces of ice formed around him. Moments later his entire body was locked within the cold prison. Still panting for breath, I threw a mound of water down over him. The force of it broke open and melted his ice prison. But when I pulled myself to a stop, freedom was of no use to him.

Another guard ran over and took his pulse. He looked up at me then over to Tannin. "He's dead," the man said, and then retreated back against the wall.

I collapsed to the floor, still straining to breathe. I guess all this magic and fighting did come naturally. It really was *in my blood.* "Give her a moment," Tannin said. "She fought well." I did fight well. So much better than I had expected. I had just killed a man. And I won't lie. I loved doing it. It made me feel powerful. So immensely powerful. And I was just scratching the surface.

Tannin snapped his fingers and I coughed up all the water that might've dripped into my lungs. Then breathing came easily to me. Completely dripping wet, I wondered how much worse this could get. Two men standing beside Tannin came and removed the body, lying seven feet in front of me, from the room. Then Tannin smiled at me and said, "Next."

But Caieta had pushed her way through her wall of guards and put herself between me and Tannin. I shook my head. "Caieta, you can't help me."

"I'm a trained Huntress -"

"Who's only real fights were in a simulated environment." I stood up. "You're not going to die for me."

Kytra appeared behind her and grabbed her arms. "I'd listen to her, Catta. That is if you wanted her keep her head." Before I could blink next, Caieta's hands were taped behind her and she had appeared next to Brad.

Tannin rolled his eyes. "Next please."

From the wall another man pulled himself away and walked over to me. He pulled his hood back. He had short blonde hair and empty blue eyes, like he had been brainwashed and left without a soul. He wasn't very tall, either. He wasn't even taller than me. Maybe an inch shorter. We stood, staring at each other.

The man took a couple of steps back and blew at me. Green gas exploded in my face. I could feel as my regular motor functions began to slow down. I was basically in slow motion. I tried to pull myself out of it but there was no way out – I simply needed to get this fog out of my face. The man put his hands up and blew me away. A gust of hot air picked me up off my feet, into the air, and slammed me into the wall behind me. The fog was gone and I could move at full speed now, but I was plummeting to the ground. I put my hands up, stopping the fall just before the collision. I hovered a couple of feet from the floor.

Slowly, I put myself down on my feet. While I was getting comfortable, the little man charged at me. Quickly, I charged back at him. He jumped, knowing that was the only way to get an advantage over me. I slid down under him, grabbing his foot and bringing him down with me. He fell to the ground hitting his face on the marble floor. I scrambled to my feet and looked down at him. He rolled over and stared at me, blood spilling from his nose. I put my hands up, hurling a blast of wind in his face. His hair flew wildly as he tried desperately to keep his eyes open.

Why drag this out? I thought. Then I wrapped the man in a bowl of hot air. I twirled him in circles in a miniature tornado made just for him. He spun round and round twenty feet in the air. I wondered how hard it was to breathe in something that. Then guilt washed over me. *He can't breathe. I'm torturing him.* I realized then why Caieta was weary of me using my magic before. It came with this element of darkness that was so exciting and thrilling. It was a power that brought conceit and ruthlessness. That's why Tannin was making me do this. He wanted me to get accustomed to my magic and thrill of murder. I pulled my hands back instantly stopping the wind.

The man fell.

"No!" I screamed. But before I could do anything the man crashed to the ground. Blood pooled around him and his eyes became just as lifeless as those of the man before him.

"Well, that was no fight at all." Tannin said trying to control his nervousness. "Next!"

"No," I said. Two men removed the little man's body. "I won't continue to do this."

"Then you'll lose. And lose again. And lose a third time. You'll be forced to stay here and choose your pledge. Of course, you get to keep your tongue so that's a plus." I scoffed. "Oh, I know you're thinking. *You can't force me to do anything.*" He mocked my voice. "*You've seen what I can do and I'm the Gifted One. I'm just getting started.* Sure. Maybe. But you still don't know where Eddie and Angel are. And this is a very big place. All I have to do is snap my fingers and by the time you find them they'll be half rotten. So, play the game." He grimaced at me. "Next!"

Another man pushed himself from the wall and walked toward me. He pulled off his hood and I found that he was a she. She had short auburn hair and dark brown vacant eyes. She had high cheekbones and small pink lips.

She stopped a yard away from me. She raised her foot slowly and slammed it into the ground. From her the marble floor broke and morphed. It rippled, jutting out of the ground was a row of rock, each one bigger than the last, creating a staircase effect. It was running straight toward me. I braced myself. It hit me in the chin, like an uppercut. I fell back. She walked around the piles of rocks and stood over me. She grabbed my arm and threw me into the thrones. She stomped toward me, demolishing the floor and destroying the thrones. One rock hit me in the ribs, another in the stomach, and a third in the head. She grabbed my hair and threw me out into the middle of the room. The little piece of fabric broke, and my hair fell down around my face. Then she reached and forced her fingers into the marble. She ripped a chunk of the floor ten feet diameter. She hurled it at me.

It would've crushed me but Tannin raised his hand stopping it in midair. He flicked his fingers and it soared into one of the marble pillars. "Enough," he said rolling his eyes. "You lose." I glared at him, forcing myself to breathe. "One of three. Choose carefully what you do from here on out." He frowned at me and glared as his eyes surveyed my body. One broken rib was puncturing my lung; I also had a fractured arm, internal bleeding, and a mild concussion. "Give her a moment." He continued to glare. I felt my rib forcing itself back into place as the hole in my lung closed. The little piece of bone in my arm melded together. The swelling in my brain receded and the blood somewhere in my gut disappeared. He was resetting the board. Like he did before every round. He was the reason I didn't drown, and he'd also be the reason I didn't suffocate.

I was just as new as I was when I walked in. But the throne room wasn't. The floor was cracked, scratched and stained with blood. One of the columns that held up the ceiling was destroyed and the thrones were reduced to rubble. Tannin didn't seem to care. "Next!" His voice echoed off the walls.

A man from the far wall stepped out. He was ten feet away from me. He snapped his finger and a little bright orange flame danced over his thumb. He tossed it at my feet. It burned away the bottom eleven inches of my dress until I simply blew it out. It hung just below my knees now. It wasn't like it didn't already look bad. That rock lady had really done a number on me.

"Fire." I said. "Fine. Let's make this quick." I pointed at his shoes. Fire sprouted up around his feet. Slowly the rubber of his shoes melted into the concrete. He realized what I was doing just a little too late. He pulled, trying to move, but it was a waste of time. Then I raised my hand slowly, making the flame burn bigger and brighter around him. He screamed aloud, and I realized I had never seen his face. The fire was so immeasurably hot that his flesh melted off of him like plastic. I just waited until the screaming stopped.

"Wow," Tannin clapped slowly. "That was quite gruesome and very impressive. You've killed three men in under an hour. I must tip my hat for you. Sorry I'm not wearing one. You may leave now."

I turned to him trying hard to keep the contents of my empty stomach down. "Caieta, let's go," I choked.

"Whoa!" Tannin raised his hands. "I said, and I quote, 'Win three… and we'll let you walk.' Not you and your friends. If you wanted to take your friends, you needed to win all five. But now you've already lost one. So just leave." He stared at me. I could tell he was anxious to see if I'd actually leave them or not. After all, I did stay this long for them.

"You tricked me."

"No, I didn't. I laid everything out in black and white. Well, I guess that's not true. So, just leave. If you can convince yourself to do it."

"Evangeline, go!" Caieta yelled. "I'll be fine. Eddie and Angel and I, we'll be fine. Just go. It's okay."

"Oh? But is it really?" Brad mocked. "Hold her," he said to the guard standing beside him. The man reached over and grabbed Caieta's arms. Brad walked over to the door farthest from me and ripped it open. Behind it hid three guards each holding a spear in their right hand, and Angel and Eddie in their left. They looked so bad. Scratched and bruised from the car accident and probably plenty more injured from what those thick-heads had inflicted upon them. But they had changed too. They both wore big white, flannel shirts and loose cotton, brown pants. Eddie had obviously been getting on their nerves because they twisted his arm behind him at a strange angle. He bared his teeth in anger. Brad walked behind Angel and grabbed his hair. "Will they be okay?"

 I gritted my teeth in frustration. They were my friends. They were the only friends I had. They would die for me if it came down to it and I stood there debating if I should run and leave them. No. No, I couldn't. I stood motionless, searching for any way to fix this horrific problem. My brain pounded against my skull. I prayed for a solution. Suddenly, a strange urge washed over me. *I have to save my friends.* I charged at Brad, ready to kill. The crowd split, two guards pulling Eddie to the left and Brad and another guard pulling Angel to the right. I came to a skidding stop in the opening. I looked to Brad with fire in my eyes. I marched to him ready to rip his throat open with my teeth. I grabbed his collar and he made a choking sound as I pulled him toward me. He let go of Angel and stood before me, his collar knotted in a ball in my hands. "Let's negotiate," I said.

"Do I look like a person who negotiates?" Brad barked.

"Does it look like you're in a position to say no?" I barked back. "Based on what you witnessed today, I could flatten your skull and leave but I'd leave this building in shambles. But I'm trying to prove to myself that I'm not a murder, so let's try avoiding the bloodshed. I don't want any more if I can help it. So, the beauty of negotiation is you can disagree with something I say without my snapping your neck! So," I pulled harder until I close enough to see the sweat building on his forehead. "Let's negotiate."

"Fine," he coughed, trying urgently to sound confident. I let go of him. "What do you want?"

"Fight me," I said. "If I win, I *and my friends* leave. You win, I marry you."

He smiled at me. "You have yourself –"

"Evangeline," Angel cut in. "You don't have to do this."

"Yes, she does." Tannin called from the other side of the room. "She's trying to save you all."

A strange moment passed. As Angel and Eddie looked over at Tannin, recognition and fear swam to their faces. Angel tripped over himself, staring him. Eddie fidgeted in his captor's grasp. "August!" Eddie yelled. "How? Aren't you dead?"

"August?" I questioned, remembering that was Angel's father's name.

"That's my father." Angel gasped.

"What?" Brad sputtered. "That's *my* father."

"Oh, about that." Tannin laughed. "For a while I lived in the Leadership. Before I married your mother, I was married to a

Huntress. She gave birth to him." He pointed to Angel. "So yeah. *I am your father.*" He laughed. "I've always wanted to say that!"

"But he's same age as me and..." Brad began.

"And my mother wasn't killed until I was seven," Angel finished.

"So, I had an affair! Big deal!" Tannin shrugged.

"So, I'm a Blood?"

Tannin shook his head, quickly. "Yes, he is." I declared. "Half Hunter, half Warlock."

"No. To get into the leadership I had to remove the magic from my blood. I kept it locked here in this building in its purest form. Just like Caieta." We all looked at her. "Your magic was removed before you went to the Leadership, correct?" She stared at him, blankly. "How did I know you were a Witch? Your father and I went to school together. Did you think I wouldn't recognize his kid? But anyway, he died before he could return it to you, so now you're magicless! Human almost. But Huntress really. So, Angel! You're not a Blood. There is not a single drop of magic in you. Not a lick. If we're being realistic, you're closer to being half human. Anyway," Tannin gritted his teeth. "Back to business. So, Brad and Evangeline will fight, and Evangeline will marry him. Begin!"

I grabbed the spear from one of the guards and turned to Brad. He scoffed. I swung. I hit him in the side with all my force.

"Ow!" He screamed. "That hurt."

"That's the point," I said.

He cracked his knuckles and glared. He stepped back and kicked me in the chest.

I fell back, dropping the spear. He tried to stomp on me, but I rolled to my side. Then I rolled back and grabbed his leg, bringing him down with me. I crawled up and sat on his chest and punched him in the face once. Twice. Three times. Then he reached up and choked me. I tried to stand up, but he pulled his leg up and kneed me in the stomach. Then he used his knee to throw me over his head. I fell to the marble floor on my chest with my legs flailing behind me. Brad scrambled to his feet and pulled me by the strings of my corset then let me fall back down. I hit my face against the marble floor. Instantly, my nose started bleeding. I pushed myself up, quickly wiping my nose and healing the wound. I glanced down at the spear. It stood between us. We both raced toward it. I grabbed it and slid under him. I raised the spear, cutting him between his legs.

"Oh!" He screeched, holding his pants. "Oh no!" He moved his hands to reveal a gash in his inner thigh. "Too close! NOT OKAY!"

"Since when was any of this okay?" I glared. I stood up and faced him, ready for action.

I charged at him. He braced himself, thinking I would tackle him, so I jumped over his head. He didn't expect it, but he was always quick on his feet. He grabbed a spear from the guard behind him and brought it up as defense. My spear broke through his, and then I broke it over Brad's head. I came down hard, twisting my ankle and left with a little nub of a dagger. He staggered, trying to keep balance in his confusion. I swung at him. He leaned back, throwing his right arm in the air to keep his balance.

I remembered this scene. I remembered it from when I was fighting Eddie in the field. Only this time I was in the superior position. I recreated the scenario but changed it just a little. Instead of throwing my hand behind him to catch him, I punched him to make sure that he fell. Then I jumped down onto him ready to thrust my wooden dagger into his chest. The fall seemed to take forever. Like I had fallen back into slow motion. Almost as though minutes ticked by as my dagger plunged into my old friend.

I mean, he was your friend, I thought. *You grew up with this guy. You witnessed his awkward phase, his know-it-all phase--even though that never left. You know him. You can't. You can't kill him. But he's not your friend now. You don't even know him now. He's as much a mystery as that cloaked woman. In an instant he went from your Ben to Tannin's Brad. Most of those phases were probably fake...He's not your friend. If you don't kill him, he'll kill you and your real friends. Then the world will be in the hands of a psychotic with identity issues.*

Before I could I figure out what I wanted to do, I was forcing the little wooden dagger into his chest.

Twelve

I heard his rib break as I forced the dagger in toward Brad's heart. I sat on his stomach holding the weapon in place. Blood pooled up out of his wound over my hands. He stared up at me, shocked.

"I, I didn't think you would," he strained. I didn't either. "You always d-did. Al-always did surprise me." I stared down at him. He watched me, studying my face frantically trying to find a solution. "Evangeline?"

"What?"

"Please? Can you, do-don't, I, I'm."

"Ben?" I whispered. Tears spilled down my face to his shirt.

"Yes. Yes, Ben." Fear raced to his eyes. Maybe I was wrong. Maybe he really was my best friend. "Remember me… like that. I was, I am a terrible friend though, wasn't I?" He smiled and glanced at Angel. "But I guess you already knew that."

I couldn't conceive of a way to making words. I couldn't conceive of a way to move. I held firm to the dagger, rigidly still. I watched him watch me. Tears flowed from my face like a river, soaking Ben's shirt. Blood was pooling around us from both the ceiling and Ben's cause of death. I watched as the last of Ben's breath escaped his lungs.

I had just killed three men before Ben, but I knew it would be his death that kept me up at night. Angel pulled away from the guard and walked toward me. Eddie looked around as he slowly made his way over to me. Caieta broke from the man and raced over to us. She looked around at all the guards watching us. They had all pulled back their hoods and were staring at me.

"Did she just…kill the prince?" One man asked.

"She just killed the prince," a woman's voice confirmed.

"Prince Bradwer is dead," another man said.

"Evangeline Welt has killed Prince Bradwer!" A third man yelled.

The pupil in Tannin's eyes slowly expanded until his eyes were completely black. Whatever darkness there was before had just become so much worse. Beside him, Kytra shook with rage. Words boiled to her throat, "You killed my son!" She raced across the room towards me but I couldn't force myself to move. I half expected Ben to wake up and laugh at me. I couldn't make myself move until he did. Kytra bulleted forward me with fury locked in her eyes.

Angel started shaking me. Kytra buried her foot in the marble with every step she took. She was out for blood. She jumped at me, baring her teeth so she could bury them in my throat. And she would've if Angel hadn't pulled me up out of the way. Kytra fell on her stomach, narrowly missing me.

I looked down at her, choking with anguish. "I'm sorry."

Angel tugged me along, as Caieta and Eddie followed close behind. We walked toward the door that Angel and Eddie had first been shoved through. But the guards blocked our path. "Move," Angel said looking the man over. "Move." The guard didn't move. "We made a deal. You all witnessed."

"She murdered the prince." The man said.

"She won."

"She committed treason."

Angel stared for a moment, then pushed the man aside. Another guard jumped in his place and stabbed Angel in the side with his spear. Angel yelled out and stared down at the wound. He ripped the spear away and shoved it in the guard's stomach. The man fell back into another one. Angel grabbed my hand and pulled me behind him. We raced down the thin corridor. The only one I had seen so far that was illuminated with electricity. Behind us, I could hear Tannin screaming for our heads. Angel pushed through a wooden door at the end of the hallway. It was a dressing room. Similar to the one Caieta and I had been locked in. The only difference was it was meant for a man. The dresses exchanged for pants and makeup for shirts. Angel pulled at the steel door, but it didn't budge.

"Move back," Eddie said stepping as far from the door as possible "I'm going to regret this later." Then he charged at the door. He threw his left shoulder into and with a loud and agonizing bang Eddie slammed into. He fell hard and blood spilled over his arm. "Yeah, yeah. I regret it. Oh, sweet mother of God that hurt!"

Then with a click the door opened. A guard stood on the other side baffled. "It's you! Hey, they're –" Angel cut him off, punching him in throat. The man struggled to breathe and fell. Eddie pulled himself from the ground and we hurried into the dark hallway. We raced through and broke out into a large concrete room. I had been there before. It was the empty room with six doorways.

"Stairs," I said. "We're looking for stairs."

Two guards came in from opposite sides of the room. That cancelled out three of the six corridors. The men charged us. I put my hand up and out shot four ice daggers into the man's chest. The other grabbed Caieta. She tripped and punched him in the face twice. He fell out cold. I had to wonder how hard her punch must really have been.

We split up to survey the other three exits. Caieta found the stairs. We raced blindly down the stairs through the dark passageway. Eddie and Caieta were ahead of Angel and me, screaming for us to hurry. We broke through into a lobby after running into a velvet rope with a sign saying, "Do Not Enter." The large room was filled with old artifacts and antiques and people. They all stopped and stared at us.

A little girl with blonde hair pointed at Angel. "He's bleeding!" She screamed.

Behind us, we heard a storm of footsteps soaring down the stairs. We decided to disregard the staring eyes as we had so many times before and sprinted towards the doors. We burst through them and down the concrete stairs out into the street. I glanced back and saw that the Council headquarters resided in the Bakersfield Museum of Art.

We ran for a good twenty or thirty minutes. We ran across the street, through a few parking lots, and finally collapsed in the middle of the park in a beautiful neighborhood. The grass was a deep green and smelled like fresh mowing. There was a blue and yellow colored jungle gym and swing set to the right of us. To the left was a basketball court and baseball field.

Angel fell first and fell hard. The entire front side of his shirt was stained with blood. I thought back to when one of the guards had stabbed him. Caieta lifted his shirt to reveal a gash from just below his belly button to right hip. "Oh, my goodness," Eddie whispered.

"What?" Angel asked. "How bad is it?"

"You knew?" I demanded.

"Yeah but –"

"Why didn't you say anything before?"

"It wasn't important."

"It wasn't import–! Yes, it was!"

"It didn't cut anything vital," Caieta said examining him. "But if we can't stop the bleeding soon, he'll…"

"Well…do something!" Eddie yelled, tears brewing in his eyes.

"With what? I have nothing with me!"

Angel was beginning to lose consciousness. "No, no, no. Stay awake. You have you stay awake, okay?" I begged. But his eyes got smaller and smaller until they eventually closed.

I got up panting and struggling to breathe. *No,* I thought. *Not Angel. Not Angel. He can't die too.* I looked around to see that the park was lined with houses. The park was smack dab in the middle of a neighborhood. I bulleted to the first house I saw. I banged on the door. "Help! Help, my friend is dying!" No one answered. I moved to the next house. I beat on the door. No answer. The next house, the next, and the next. No answer. Then before my fist could even hit the next door, it swung open. "Help, my –" I began. "Benzi?"

Benzi stood at the other side of the doorway with a girl I somehow recognized. "Evangeline," he said slowly. Then he reached out and pulled me off my feet and into the house.

Thirteen

I fell on the floor in the little hallway that led to the living room as the door clicked shut behind me. I stood up quickly, ready to fight.

"Come on," I yelled. "Let's go! Make it quick. I don't have time for this."

"Whoa," Benzi raised his hands above his head. "I'm just trying to help." I scoffed. "Really. It's true. I considered what you said and –"

"Who's she?" I pointed at the girl. She had thick black hair that she had tied in a tight ponytail in the back of her head. She had big, muddy brown eyes and small pale lips. She wore black leather pants, a black V-neck, and black tennis shoes. She was a Huntress.

"This is –"

"You know what? Sorry, but I really don't have time to care!" I pushed around them back to the door and ran over to my friends. Benzi and the girl rushed out of the house behind me back into the park. I fell down at Angel's side. He was semiconscious.

"Oh gracious…" The girl said. "Okay, move back." The girl surveyed his wounds. "You've already stopped the bleeding?" She looked up at me. "Where's the wound?"

I pulled up his shirt to find the gash in his side was now just a huge scar. "I don't understand. Did you –" I turned to Caieta.

"I didn't do anything." She said quickly.

"Well, what happened?" The girl demanded.

"Magic. Was it magic?" Eddie asked.

"Magic!" The girl exclaimed. "Who has magic?" She stood up and looked at Eddie and gaped at him. "Edmund? What are you doing here? I thought you were in Ohio."

"Went and came back. Why are you here?"

"Benzi pulled me off leave. Said he needed some help."

"Leave?" He asked in disbelief. "*You* were on leave? When do you ever take leave?"

"When I'm commanded to. Apparently, I'm over worked and that can violence." She glanced at Benzi. "No hard feelings by the way, right?" Benzi rolled his eyes.

"Oh," Eddie laughed. "That would explain the leather pants."

"Shut up. Now back to this magic stuff." She turned back to us. "It's obviously not Angel due to his unconsciousness and his Huntership. It's not Eddie, Caieta, Benzi, or myself also due to our

Huntership. So that only leaves you." She glowered at me. "Are you a Witch?"

"Yes, I am." I said standing up.

Suddenly she lunged at me and before I could blink I was dangling from the ground by my neck. "You are foolish to be in our company," she declared. "We are the –"

I kicked her in the chest throwing myself away from her into the grass. She fell back too. But just as quickly she was up and jumping at me. She would've tackled me, but she stopped in midair. Angel was awake and had caught her just as she leaped from the ground.

"What are you doing?" She demanded. "Don't you know this girl is a Witch?"

"Yes," Angel said rolling his eyes. "I also know she's the only reason I didn't bleed out in the grass." He put the girl down and smiled. "It is great to see you though, Loyce."

"Did you just *smile* at me?"

"No." He frowned.

"Wait, Loyce!" I exclaimed dusting myself off. "You're Eddie's sister?" I gaped at her. "Well, that makes sense." I looked at Eddie and laughed. "Oh crap! Your arm!" I yelled.

We looked over at it. It hung limp at Eddie's side. "Oh man."

I walked over to him and grabbed his shoulder. I felt around the injury to see just how bad it was. It seemed like it had popped out of place and then his actual shoulder bone shattered. "Alright. This might hurt."

"Just do it," he said, biting his lip. First, I squeezed his shoulder, forcing the bone to heal itself. It made a couple cracking sounds. "Well that didn't –" he began. Then I popped his shoulder back into place. "Sweet mother of God!" He grit his teeth. "That was easy," he huffed.

"Wait," Loyce said. "Why haven't you killed her? She's a Witch."

"There's that," Caieta said. "But she's also Huntress."

"You're a Blood?" Benzi questioned me. I nodded.

"No way." Loyce said gapping at me. "You're the girl. The Gifted One. Every Hunter and every Warlock in the country is looking for you. If I take you back to Mathrel –" She nodded at me.

"Now, you see why I needed your help?" Benzi asked her.

"No, I don't." She said forcefully. "What? You couldn't do it yourself? She's just girl."

"We're not going back to the Leadership, Loyce." Angel said.

"What? Why not?" She questioned him.

"They're traitors." Benzi said quickly. "They helped her escape."

"That's not true." She looked at Eddie. "Right?"

"We broke her out of Room 33," he confirmed.

"What?" She screamed. Stepped at me. "For a Witch?" She looked back at Eddie. "You threw away your whole life!"

"There's more going on than you understand," Caieta said.

"I know the stories. And she's dead, everything will be put –"

"She holds both prophecies," Angel said.

In unison Loyce and Benzi both turned to me. "What?"

"Yeah," I said. "I guess I'm your *Chosen One*," I forced a smile. "Nice to meet you."

Loyce stared at me and shook her head before turning and heading back to the house. Benzi ran after her.

I rolled my eyes and turned to Angel. "Why didn't you say anything? You could've died."

"But I'm alive. There's nothing wrong with me." I glared at him. "Why are you angry?"

"If you had died... if you had died it would've been my fault. We're supposed to be a team, but I consistently fail you."

"That's not true," Eddie shook his head.

"I think you said it best. I've gotten you all into this horrible, wicked disaster. I'm dragging you down."

"You know I didn't mean that."

"That doesn't make it any less true." I frowned. "You should just go with your sister. I can handle this myself."

"Are you kidding me?" Caieta said. "We're not going anywhere. Neither are they. They're gonna help us now."

"Maybe," Eddie said, shaking his head. He turned and began towards one of the houses lining the park. We all followed him. We filled into the house and through the thin hallway into the living room. The house had a gray theme. The suede couch, which was facing the TV on the right, was a neutral gray color. The two recliners surrounding it were a darker gray. The coffee table was black, but the walls were the lightest shade in the room, although, still gray. The curtains hanging in front of the door leading to the backyard were just a soft gray.

Immediately, Benzi raced up the stairs behind the couch as we arranged ourselves among the couch and chairs. Caieta sat in one of the recliners, Eddie sat in the other. I ended up on the couch between Angel and Loyce. I sat down just to stand back up.

"I can save Ben!" I exclaimed.

"What?" Loyce asked.

"If I could somehow save Angel, I can bring Ben back. I can't believe I didn't think about it! Tannin kept resetting my wounds, I can do the same to Ben."

"No, no, no." Caieta stood shaking her head.

"Who's Ben?" Loyce asked.

"He's already crossed over," Eddie said.

"Who's Ben?" Loyce asked again.

"I was dying," Angel clarified. "Ben's already dead. While a person's dying, you can do everything you can but once they've crossed, they're gone. There are serious consequences to do anything more. Just because you brought back the body doesn't mean you brought back the person. Even the demon king himself, wouldn't dabble with the dead."

"Who's Ben?" Loyce asked a final time.

"Prince Bradwer," Eddie answered.

"Prince Bradwer is dead?"

"I killed him," I declared.

"You killed Prince Bradwer?" She smirked at me. "Mm, I might actually like you."

"It was an accident," I said slowly.

"Accident? How does one *accidentally* kill the Warlock Prince?"

"Or…it was on purpose but…it wasn't supposed to be. I –"

"Right…" She smiled at me.

I rolled my eyes at her, I fell back into the couch, and I threw my head back. Seconds later, Benzi came back down the stairs stuffing something in his pocket and holding a ball of clothes. He threw it at Eddie.

"Put those on." Benzi said. "You can't be running around in peasant clothing."

Quickly Caieta, Eddie, Angel, and I changed into jeans and t-shirts. The jeans hung a little baggy on Caieta and me, but not by much. After which we explained to Loyce and Benzi that we need to get to Quebec. They weren't exactly thrilled by the idea of taking the 50-hour trip but Benzi led us out to his garage. Two cars sat in the dark, cold room. The first was a black minivan; the other was a black truck. We ended up taking the minivan considering the magnitude by which the group had grown. Angel and I sat in the very back, the third row. Eddie and Caieta sat in front of us, Benzi drove and Loyce sat in the passenger seat. Then we embarked on the journey that would take more than two days to complete. Or so I thought. With Benzi driving, we could leave late and arrive early. Have you ever heard of the term *lead foot*? Well, his had silver and gold too. We were out of Bakersfield and in Las Vegas in less than four hours. By the time we had to stop for gas, my stomach had found a new home in my throat. Caieta went into the station to buy aspirin while Eddie actually puked. Angel was also gifted with stomach sickness, but Loyce seemed to be perfectly all right. She went into the station, bought some Oreos, climbed back into her seat, and ate herself delighted. Five hours later we found ourselves in Price, Utah. There we had to take a second to stop and relieve ourselves. After that we took another five hours to get to Denver. There we banned Benzi from driving. Of course, he protested because it was his father's car but we insisted.

While in Denver we stopped to rest at a park. It was a community park surrounded by an empty parking lot. A pool of wood chips promised safety from the high jungle gym and the oh so dangerous swings. It was also nearly midnight and the only light that spilled over us was that of the moon. The six of us divided ourselves up among the playground. Eddie and Caieta went to the swings, Benzi and Loyce sat at the edge with their feet in the wood chips, Angel and I went to the top of the jungle gym and sat under the dome. I pretended that I wasn't on the edge of hurling as Angel explained to me the Benzi was a better liar than he was a Hunter.

"I just mean," he explained. "Benzi will say and do anything it takes to get the job done. Even if that means pretending to help us." I stared at him. "Just beware of him is all. He is his father's son."

"I already know who Benzi is." I looked down at Benzi and Loyce. "He explained pretty well in his elaborate speech on the plane. Based on what he said, I know he wants me dead. In his case, the apple fell right next to the tree."

"But you changed me."

"No, I didn't. People don't change. Not unless you tamper with their mind like Caieta did to Eddie. No, this was already who you were."

He smiled at me in the moonlight, and I wondered at him. I wondered if this would always be our life. I wondered if we'd always be running from state to state from someone else every time. I looked down at Eddie and Caieta. Eddie glanced up at me and smiled. I smiled back at him. Then, I was washed in a sense of suddenly anxiety. "Looks, like Eddie and Caieta are spending a lot of time together."

"They were really good friends. Best friends," he sighed

"What? Are you jealous?" I mocked.

"Only if you are."

"What?" I laughed. But he stared at me longingly. "Wait… wait. What?"

"I meant what I said before, Evangeline." I shook my head, confused. "You are -"

"No. Angel, you're wrong. I literally have the power to decimate the world. I have little control over it and I'm pretty sure if I start I won't be able to stop. Because, I think, I won't want to." He stared me. "Angel, thank you for helping me. Really. But you could be wrong. You don't know me."

"I want to."

"Why?" I shook my head. "Actually, don't answer that."

Angel looked up into the sky. "I didn't mean to make you uncomfortable." He sighed, "I just wanted to say it, you know?"

"I just don't want you to get your hopes up about me."

He looked over at me. "You don't actually think you're a monster. Do you?"

"I think I've killed people, Angel. I think I did it easily, willfully, and with enjoyment. If that doesn't say psycho, then I've been watching the wrong movies."

Suddenly, Caieta stood up. She turned to face me and shouted excitedly, "I can train you!" I stared down at her. "I don't have my magic, but I know how to use it. I could teach you how to use yours effectively and safely."

"Wait a minute!" Loyce yelled. "What do you know about magic training? As a Huntress nurse, you're taught how to deflect it. Or in your case, how to treat its effects. So as a *Huntress,* how can you teach her how to use it?"

"I'm a Huntress, but I was born a –"

"Witch?"

She stared at them panicking. They stared back judging. Finally, she nodded.

Seconds later, Benzi and Loyce were in the woodchips. Benzi tackled Caieta to the ground. Angel and I raced down the jungle gym to her aid, and Eddie jumped on Benzi, Loyce stood back, grinning to herself. Caieta didn't need help. She pushed Benzi and he rolled away with Eddie. Caieta stood up quickly, readying herself for his counterattack. Benzi shook Eddie off and charged at Caieta. She held her foot up, so he'd run into it. He coughed as his stomach swallowed her shoe. He fell down onto his back.

"I cannot believe you!" She yelled. "You know, actually, I can. I should expect it! You! Your empty words!" She was suddenly flaming angry. "And your false gestures, fooled me again! You're stuck in your ways like a stubborn beast. I tried to pretend that your face didn't disgust me or that your existence didn't boil hatred within me, so that Evangeline might find a way to trust you if she needed you, because your sadistic self-respect may come in handy! I wanted to give her that opportunity! But you couldn't even pretend to be innocent! …You never were, were you?

"Have you forgotten? We grew up together, you and me! I studied beneath you. But now you want to kill me because the way I was born is not as you expected? Fine, fine! Let's go! Just remember, we trained together." Then, she jumped, kicking him in the face, and then again. His head flew back, blood spilling from his mouth. Before he could regain his stability, she kicked him in the stomach. He fell back, into the woodchips. She marched toward him, her feet digging into the ground.

I charged between them, placing myself in front of her. "Caieta." I raised my arms. "Stop."

She pulled her glare from Benzi and stared at me. "You don't know, Evangeline. You only know the pieces of me you've seen in the, what, eight, nine days? You could only discover fractions of who I am and my lonely past. I've had to endure this guy's shit for more than ten years!" She spat out words like a machine gun spits out bullets.

"What are you talking about?" Angel questioned.

She turned to Angel. "Well, while Mathrel was favoring Loyce over his own son, and you and Eddie were out playing superhero, that bastard was taking his aggressions out on me! I spent my Saturdays fending off teenagers he bribed to beat me up. I spent Sunday nights tending to my bloody noses and bruises because he just *had* to be my sparring partner Sunday afternoons! AND I bet you he didn't even know my name!" She glowered down at Benzi over my shoulder. She stepped back and frowned at the ground. "And I know why you did it. Why you're doing it. Why you're such a jackass. Just because you could never live up to your father's expectations."

"Excuse me!" Benzi was on his feet instantly. Immediately, I put up my arms to create a barrier.

"Just because your father favored some scrawny little teenage tomboy over his eleven-year-old son."

"You shut –" Benzi began but Caieta continued.

"Oh, poor daddy's boy. He'd do anything for the love and affection of his father. To prove he was tough enough for the job. But he never would be."

"Shut your mouth!"

"Or what? Huh? You know it's true. You're the sin that killed his wife. The only person in the world he could express real emotion for and she died bringing you into the world. And you hate yourself almost as much as he hates you for it."

"Stop talking," he said through his teeth as tears brimmed his eyes.

"Is it not true? Your dad, your dad's dad, your dad's granddad. No one knew their names. Think! Mathrel is your surname, yes? No one knows the first names of those in the Mathrel line. Not even you. But everyone knows you're Benzi. Benzi Mathrel. The great son of the commander. If he really thought you were good enough to succeed him, he would've never told anyone your name. You will *never* be worthy of your name."

Benzi charged at her. Caieta pushed me out of the way, towards Angel. She braced herself, planting her feet for impact. She waited for him. Then, when he was just a step away from her, she jumped, letting him run into the jungle gym. He fell back hard. Blood spilled from his nose over his lips.

"Stop!" I yelled, pulling myself away from Angel. I ran over to Caieta and grabbed her. "Forget him," I said. "It's Benzi. He's gonna be Benzi. You're old enough to kick his ass now, but that doesn't mean you should."

Angel had grabbed a hold on Benzi. We all spent an awkward moment standing around, looking at each other.

"I wasn't scrawny," Loyce finally said.

"You were the skinniest fifteen-year-old anyone had ever seen," Caieta replied.

Then a quiet sobbing caught everyone's attention. "We shouldn't be fighting," Eddie said. We were all taken aback to see him crying. It was wildly out of character and something I thought I would never see. Not just because he was crying. But because it was Eddie. Eddie. Crying. It didn't seem right. "We're all supposed to be on the same team. We're not supposed to fall apart."

Horror rushed over Caieta as she came to the realization of something. "What the –" she began.

"What the hell did you do to my brother?" Loyce barked. "What did you do?" She marched over Eddie and slapped him across the face. "Pull yourself together! You're a Markus. Act like it." Eddie wiped his face and nodded.

We stared for a minute, before we gathered ourselves and got back on the road. Benzi denied anyone else the right to drive to save the last bit of pride he had. So, we spent six to seven hours in the car at a time. Around ten in the morning we were in Des Moines, Iowa, but by the time the day ended we were in Detroit, about an hour away from the Detroit River.

My head hurt, and my stomach hurt. When the car finally stopped we, all fell out like acorns escaping their oaky captors. We collapsed on the sidewalk outside a gas station. Angel coughed and stood up. He stalked over to Benzi and Loyce, who were conversing nonchalantly. He stood in front of Benzi and said something I couldn't hear. Benzi said nothing. Angel repeated himself, and Benzi nodded. Then Angel put his hand in Benzi's pocket and pulled out the car keys. Benzi frowned as Angel waved us back over. We climbed back into the van. Angel in the driver's seat, myself in the passenger's, Loyce and Benzi behind us, and Eddie and Caieta in the back.

There was obvious tension and morning was nowhere in sight. We were all very tired and jet lagged if that was even possible. Exhaustion ran through us like an electric current and fatigue was eating us alive. It was vibrant, and strong, and nauseating. Angel made the call. He drove us to a hotel, ignoring all protests, and checked us into two adjoining rooms. Caieta, Loyce, and I would share the first room and the boys would share the second. There were two beds in each room. Loyce quickly claimed the first, and Caieta offered to take first watch, so I took the second bed. I crawled under the thick, white comforter and quickly fell asleep. I then wished I had never closed my eyes.

I, suddenly, stood in the middle of a large woodsy opening. One similar to where Angel and Caieta began my combat training. The only difference was this one was a lot bigger. I stood in front of a crowd. Two crowds. One dressed in black, the other in thick cloaks. I stood giving them a speech. My hair fell straight down my back. My hair had never been so straight, and it was white. Pure white, like unadulterated snow. I looked at them through fiery red eyes. I coughed once, then twice, then a third time. Blood splattered to the floor from my mouth. Then I fell. I coughed again, and it was gone.

My eyes shot open and I was back in the dark hotel room. Caieta was sitting on the floor next to the door that adjoined the rooms. Suddenly the door clicked open and Eddie's head popped in.

"Hey, Boo Bear," he said.

"What?" Caieta demanded.

"Do you remember when I called you that? That was so cute. Should I start again?"

"No. Eddie, no. You shouldn't call me *Boo Bear* and you shouldn't call me *princess*. No. We're not kids anymore. And when we were, those names were not terms of endearment. You teased me because I was one of two of the only girls that trained in physical combat. We joked like that then, but now…" she trailed off staring at Eddie in the dark. "I used to think that people never changed. And…" She shook her head. "They don't. And I know it's impossible for ten years to go by and *things* not change. But come on, to this extent? You were so hard. So rough and tumble when we were kids. You weren't exactly nice, or calm, or sane. But I thought you were the coolest guy ever, and by association I was too. Then I *met* you again and you were just plain old mean. And spiteful and suspicious. And now you've got your memory back and …"

"What? Just tell me."

"You're so weak. You're like the shell of your former self."

"Weak? I ran to your aid when Benzi attacked you."

"No, you fell on him, putting pressure on me."

"But… back at the Council –"

"At the Council you did nothing but aggravate them. You were annoying at most and gifted yourself some pretty gnarly scars." She grabbed his face with one hand and surveyed his injuries. "Evangeline can fix it in the morning."

An awkward moment passed.

"About, Evangeline," Caieta said. "When her seventeenth birthday comes by do you think… think that –"

"She'll pick the dark side? If I were using the instincts I was taught to use, I would say yes. I would say we should kill her now. Using what I've learned in the last week, I would still say yes. But… I would also say we could plead with her. But you don't want to hear the weakness in me."

"That's not what I meant. You're just not you anymore. But we're talking about Evangeline."

"She's not either. Your expectations are unrealistic and unattainable."

"No, they're not. Just because you can't…We'd just better pray Evangeline is better than you."

Eddie grabbed her hand. "Is that really what you think?" Tears bubbled in his eyes.

"Are – see?" She pulled her hands away. "Why are you crying? Eddie," she rubbed her faced, fighting for the right words. "I don't want to tell you not to cry or emasculate you but… what happened when you regained your memory. You don't cry. Never have you ever cried. People said you came out of the womb stone faced. And I'm not saying don't cry, or that men shouldn't cry. I don't mean that. Express yourself. Whatever. I'm all for it. I am. Really. But you're not… you. Something is wrong. I preferred the Eddie that stared hatred at me. Because then at least behind those eyes was someone I knew. I hope I don't sound mean but –"

"Well, I hate to disappoint you again, but you do sound mean." Then he disappeared behind the door.

Caieta leaned back against the wall and her, normally big, eyes drooped. I listened to her breathe for a while. Then I decided to climb out of bed and crawl over to her. Even in the dark I could see the depression on her face. She sat with her legs crossed and her hands in her lap. I put my hand on her knee.

"I can take over if you need to sleep," I said. "After all, you haven't slept in three days."

"Neither have you. You sleep –"

"Caieta do you want to talk? It's just… we all know Benzi's an awful person so why engage him? Of all people, I thought you'd be the last."

"Are you serious? He attacked me!"

"I know, I know. That's not what I meant. I just mean, you seem to be on edge. I don't know, maybe you're sleep deprived, but you don't seem like you."

"No, I'm fine."

"Fine, fine. Let's pretend that's true. Maybe I just need time to think myself."

"You can think in bed."

"Damnit, Caieta! Just go to sleep!"

She gaped at me and then nodded." She crawled away and got into the bed.

I leaned against the doorframe and stared out the window. The moonlight danced over the street like wind gliding over water. I stayed that way for three hours and watched the sun rise. Then, Angel ripped open the door to his and Eddie's room. He grabbed my arms and pulled me to my feet. He covered my mouth and carried me away. I thought he was kidnapping me. He carried me out into the hallway. He continued down the hallway. He carried me to the elevator and put me down only when the doors when shut. "What's going on?" I demanded pushing him away.

"Loyce and Benzi," he said. "They're missing."

"What? No. I sat at the door most of the night."

"So, did I. But I got up to speak to Benzi and he was gone. Then, I remember just how skilled they were at everything. Including stealth."

"So, what's the big deal? Did they take the keys?"

"No but If they double-crossed us, the Leadership and/or the Council will know our location in a matter of hours."

The doors clicked open and we rushed around the corner into the lobby. What we found was quite a sight. We saw Loyce and Benzi sitting at a table with a plate full of food. They were eating breakfast. I gaped at them for a moment then suddenly started laughing. They turned to look at me and Angel pulled me back around the corner. He shushed me again, but I couldn't stop laughing. We turned back and started running through the hotel. We escaped into the stairwell, racing up the steps. I went all the way up to the sixth floor and collapsed on the stairs.

"Double-crossed us!" I laughed. "You thought they double-crossed us!"

"It's really not that funny," Angel moped.

"Yeah I know. It's hilarious! They were eating breakfast!"

"Okay, okay. But how was I to know? Those two are so suspicious. I mean, who sneaks out to get breakfast?"

We took the stairs back down to our floor and tiptoed back to our room. Neither Caieta nor Eddie had moved an inch since we left. I fell down against the doorframe and continued to "keep watch." Angel wanted to keep the door open that joined the room now that it was morning. We sat in the doorways, whispering to each other until Benzi and Loyce returned and woke Eddie.

Immediately when Eddie got up, he decided it best to wake Caieta and be on our way. He was very forceful and demanding. He shook Caieta awake, took the keys from Angel, and we continued our journey to Quebec. Everything seemed well and there was no conflict between us at all. At least not until Eddie realized he didn't know where we were. Somehow, we found ourselves on the coast of the Detroit River.

"Seriously, Eddie?" Loyce demanded. "Where are you taking us? We're not going swimming anytime soon." Eddie sighed down at the wheel. "I'm just saying," Loyce went on. "If it's such a big deal to get to Quebec, then it's a waste of time to be here."

"I know," Eddie sighed.

"I don't get it."

"It's really not that big of a deal," I said. "Let's hang out for a while."

"I'm okay with that," Angel said nodding. We all turned to look at him, gaping. "What? Was that out of character? Should I have perhaps objected just to listen to your whining, and eventually agreed because I've realized that I actually want to myself?" He pushed open his door. "Fine, I object. Now, I'll –" Before he could finish his sentence he was pulled out of the car to the concrete.

Immediately Loyce and Benzi were out and surveying the scene. Caieta and Eddie were right behind them. I crawled out of the back seat and pulled myself out of Angel's door. I leaned over him. "Are you okay?" I asked him.

Instantly, he stood up and grabbed me. He pushed me back into the car and closed the door behind me. He mouthed, "stay here," through the window. Although, I was the one with all the deadly powers. Still, I stayed put. He joined the others in circling around the car. They met up in front of my door when they found nothing suspicious. From the extensive research they did in under a minute it appears Angel had just fallen out of the car. But then, a thought came to me, and it appeared that Angel came to the same inquiry. Had anyone checked under the car?

    I concluded that no one had checked when the door on the other side of me pulled open and I was ripped out of the car by my collar. My back hit the ground with a crash. I almost thought I broke something. Suddenly, leaning over me, there were three men wearing thick, heavy black cloaks. *Warlocks,* I thought. I quickly found that nothing was broken when I jumped my feet. Eddie, Caieta, Loyce, Benzi, and Angel had surrounded the men in seconds. The ratio of two to one put us in favor. But, I thought that even without the advantage we'd be more than fine, considering the fact that each one of us had destructive fighting skills either built or pounded into us.

    I thought that way until one of the men pulled back his hood. He had thick, black hair that laid flat against his head. His eyes were a deep blue color, but dull, like a crayon. Below his right eye, but above his cheekbone, were three marks branded into his skin. They weren't English, or anything of this current world. I recognized the first and last one. I remembered seeing the first on the cover of Mathrel's book the first time I went to the library. I couldn't put together where I knew the other one from. It wasn't exactly something you saw on billboards.

    The man smiled at me through his permanent frown. "Do you recognize this?" He pointed to the mark farthest to the left. The one I was having a difficult time recalling. "This was the mark on your mother's arm. You know, a little birdy told me she's not actually dead at all."

    I stared at him a moment, visualizing the mark on my mother's arm just above her wrist. "What?"

    "You deaf?" He said. "This is the-"

"I heard you," I said through my teeth. "I have to wonder what game you're playing if you think telling me that was your best idea."

"But you don't even know what I'm playing, do you?"

"...Are you testing me?"

"You can be sure that I am."

Rage boiled in my face. I felt the red spread from my cheeks. I planned my next steps meticulously in the following seconds. But all logic flew out the window when I glanced again at that hideous smile. I charged at him, jumping and kicking him in the face. The scene had hardly shifted. My friends held their position and the air no longer blew my hair abruptly. Time had frozen. The only difference was the man's face swung to the left and his stiff hair fell out of place. I thought that I had the upper hand. That I had left him distraught and confused. I quickly found that I was wrong. Before I could blink, I was falling back, almost as if I was about to do a back bend. I realized that the only reason I hadn't hit the ground was because the man was holding me by my neck. The man was choking me. Any plan I might have thought to form became blocked when my airway did. I grabbed his hands as burning pain spread up my throat. Even coughing failed.

It registered with me that if this continued, I wouldn't live very much longer. I jumped, wrapping my legs around the man's arms. The weight brought us both down and I fell on my back again. I squeezed my legs together until eventually he lets go. I used my knees to hit him in the face. Blood spilled out of his lower lip. He stood up with my legs still wrapped around him. I let go of him. Falling down for the third time. Before he could jump at me again Angel was there. He pulled me out of the way to my feet. The man's fist destroyed the pavement.

I supposed the little game we had been playing was over then. Caieta and Loyce moved on the man to the far left, and Eddie and

Benzi on the man to the right. That only left Angel and me to deal with the guy with awkward hair. He snarled at us. He stuck his hand out and from the shore behind us, a wave shot up overhead. *We're using magic now?* I thought. *How fun.* He brought the water down over us, and just as quickly I made a bubble around Angel and myself, almost like a glass dome. Slowly, above our heads, our shield began to crack. Then, the water seeped away, and our bubble popped. I couldn't see too well how my friends were faring, but Angel and I worked like a well-oiled machine. We worked like Bonnie & Clyde, or Frank & Jesse James. Bad examples.

Anyway, with my magic and Angel's combat training, he couldn't take us both. In a matter of minutes, I had another dead man's blood on my hands. I looked around. My friends and I stood staring at each other awkwardly. Blood dripped down Caieta's arm and stained Loyce's fist.

"Well," Benzi said wiping his hands on his jeans. "That was wildly unexpected." He walked past me to the edge of the dock. He leaned down and put his hands in the water. Red polluted the already filthy water. Loyce, Caieta, and Angel followed behind him. Eddie climbed back into the driver's seat. I crawled into the seat behind him. I wiped my hands on my knees and sighed. Eddie dropped his head on the steering wheel.

"I'm sorry," he said.

I looked up at him. "For what?"

"This is my fault. If I didn't get us lost -"

"Relax. You had nothing to do with anything. They led us here on purpose. It wouldn't have mattered who was driving."

Benzi pulled open the door and crawled into the seat behind me. Loyce followed him. After a moment Caieta got in beside me. Angel got in the passenger's seat. We continued on our way.

"Eddie," Benzi said from behind me. "Thanks for back there. That could've been the end of me."

"No big deal," Eddie said.

"Huge deal. I almost died. So…thanks."

"You're welcome."

"Um… Caieta," Loyce said. "Thank you too."

"No thank you. You ended the guy. If you hadn't, I probably would've suffocated."

I smiled at the idea of our newfound alliance. Maybe the death of a few Warlocks was just what we needed to be united as a team. I nudged Caieta and smiled. Then I leaned back and in seconds, I was asleep.

I was standing in a long corridor. There were lights embedded in the wall to light the way. I dressed in futuristic space-like jumpsuit. Something right out of a sci-fi film. My hair was snow white down my back. I was talking to a girl, probably no older than 14. She was dressed similarly with her hair pulled back into a ponytail. She stared at me for a moment.

I woke with a jolt. Angel had a grip on my arm. We were in Quebec. I'm not exactly sure how we slipped through customs, but I didn't ask questions. It was dark, and we stood in the parking lot of a hotel. Angel pulled me out of the car and stood me on my feet. He scanned my face as I peered down at his shoes. "Are you okay?"

"I… I just had a weird dream. The sad part is it was only a dream." He stared at me blankly. "That's not in my future."

"What are you talking about?"

I sighed, "I have this gift. I have premonitions. I've always had them, but they occur more often now. But what I just saw was not a premonition. One of the sweetest thing I've seen in a long time and it's not mine." Slowly, I raised my gaze to look at Angel in the face. He gaped at me. "What?"

"How is that possible?"

"What? Premonitions? Ben said that Witches –"

"No. Premonitions are not a magical occurrence. Witches don't have that by nature. And neither do Hunters. Premonitions are a human trait. Very, very, *very* rare and only found in human females." I stared at him. "Evangeline, somewhere in your ancestry is human blood." I continued to stare.

Suddenly, my memories flashed through my mind. I remembered killing the Warlock. Loyce's sideways glance at the park. Killing Ben. Next, Tannin pulled me from the crate. Benzi kidnapped me. Earlier had come Richard's confession. Caieta saved my life. I remembered with fondness sitting on the beach with Angel. Eddie pulling my hair. I remembered when I first used my magic and blew Ben away. I remembered when Ben was bashing against my door. I remembered sitting in the parking lot staring at Angel and Eddie, wondering why they hated me. I remembered Kytra, and thinking she was a history teacher. I remembered the last movie I saw with my mom. I remembered my dad's funeral. Finally, I remembered my first premonition.

I was eleven. I had a dream that a girl in my class, Josie King, would break her glasses by running into a wall. She had just gotten those glasses. They were bright purple and made her eyes look too big for her face. A week later, I saw her running by me down the hall. She tripped. She fell face first into the wall that divided us from the cafeteria. When she stood, her glasses clattered to the floor, destroyed.

I looked up at Angel. "Ben said…" I wondered how much Ben really did know. How much he had hidden from me. How much I'd never know. How much he'd taken with him, to his grave.

My attention was torn back to the hotel. Eddie was yelling for us to hurry in. I nodded slowly. He turned and went back inside. "I don't understand," I said.

"I don't either," Angel said. "It was probably your father's side. However unlikely, there's a better chance that a Hunter would marry a human than a Warlock would… It's interesting that we can barely tell each other a part but are so adamant to stay away from one another."

My train of thought halted. Immediately, my worries shifted to the insanity that had been tangled around me. Eddie walked up to us. He handed Angel a room card. "Room 17." Then he went back to hotel.

"Why do you think that is?" I asked.

"I really couldn't tell you. I don't know."

Angel turned to start towards the hotel, but I didn't move. "Angel, why did this war start?"

"Because Warlocks wanted to destroy humanity. Thus, started the Witch Trials and the war. They wanted revenge, they're just evil."

"Is that all? No other reason why?" It was hard to believe that anyone could *just be evil.*

"Um, um." He looked away from me. "As far as I know." I stared at him a moment, he didn't look back to me. "Really, I don't know."

"Really? Or is it that I'm not supposed to know? Or that *you're* not supposed to know?"

"I really don't know," he said again.

"Then why won't you look at me?"

His eyes darted to meet mine. "I'm looking at you."

"Angel?"

He sighed, "Okay. There are these books in the library that only Mathrel is supposed to know about. I saw him reading one of them one day, and the next day, I snuck in and read one. I am not supposed to know half the things I do. And I wasn't supposed to tell my mother. That's why she died, why she was killed." I reached out and grabbed his hand. He smiled at me. "I never told anyone that. But, the things I found out could rip apart the Leadership. Everything that we stand for is a lie.

"Back then, when the war started, there was a series of crimes. Just like any other time period in any other country. But when children start getting hurt, that's when things really blow up. I read that two boys, teenagers, one a presumed Warlock, started a fire that killed eight human boys. There was no evidence or witnesses that proved that they were guilty. But it was their word against the mayor's son's. So, the two boys were hung. The lack of evidence made a lot of people mad.

"It was reason enough to start a war. Especially because there was evidence and proof that the person who set the fire was actually the Mayor's son. He and his friend had gone out to the church that night, playing with torches. They also brought a little liquor, which they couldn't hold. One thing led to another and their clumsiness killed those boys. And at the time, Degrick Carter was at the head of the Warlock community and Boris Waters was the mayor, and he was great friends with the judge, Danforth. Who just so happens to be known for starting the Witch trials. Waters later became known as Mathrel and it was Carter's boys who were hung." He raised his eyebrows and shrugged. "That's what really started the war. That's why they wanted to end humanity."

"But when did the prophecies come about?"

He sighed again, "At the time, hardly any Witches existed. Not nearly as many as today. There was maybe one in every other town. Except Salem, which held three. A mother, a daughter. But, they were never even accused. However, there was a second daughter. Older than her Witch sister, the one who gave birth to third witch. She was accused. But only because she was blind."

"She was a Sense?"

"Yes, we know that now. But back then, only her mother knew. And she went to her grave with that secret. But their Senses were different than ours are. Just as everything else changes over time, so did the power of the Senses. Bibi can see the future and only tell it. However, back then, they could see the future and change it. We don't know what was originally meant to happen; only she did. But we know it wasn't this, what's happening now. She stood up, ready to hang, and swore that the power of her lineage would only grow with time. That one day a daughter of hers would be born with so much power, she could destroy the world. And that daughter is you.

"What was her name?" I demanded. Angel shook his head. "What was her name?"

"We don't know. That died with her body."

"Does Eddie –"

"You can never tell him."

"Why?"

"He spent his whole life thinking that he was fighting for the greater good, and then you came along and told him that it was just unnecessary violence. If he finds out that it was Leadership that started all of this, his conscious would burn a hole in his head. Maybe not a couple of weeks ago, but lately he's been so…"

"Sensitive?"

"…Just promise you won't tell him."

"I won't tell him."

Fourteen

Angel and I walked quietly to the room. He unlocked the door and pushed it open. Loyce and Eddie were sitting in the middle of the floor talking. I'm not sure what they were talking about, but I assumed it was private sibling stuff because they quickly became quiet when we entered. Loyce patted Eddie's knee and stood up. She went into the other room and kicked Benzi out. I followed Loyce. This time there were three beds. I took the middle one and fell asleep on top of the comforter.

I woke before morning broke. No one had been put on guard, but I didn't think it mattered. I lay still, staring up at the ceiling. I wondered what I'd be doing if I wasn't Evangeline Welt the Prophecy Child, but just Evangeline Welt. Most likely, I'd be tiptoeing down stairs to get a snack. I sighed remembering the last time I had done that.

When the sun rose three hours later, Loyce gathered us up and shoved us into the car. We drove for an hour without any real idea of where we were going. But it wasn't very long before we pulled up to a small gas station with only one pump. I pulled myself from the passenger's seat and yawned. "I think it's one of those really old ones where you have to have someone come out and pump it for you," I said.

Caieta nodded and began towards the little shack. I followed her. She pulled open the door and then stopped in her tracks. I walked right into her. I looked over her shoulder and gasped. "Sweet mother of Jesus," Caieta gasped.

"Caieta!" I yelled.

"I'm sorry, I'm sorry." She continued inside, walking up to the cashier. He was a tall man with deep brown, almost black eyes and had curly hair to match. "I have a feeling that you're the man we're looking for." And she was probably right. The only thing about this guy that could've thrown me off was his mouth. Instead of two lips he had a thick piece of skin that welded his flesh together. The tissue was darker than the rest of his carmen skin. The stress marks were visible where the extra tissue had been forged.

I do believe I am. A voice echoed in my head. I looked around wondering who could have said that. *What are you looking for?* My gaze settled on the man. Knowing there was no way for him to say anything, I wondered if there was someone behind him. Someone not so tall, or mute. *Stop looking.*

"Holy jumping Jesus on a breadstick," Caieta said. "That's you."

My mouth fell open. "Oh my God, it *is* you." I stared at him a moment. "How is that possible?"

Telepathy. Now, come, gather your friends. I don't like to waste my time. Let them all be amazed. Hurry. I turned and yelled for Loyce to hurry. The rest followed her. They all stopped and gaped when they saw him. *Yes, yes. How wonderful. Now, I'm –*

"Are you talking in my head?" Eddie gasped. "How?"

Telepathy. Did I not just explain this? Nonetheless, I am Isaiah. You can call me Mr. Isaiah. Not anything else.

"I suppose you know why we're here," Loyce said. "Because I don't."

I do. I'm going to give you a list of instructions. Follow them to a T. It will be up to you to follow them or not. But you're the ones trying to save the world, so I'd suggest you do as you're told. Listen clearly. I don't like to repeat myself. He looked us over once. *Very well. First, go to Montreal. Ask around for the location of the Well of Fears. Some will try to tell you it's a myth. Most believe that it is. Others will deter you from going. Ask them where it's located. Tell them you can withstand the fear. When you arrive, one by one you must each jump into the pool of water. When your deepest fears are revealed, only Evangeline and the swimmer must be there to witness.*

"And if you don't have any *deep fears*?" Loyce asked.

Everyone is afraid of something. Some people are just better at hiding it. You are the best I've seen so far. But the winds bring me the truth.

"The winds?" I asked.

The nature around me tells me the truth. Everything I need to know is whispered to me through silent voices.

"But how would witnessing their fears help us?"

199

They are all tied back to you. I gapped at him. *After that, wait until the next morning and on the banks of the pool, begin training. Combat training for five hours. Five hours approximately. There's no need for exact time. But try to be close. Then go to Warren, Vermont. Have as much fun as you can before midnight because there you will endure the Sweat. This is what we call an internal struggle that takes all of the body and mind to make a decision.*

"We?" Benzi demanded.

The Senses. It is what we went through to become as we are. Be careful Evangeline, it can literally destroy the weak.

I panicked slightly. My birthday. I just remembered that's when it all starts. And it was just a few days away. I'm not sure I was ready for it all yet. But it's not like I really had a choice.

I sighed and glanced over at Loyce who made a face and rolled her eyes.

Excuse me.

"What..." Loyce gasped. "Can you hear my thoughts?"

The man nodded, she stared at him a moment. *And you should be warned. One of you will die before your quest is through.*

"Wait, what? I was joking."

I'm sure you were. But I'm not. And I'm sorry to say I have not the slightest idea of whom.

"What do you mean?" Benzi demanded.

I mean God only gives me the information you need.

"Well, Mr. Isaiah, thank you." I said, trying to figure out how I could possibly prevent the death of one of my friends. "We'll get out of your way now."

Actually, Ms. Welt, may I speak with you and Mr. Markus alone?

Eddie looked at me cautiously. I smiled at him and turned back to Mr. Isaiah. "Of course." I watched as the rest of our crew exited the little shack. "Is there something wrong?"

Your friend has not always been the way he is has he? He was a different person when you met him? Eddie. He's...strange. Yes?

"Me?" Eddie questioned.

I am not trying to come across as creepy or mysterious. But I know I'm always viewed that way. I am just trying to bring up the topic as gently as I can.

"Just say it. I'm prepared," Eddie said.

Help him. Eddie and I glanced at each other. *We all know that this is not Eddie. The Eddie Caieta knew back when they were seven, that was not him either. You need to fix him, and you need to help him.*

"What do you mean?" Eddie questioned.

The Eddie you met did not know Caieta and he was... aggressive, to say the least. But Eddie with the memories of Caieta, he is not anything.

"What is that supposed to mean?"

In the time between seven and eight he had no memories of her. The softness you are noticing about him now that is cute, it was based on his memories with Caieta. But those were gone and that is what made him mean. But then those empty memories were completely replaced with nothing but memories of her, only her. It's made him, if you don't mind, pathetic.

"Pathetic? I'm pathetic?"

Soft. Irrational. For him seven to eight is a sensitive group of memories. For some people it might be ten to twelve, others one to two. So, altering his memories in that time frame has completely changed his identity. It's broken him. There were other memories in that time frame, but now he can't remember them. They were moved aside, if you will, by the memories of Caieta. You must help him see them. Find a balance between Caieta and whatever else was there. Fix him, for everyone's sake. I nodded.

"I am right here!"

And the Sweat is heavily reliant on the mind. If the mind is not right, the Sweat will last for days, or even weeks. It is very painful, physically and emotionally.

I nodded again and watched as he went into the back room. I looked up at Eddie, his hands stuffed in his pockets and his hair falling into his face looking at me with one eye.

"So, I'm not me," he said. "Never really was, was I?" I stared at me silently. "What if I don't like who I'm supposed to be? I liked who I was before. Before Caieta, before you. I've had seventeen years to get used to him. Now I got to start all over?" He stared at me a moment. He did that things where he saw into me. Into parts I didn't want to him. "Do you think you'll like me?" I nodded. He mimicked, "Ok, then do it."

I put my hands on his temples and closed my eyes trying to envision anything that would help. Eddie's soul, his mind, something, but I couldn't get a visual. Then I heard whisper in the back of my mind. I asked myself, where are Eddie's memories? Suddenly I was searching through his brain. The frontal lobe, the occipital lobe and then I was watching memories.

I watched mini Eddie and Caieta sitting on the swing at the park. But I also saw a faded vision of him pushing a kid off the swing so Caieta could get on. I saw them later watching TV, laughing with their feet on the coffee table, but once again I also saw a faded picture of earlier Eddie, pushing the books of homework off the table. I saw them practicing Kung Fu in a dojo and another faded picture of breaking his Sensei's hand. I pulled all the faded pictures through. Of everyone and everything that had been hidden, pushed back by the memories of Caieta. And then I jumped back, pulling my hands away. Eddie was frozen still for moment, not moving at all. "Eddie?" I asked. He stumbled, falling to his knees. "Are you okay?

"Wow," he said. "That was intense. I just had a flashback. A few."

"So, you're okay?"

"Yeah, yeah I'm fine." Then he stumbled a little and blood came streaming over his lip. I grabbed his arm and helped him catch his balance. Then he wiped the blood from his nose and looked at me. I could tell something had changed. A new determination was in his eyes and it was gorgeous. "Can I tell you something? Something I was afraid to tell you before? And something I didn't think you deserved to know before?"

"Sure," I nodded vigorously.

He looked at some of the cans on the counter than back at me. "Two weeks. I've known you for two weeks and in those two weeks I've changed my personality more times than I have my pants. I don't know if it's my memories that are jacked up or what, but I know now what I want to say is the truth. My truth."

"Don't get all sentimental on me." I looked down at my feet.

He stepped closer, reaffirming eye contact. He looked so serious, so passionate. It made me anxious. I recognized the look from the park when he had nearly killed me in combat. "I feel an obligation to you, more than that, I feel a need for you. To protect you. To carry you. And I know you don't need protecting, or carrying, and I know you sure as hell don't *want* it. But I want to. It's this overwhelming desire. It's always been there. From the moment you nearly fainted in the parking lot of your high school. I wanted to run over and catch you." He knit eyebrows in frustration. "But I couldn't do that. Because where I'm from that's illegal. Because you're a Witch who didn't deserve to be caught. I couldn't want to catch you. I couldn't even think about catching you." He looked up and sighed. "Then my mind changed, and thoughts changed and pieces of me disappeared." He looked back down at me. "Then it was *I* that didn't deserve to tell you. I didn't deserve someone like you. You need someone like Angel. Grounded and leveled headed. He's perfect for you and," he laughed, "cares about you just as much. I was scared to tell you." Then he looked down at my lips. "And now I'm here. And my mind has changed again. And I have a feeling that it'll be the last time it changes because I don't want it to change again." He looked back up into my eyes. "So, listen to me very carefully, Evangeline Welt. No matter what you decide to do, no matter… I will stand by you until the day I die. Because I couldn't breathe anywhere else."

I was very aware of the overwhelming intensity of that moment. And the quiet that was lingering between us. He stared at me for a long moment, and I hated how good he was at keeping a neutral face. I could guess what he wanted me to say, I could also guess what he expected me to say. But I had no idea what I actually wanted to say. Or what I wanted to do. A part of me said, *hug him*. Another part said, *kiss him*. But then there was another that said I should go consult Angel. And a whole other part that said, *ignore all of this and just get in the car*.

"Um," I finally stuttered, pulling my eyes away from his. "I don't know what's going to happen in the following days…if I'm…or if…I just…"

"Keep me posted?"

I looked back up and nodded. "Yeah. Yeah, I'll keep you posted." He nodded once and continued to stare at me. "You know," I said quickly. "I wish you were easier to read."

He laughed to himself. "I wish you were too." Then he bit his lip and left the little shack. His demeanor, his walk, and his attitude had completely changed. I prayed that this was the man he was meant to be. That he was untampered with and could grow into himself.

I followed behind him when I regained control over my nerves. Angel ran up to me, ready with questions.

"What just happened?" He asked.

I smiled at him, "Nothing."

"You've got to give me something."

I patted his arm. "Sometimes nothing is something." Then I continued out to the car.

Angel laughed behind me. "I don't like how great you've gotten at this 'cryptic' thing."

The drive was hardly memorable. I didn't think boredom could get that bad, but of course it did. And it was only three hours. The radio stations didn't work up there. The car games were cliché and useless. And everyone preferred not to talk anyway. I got so mind-numbingly bored, I'm pretty sure my brain started eating at my skull to entertain itself.

We pulled off the road, into another gas station, and Angel rolled down the window. A soft breeze swept into the car and wrapped around my face. He beckoned to the guy across the lot. The man ran over to the car.

"Is there something I can help you with?" the man asked.

"We read that there was a legend. About the Well of Fears."

"It's a myth."

"But if it were real, where might we find it?"

"It's not."

"I hear you, but *if,* where would it be?"

"Um… I really don't know. Sorry."

The man walked away, but just as quickly as he disappeared, a woman took his place. She had deep dark hair and hazel eyes that barely made it over the window. "Why are asking about the Well of Fears?" She demanded, pushing herself up at Angel's window.

"We need to find it."

"Why? You don't need to go there. That place destroys people. You need to stay as far away from it as possible."

"But where is it?"

"Go back to where you came from."

"Tell us. We can handle a few frights."

"Frights? These aren't spiders and the Boogie Man. These are things that taunt your thoughts and stain your sanity. Your innermost, most terrifying fears. These are things that haunt you the most; the things that make you question your existence. Believe me, you don't want to go there."

"Have you been?"

"No. But I know someone who has."

"We have to get there. Believe it or not, the fate of the world depends on it."

"Subtle, aren't we?" Loyce said.

The woman sighed, "Fine. When you leave this road turn left. You'll see a sign that says dead end continue on the road for about another two hours. Eventually, you'll come across a street with no sign. Turn right. You'll follow that until you get to the T in road. Turn right onto the dirt road. From there it will lead you to the Well of Fears. It's a little lake. Visit at your own risk. Just know that you've been warned." She turned and walked away. I could see her pink jacket and matching boots, then.

"Well," Caieta sighed. "That was interesting."

Angel pulled out of the lot and continued down the road. After a little while, boredom washed over me like rain. Street after street and sign after sign, with little progress seeming to be made. Random events crept through my thoughts. Then, an interesting fact made an appearance in my mind.

"You know, I just realized," I said. "Eddie and Loyce are the only ones with parents who'd worry they were missing."

Eddie turned from the window to look at me. "Just because we have parents doesn't mean they'll care that I'm missing. It just means I have access to my bloodline."

"What?"

He rolled his eyes. "My parents don't care about me. Loyce maybe, but not me."

"I – I don't understand."

"He's trying to say," Loyce sighed. "That our parents only had kids because that's what was expected of them."

Silence spilled on for a while. I wondered why I had even brought up the idea of parents. We all seemed to know everything about each other. But the more I thought about it, the more I realized that wasn't true. I knew enough about Angel, still not very much. I didn't know what he did after his parents died or how long he mourned. I didn't know how Caieta's parents died or why she was so mad at Benzi. But I thought I could put it together. I didn't know why Benzi was so protective of himself. I didn't know why Eddie's parents hated him or why Loyce was so absent in his life. And more over I didn't know why these were the five people to accompany me on my journey.

    Eventually, Angel turned. He reached the end of the paved road and began on the dirt. The dirt road was more intense than I expected. It was unkempt and laced with rocks and twigs. It was barely even a road, with all of the overgrowth. I could see why people hardly visited. Why risk popping a tire or destroying the undercarriage? But the woman wasn't lying. Twenty feet from the road was a small lake. More like a pool. It couldn't have been more than 50 feet in diameter. And the only thing that separated us from the pool was an old, wooden pavilion, once painted white, but now faded grey.

    We all climbed out of the car and filed into the pavilion. Hanging inside the dome was a black chandelier, also faded grey. We started looking for a light switch. Caieta wasn't the one to find it.

    "Guys," she said. "I think I found something. And it's not a light switch."

    We gathered behind her to see what it was. Carved into the wood:

> Do as you dare.
> I do not care.
> Jump in the water.
> Meet your maker.
> To witness the fear.
> Just stand near.
> Watch the waves.
> Watch them behave.

Written below it in sharpie was:

In other words, if it's your fear you wish to see, jump in the water. If you're just watching, sit at the edge and stick your foot in the water. You should be warned, what you see could rip you apart.

We all gaped at each other for a while, debating how this could really benefit us.

Benzi stepped up then. Claiming that he could withstand any trial, he volunteered to go first. He and I sauntered over to the pool. He sighed. Then he looked back at Loyce and pursed his lips. He looked down at the pool, glared, and proceeded to pull off his shoes. He pulled the knife on his ankle off. Then pulled off his shirt. I had been right the first time I saw him in Ms. Yang's class. Benzi's chest was just as perfect was his face. I wondered than if the Leadership only bred beautiful boys.

I looked away, sitting down at the edge of the pool. I pulled off my shoe and stuck my foot into the water. It was chilling. The blood in my veins froze. Ice crystals spread up my leg. My foot turned blue. I pulled my foot out screaming.

"What?" Benzi panicked. "What is it?"

My foot was perfectly fine. Wet and cold. But fine. "I…" I looked up at him. "For a split second. Barely a second. I thought the water was cold. Freezing. It twisted my subconscious thought into a very real and inescapable terror."

Benzi starred down at me, realizing what I was saying. I dropped my foot back into the water and watched as my toes turned black, but I did not draw my foot out. Benzi watched. I could tell he was trying to see what I could see, but he failed. He took a deep breath and plunged into the water.

Fifteen

I was standing in a large grey room. Fog hid the floor and ceiling from me, and light spilled in faintly from an unknown source. I wandered around until I remembered I traveled with Benzi.

I started yelling for him. Then I tripped over something. I felt through the fog until I found it. It was Benzi's dagger. The one I had just watched him pull off his ankle. I dropped it instantly. I was shocked to find it was the handle that was covered in blood, not the blade. I screamed for him louder, forcing more air out of my lungs every time. I was running. Suddenly, he was in front of me.

"Evangeline!" Benzi yelled into my face. "It's you! We have to get out! We need to go!" Blood dripped down over his right eye and down his face. His left cheek was ripped open with wide claw marks leaving huge empty gashes in his flesh. His shirt was ripped open and the skin on his chest and stomach were also torn, revealing the pink bloody tissue inside. But the worst and most terrifying sight was his arm. His left forearm had been torn away, leaving just a bloody stump. I screamed back at him in a loud shriek. "We have got to go!" He repeated. "We have got to get out!"

"That's not me!" A voice called from behind me. A voice not unlike my own. "She's the monster! Get away from her!" I looked around Benzi and saw my own panting reflection staring back at me. Benzi jumped away from me, screaming. He stumbled back but didn't go towards her. The other Evangeline. I called her Eva. The version of me that I didn't want to be. The worse version of me, personified.

"Who are you?" He pointed at her, tears spilling out of his one good eye. "Who are you?" He asked again, this time pointing at me.

"I'm Evangeline!" I yelled.

"No! It's me!" She yelled. "I'm Evangeline! Hurry!"

"It's me! It's me!"

"I'm Evangeline!" She barked at him. Her false fright momentarily turned to anger.

"No! You're Eva!"

"Yes!" She smiled. "That's what I've been trying to say! Come on! I'm Eva!"

"Eva?" I barked. "Eva's the half of me that I don't want to be!"

She gaped at me a moment, then her frown curled into a smile. "She's the half that you need to be." Suddenly, her hair turned red. Spreading from her roots to the tips and dripping down her spine. Almost like blood was growing from her scalp. Then her eyes disappeared in an ocean of black. And her nails grew twice their length to make claws. Benzi screamed in panic. Eva yelled at him to shut up. Suddenly she was standing inches away from him.

Mathrel was standing behind Eva.

"Father," Benzi cried. "Help me!"

"What!" Mathrel laughed. "Why would I do such a stupid thing? Now that I finally have a child that I can be proud of." He draped his arm around Eva, who flicked it away immediately. "You're not my son. You're a failure that needs to be done away with."

"Father. Please. Plea–"

Eva forced her hand into Benzi's mouth and when she pulled away she had his tongue in her fist.

"Oh God!" I yelled. "Oh God!"

"Finish him," Mathrel said.

"No! No!" I tried to run at them, but I couldn't move.

Eva looked at me and laughed. Then she threw the tongue over her shoulder. While still watching me, she pushed her hand into one of the gashes in Benzi's stomach. She twisted her hand around then pulled out a string of intestines. I screamed in terror. Eva threw his organs at me. They hit me in the face and fell around my shoulder. Benzi fell into the fog. Eva thrust her hand down at him. She pulled away with a bright red ball of meat in her hands. It was his heart. She brought it to her lips and took a big bite out of it. She laughed at my disgust. "You just have to accept the darkness that already lives in you!" A scream echoed from her feet. A tear fell down my face as I realized Benzi was still alive to endure this torture.

"My child," Mathrel said, patting Eva on the back. "Take her."

Eva charged at me. Pain and fear kept me from running. She tackled me into the fog. But instead of hitting the floor I was back on the dirt, panting for breath. Benzi was beside me, sobbing and soaked. He looked up at me and screamed. He pushed away from me, rubbing his face and chest.

I crawled for breath. "Benzi!" He kicked me farther away from him. I fell on my back.

Angel ran out to me. "What are you doing?" He pulled me to my knees.

"Get away from her!" Benzi yelled.

"What is wrong with you?" Angel looked back at me. I was shaking, and tears spilled down my face like waterfalls. "Are you okay?"

"Is he okay?" I demanded, trying to shake Angel's grip. "Are you okay?"

"Stay away from me!" Benzi yelled.

"What happened?" Eddie yelled, pulling Benzi to his feet. Benzi stopped panicking then. He ran his hands over his face and chest one more time and then looked down at me. His face was red and blotchy from the tears that had already escaped his eyes.

"That wasn't me," I said.

"What happened?" Eddie demanded again.

The Benzi jumped at me. "You demon!" Eddie and Loyce held him away. Angel turned so that he was between and Benzi and me. I realized then that my body was limp; the only thing keeping me upright was Angel. Benzi shook Eddie and Loyce away from him "I'm fine! Okay! I'm fine."

I pulled myself up and took a deep breath. I had to cover my face in my hands and remember: *That was a fictional reality. It was created and enacted in Benzi's subconscious. It was not me or my future. It was an illusion.* I pulled my face from my hands. "Benzi?" He looked at me, his eyes bloodshot. "That was not me and it will never be me."

He nodded. "Yeah." He sucked in a deep breath. "You're Evangeline. Just make sure you stay *Evangeline*." He turned and went back to the car. He got in, closed the door, and buried his face in his hands. Eddie and Loyce looked at me.

"What happened?" Eddied demanded a final time.

"We entered Benzi's innermost thoughts and I witnessed his deepest fear while he lived it." I swallowed. "That lady wasn't wrong. What you see in there could destroy a person." I shook my head. "I can't do that again." I ran my hands over my chest and neck. "I was there. I felt it. I touched it...I was so scared. And they weren't even my thoughts." Tears poured down my face. Eddie sat down in front of me and nodded. "I can't."

"You broke Benzi," Loyce said. She shook her head at me. "I'm not getting in there. If that puddle can destroy Benzi, we have a problem! I won't do it!"

"Mr. Isaiah said –" Angel began.

"Screw Isaiah! I will not –"

"I'll go next," Caieta cut in.

I shook my head at her. "You don't want to. It's –"

"I already know what I'm afraid of. I haven't gifted myself with the illusion that I am fearless. Besides, I'm sure that mine are the softest out of the five of us." She took my gaze and broke it. "I won't take no for an answer." I stared at her. She nodded at me. I nodded back. I turned and stuck my foot in the water. Angel, Eddie, and Loyce retreated to the pavilion. Caieta peeled off her shirt and shoes and dove into the water.

I was back in the foggy room. I peeled myself from the floor and began my search for Caieta. I felt like I was running for hours. I was no closer to an exit or my friend. I could barely tell if I had even moved. I stopped and dropped to my knees, panting. I caught my breath, stood up and turned around.

Behind me Caieta was on the floor, screaming. I raced over to her. As I approached, I saw what she was screaming at.

They were all dead. Piled on top of each other. Partially dismembered and severely injured. Benzi, Angel, Loyce, Eddie, Bibi and six other people I didn't know. Blood stained their skin and clothes.

"Nice of you to join us." Eva was standing on the other side of the mound. She looked different in Caieta's mind. Her hair was black. But it was tied up in a tight bun at the top of her head. Her eyes were boiling red and her lips were black. Like an infection had changed the color.

Caieta pushed herself to her feet. "Why would you do this?" She barked.

"Well," Eva shrugged. "Why not?" Caieta leaped over the bodies at Eva. Caieta hit the ground where Eva had stood, but Eva no longer stood there. She was on the other side of the pile. Standing in front of me. "Watch this," she whispered to me. Then she turned back to Caieta. She leaned over the pile and grabbed Caieta's neck. She pulled her back over her friends, choking her. She fell to the floor at Eva's feet.

"You were my friend once! Remember?" Caieta yelled.

"No," Eva shook her head. "She was." She pointed at me.

Caieta looked up quickly. "Evangeline! You've got to help! You have to –"

"She has to do nothing!" Eva grabbed a fistful of her hair and pushed her face against Loyce's head. "You have to say your goodbyes! Go ahead! They're dead! Mourn!" She pulled Caieta's head back, blood staining her right cheek. Tears trickled down her face. Eva forced her head against one of the women I didn't recognize. "Come now! Don't tell me you won't miss Wanda!" The woman was probably in her early thirties. She long blonde to match Caieta's and blue eyes. "Come on!" Caieta tried hard not to show her pain but it was carved into her face as if it were stone. "Not them?" Eva pulled her face up and turned her to look at the rest of the room.

Suddenly we were surrounded with heaping piles of dead bodies. Thousands and thousands of dead people. Some we knew. Some we didn't. "This is everyone in the world!" Eva yelled. "Take your pick!" In my panic, I screamed. Eva turned to me and snarled. She threw Caieta against one of the piles. Like they weren't people. Like they were laundry. Like they were nothing. Then she smacked me in the face. "Prepare yourself for the future!" She hit me again. The force threw me off balance.

But instead of the ground, I hit the dirt.

I looked up at Caieta. She was rubbing her face and panting. Her wet hair had broken free from the bands that were holding it back and fallen down over her shoulders, clinging to her stomach. She pulled her hair behind her and stood. She slowed her breathing, pulled on her shirt and shoes, and turned to look at me. She spoke slowly. "Evangeline." Her voice rang with sincerity, but her eyes bred hatred. "I know that you have outrageous powers. I know that you are capable of many things. I know that you are strong and noble. I know that you are brave and courageous. But," she ran her hands through her hair and pulled. "If you lose it and become Eva, do not be offended if I kill you." I nodded.

She rubbed her face again and went to the pavilion. She turned sharply, swinging her arms around to hug Eddie. He was surprised by the contact. She whispered something to him. I doubt that Loyce or

Angel heard. If they did, they didn't take notice of it. Eddie frowned and hugged her back.

Eddie peeled himself from her grasp and looked into her eyes. He said something that shook Loyce's attention. She gaped at him, surprised by whatever he had said. Angel shifted uneasily. His facial expression hardened. Caieta nodded. Eddie sighed and walked down to me.

"I guess I'm next," he said.

I stared at him as he shed his shirt and shoes. He was different. He wasn't the guy that had kidnapped me. He wasn't the guy that hated Caieta. He wasn't the guy who started crying at the park. He was someone else entirely. And I wasn't mad about it.

I looked down at my foot. It still sat in the water. This time blood sprayed from various wounds polluting the water. I had to remind myself that it was an illusion brought on by the cursed pool.

I looked back at Eddie just as he jumped into the water.

The room was a lot darker. As if there was no sunshine, and the moon failed to glow. The fog was more concentrated and burned my throat.

I didn't have to look for Eddie. When I stood up, I saw him sitting on the floor next to a throne. It was stone, spattered with black paint. Red stained the surrounding floor. I hoped it was paint. Eva was sitting on the throne. Eddie imagined her with long red hair. It came all the way down her spine and fell to the floor. She had it tied back in a loose ponytail at the base of her head. Her pupils were red laced with black and brown. Her lips were pale white; the color of unrealistic, movie-made snow and patches of her hands and fingers had turned black and her nails grew out thick and brown like talons.

"Do it now," she said. "Stop stalling."

"I can't. I can't do that." I took a long look at Eddie then. His hair was slicked back with some sort of shiny mousse and a thick grey scar stretched from the left side of his forehead to his eyebrow. "I just can't."

"Why? Just look at them." She pointed at the three women tied up in front of them. "Your mother never liked you." I assumed the woman with deep brown hair was his mother. "Your sister was never around. And Caieta…well, she really hasn't done anything, but it's not that big of a deal."

"I can't do it! My sister! My mother! Caieta! It's Caieta!"

"You've done worse." He shook his head. "No? What about all those innocent Witches you've killed? Is that not worse? Or better yet, Mia."

"I didn't kill her!"

"You knew the consequences of your actions! You knew she would die! And what about Angel? Wasn't it your dagger that punctured Angel's heart? Wasn't it you who did that for me? In my honor?"

"M-me?"

"Don't play dumb. You and I, we're two of a kind." She patted his head. Pain spread across his face. "That's why we're best friends." She ran her hand over his face.

"I killed him?" Grief rose in his voice.

"You killed him! *You* killed him!" She grabbed his face and turned it to look at her. "For me! For us! You're more than just a man, you're a murderer! Me and you, Eddie! You and me. Always." Then she pulled him in and kissed him.

My eyes popped out of my skull. Sincere and utter shock ripped through me.

He pulled away from her and stood up. He walked away, rubbing his hand over his face. "No! This isn't you!" She followed him. "This isn't you!" He turned back to her. "What happened to you?"

She rubbed her hands over his cheeks and down the back of his neck. "This is me. The best version of me." Then she turned, throwing her hands out to flash an image of the glowing earth. "This is all mine. The world at my command because of this power that I wield. All ours."

"Eva," Eddie said as he pulled a dagger from a loop in his belt.

"Edmund!" Eva laughed.

When she turned back around, he plunged it into her heart. Shocked, she looked down at her chest. Blood spilled from her wound. Then she looked back up at Eddie and collapsed. Eddie slid down to catch her. She coughed up a pool blood and then succumbed to her demise. Eddie clung to the Witch's body, holding her to his chest. "And I'm so sorry that I failed you," he said.

I watched in paralyzing sadness. The next time I blinked, I was back on the shore. Nightfall was edging in and the air, that had already been cool enough, was chilling. Eddie and I were still gaping at each other when I realized where we were.

"Your deepest fear," I questioned. "Is killing me?"

"I won't do it. I can't. Not… not for real. I meant what I said," he said. "Back at the shack."

I shook my head. "Eddie –"

"Forget what you saw in there."

"Eddie –"

"I will never –"

"Shut up!" He clenched his jaw. I racked my brain for the words to say so he'd understand what I was feeling. "I…" My mouth hung open for a minute. "I want… I want you to do it." He shook his head. "If I lose it. I want you to kill me."

"Evangeline –"

"I want you to do it! I don't want you to become that person. A planet of people or one evil person. Please, remember that."

He pulled me in and hugged me. His shirt was wet and cold, but I hugged him back. Then he nodded and stood up. He walked over to Loyce. She shook her head. He said something. She shook her head again. He said something else. She sighed, pulled off her shoes and threw them at Eddie. Then she walked down to the pool and glared at me.

"I genuinely hate you," she said. I nodded. She frowned at the water and jumped in.

It was like I had just left off at Eddie's fear. I was standing exactly where I was before. Eddie, Loyce, Eva, Caieta. They hadn't moved. The only difference was Eva's hair. Instead of red it was black. And she wasn't dead. Those were the only differences.

"What are you doing?" Loyce screeched. "Get away from her!"

Eddie pulled away from her and looked at Loyce. "Shut up," he said slowly.

"Get away from her!"

Then Eva was up. She walked over to Loyce and grabbed her throat. Immediately, pain stretched across her face. "Did he not say, 'shut up?' Or are you deaf?" Eva pulled her hand away to reveal a burn mark in the shape of a hand. She smirked at her. "Anyway, Eddie. Do it. Now." Eva strolled over to Eddie's mom and stroked her face. Then she stood behind her. She wrapped her right hand around the woman's throat. "Like this." Then she used her left hand to grab the woman's stomach. She ripped away flesh and dropped it to the floor. The woman screamed in agony as Eva did it again. Then she pushed her hand into the woman's stomach, pulled out a handful of mush she found inside and flung it at Loyce's feet. The woman screamed continuously until Eva snapped her neck. Her body crumpled to the ground like a lifeless toy. "This one next." Eva walked over Caieta. She pulled all of her hair out of her face. "Her. Hurry."

Eddie pulled himself to his feet and strolled over to them. He stood in in front of Caieta, staring down his nose at her. "Why me?"

Eva pulled at Caieta's hair in her frustration. "I told you before. We are two of a kind. So, do it. Now." He nodded.

"Don't do it!" Loyce yelled. But Eddie paid her no mind. He pulled the dagger from his belt loop and plunged it into Caieta's gut. He pulled it up and down, ripping a hole in her stomach. He dropped the blade, watching as the blood ran down her shirt and jeans. Then, just as quickly as he had stabbed her, he thrust his hand into her gut. Caieta didn't scream. She didn't beg. She just tried hard to stifle her agony.

Eva let go of her and began jumping. "Finish it! Do it! Kill her!" Eddie twisted his wrist and with a single burp, blood poured from Caieta's mouth and she was gone. She fell quickly. The fog cleared around her body. The puddle forming around her grew bigger with every second. Eva laughed. "Do the next one." He tore his gaze from Caieta. When it dropped to Loyce she was frowning in shock.

When she realized that she was the next one, she screamed. "Stay away from me!" She turned to Eva. "What have you done to him?"

"I did nothing wrong. It was you who abandoned him!"

"I was trying to protect him!"

"Protect him? You left him with parents that hated him for just being born. And unlike Benzi he can't win back his father's love by being the best. And even he fails at that. Eddie's parents will eternally hate him and only you could've changed that. They worshipped the ground you walked on. And you thought leaving him would help!"

"I thought if I wasn't there they could love him. I was wrong."

"You were pathetically wrong! *I* helped! I made him strong! I made him what he needed to be!"

"You demon!"

"Don't call her that!" Eddie pulled Loyce's attention by physically pulling her shirt. He shook her back and forth. She gasped at his severity as her hair flew around. "Listen to me," he barked. "You're not in charge. I am. This time I make the rules and you follow them." She nodded. He threw her back, flicking his hand like she was trash. She wobbled off balance. Eva grabbed her hair to make sure she didn't fall. Loyce struggled with her restraints uselessly. Her arms were tightly bound behind her back and her knees were taped together. Eddie went over to pick up the blade, wiping it on his jeans. A streak of blood stained his thigh. He turned back to Loyce. Her eyes bulged at the sight of his intentions. But the next time she blinked we were back on the shore.

Her eyes were still big when she looked at me. I stared back at her. She rolled her eyes. "It had nothing to do with you. It was about me."

I stared at her. "I know."

"It's about *my* fears becoming a reality. You were just the gasoline to the fire."

"I know."

"Maybe Eddie's was about you. Maybe he meant what he said to Caieta. Maybe he does. What I fear from you isn't what you'll do. It's what I'll have helped you to do." I nodded. "It was my sins coming back to bite me. It was all I've done to him. All I haven't done. My fear was that I created a monster in my brother. That I, and my mother, and my father, might have destroyed him. That he might look up and find a kindred spirit in evil. That he has nothing else to lose but his life." She looked away from me then.

I realized that no one's fear actually had anything to do with me. Eddie was afraid of betraying someone who put their full faith in him. Someone who finally cared enough to believe in him. He was afraid of failing them. I was that someone.

And Caieta. Her mother and father were already gone. Eddie left her when they were seven. She was afraid that she would have no one left. No one but the monster that had killed them. Benzi wasn't even afraid of me. No. He was afraid that his father's hatred would turn into betrayal. How much hate is too much?

Any of it.

"I was a terrible sister," Loyce continued. "I know that I was. But I'm a girl in the Leadership. We're expected to be cooks, and nurses, and wives. It's like the 1950's. But I didn't want that. I wanted power, so I trained with the boys, and I wanted respect, so I became Mathrel's student. And I was more than just a Huntress. Before I was sixteen, I was being treated like a war goddess. The only issue was the person I most wanted to celebrate with, had been excluded from my life and left with a mother who ignored his existence. I thought that by my leaving, I was killing two birds with one stone. I could chase my dreams and my brother would find happiness at home. I was wrong. How could I do that? How could I be so selfish?"

"You're not his mother," I said.

"I wasn't his sister either. I wasn't there. And the worst part is that even when I found out, I didn't come back. I was so desperate for power and respect, he and I might as well as be strangers." She stood up then.

"That's not true," I shook my head. I thought about how similar their nightmares were. "You guys are two of a kind."

I watched as she walked over to Eddie, took her shoes, slipped them on, and sat down. Angel came down to the pool.

"My turn then," he said, resolutely.

"I suppose so," I nodded. He pulled off his socks, shirt, and shoes and dropped them on the ground. They made a pile next Benzi's. I looked back to at Benzi to see he was still sitting in the car. He was staring at something in the floor. His gaze never broke and his expression never wavered. He was a statue. A statue with contempt carved into its face. I was studying the fall of his hair around his face when suddenly I was no longer there.

I was, again, in the foggy room. But that was no surprise to me. What did surprise me was Angel. He was sitting on the floor in front of Eva. In his version, her hair was black and cut short in a messy bob, like she'd cut it herself with a jagged blade. Blood streamed from her eyes like tears and sweat was building on her forehead.

"No!" Angel cried up at her. He grabbed her feet and pulled them off the ground. She came crashing to the floor with a thud, hitting her head on the ground. Angel jumped over her, grabbing her throat and strangling her. When she died, we were back on the shore. Angel rolled over so he was on his feet, ready to fight me.

"I don't understand," I said. He dropped his stance. "What did that mean?"

"It meant that I'm afraid that I was wrong. That Mathrel, a man more than twice my age, actually knew what he was doing. That perhaps you are evil and you want to see the world burn. That you're putting on this show until you come into your full power at seventeen."

"That doesn't sound like a *subconscious* fear."

"It's not!" He shook head, his overgrown hair flying around his head. "It became a very conscious fear the moment I decided to save your life! What if you're a monster? What if you decide to kill everyone? What if I helped a genocidal maniac? What if I should've let Mathrel kill you?"

Pain rushed up my throat. "Do you really think should've? Do you really think I'm capable?"

He leaned down into my face. "You seem increasingly capable with every day." I bit back the urge to cry as he turned to look at pavilion. "But no. I don't."

I watched as he marched around the already sleeping Eddie, Benzi, and Loyce. Caieta sat on the stairs. She was watching me, but she didn't say anything.

They thought it was possible. No matter how unwilling they were to admit it. They were all aware – no, they were all sure of the likely possibility of me being a bloodthirsty demon. Maybe it was more true than I realized. Maybe I was more like Eva than I thought. Perhaps, just maybe, I had gotten a glimpse of my future.

I looked away from them and lay on the shore. I slept there. I would come regret not moving. I had left my foot in the water.

Sixteen

I was almost entirely sure that I was dreaming. My certainty came from two facts: first, I was sitting in the dark, enveloped in fog. The same room in which I had witnessed all of my friends' fears. And second, I was staring at Eva. Her presence alone was solid evidence toward the dream theory. In my vision of Eva, she looked hardly so gruesome. She looked like a ghost with long black hair falling behind her like water. Her mouth, painted red, gasped at just the same moment I did, revealing the jagged fangs behind her lips.

I was about to tell her off. Tell her that I was nothing like her. That she could go to hell. But she opened her mouth when I did, so I stopped to listen to whatever threats she was going to dole out. She paused too and we both glared at each other.

"Hey!" It wasn't Eva who yelled and we both turned to see who had intruded on our conversation. But I didn't have to look to know who it was. This was one of the only voices I'd heard over the last two weeks. A voice I'd heard yell and cry. The voice that confused me constantly. A voice that had vowed to stand by me, but I prayed wouldn't, if I was to become Eva for real.

Eddie.

Even though I was glad to see him and welcomed his assistance, I panicked as he made his way towards us. I panicked because Eva could obliterate him in seconds if she was as powerful as I thought. What was I supposed to do if she decided to snap her fingers and make him pop? Nothing in this state. The fog kept me from being able to move very well. What was he expecting to do? I know I had told him to kill her, but I thought I could handle this myself.

Still, he marched toward me, paying her no mind, like she wasn't there. In that moment, the only magic I wanted was the gift of telepathy. So, he could hear the warnings going off like a siren in my head. I shot a look back at Eva and saw that there was nothing I could do. She was already turning to look back at me, sharing my glare as we both developed a strategy. Eddie, holding his familiar stare of calculation, pulled a dagger from his back pocket and brought it down over me. I grabbed his arm before the blade reached my chest and looked at Eva, sure that she had him under some sort of mind control. But her expression surprised me. Instead of looking amused, she was staring at me, horrified and confused. As if trying to understand what I was doing. And she was standing in such a strange position. One hand held awkwardly above her body, stretched out and then curled around someone's wrist.

Only then did I see the huge wooden frame that enclosed Eva's body. Dumbfounded, I pushed Eddie away and reached out to grab Eva. She mimicked my movement exactly. Mirrored it. But where our hands should have met, there was only glass.

In an instant, my dream became a nightmare. There was no Eva. That was me. Me in a mirror. Ghastly and evil. Eddie stood beside me, hardly in the frame. He grabbed my wrist and said,

"I'm sorry that have to kill you."

I woke with a gasp. My eyes opening to darkness. I thought I was still asleep until I realized that my lungs were filling with cold moisture. Oxygen was being replaced with water. I looked around my suffocating prison to realize that I couldn't tell up from down.

Suddenly a hand grabbed my ankle and started pulling me down. Or maybe it was up. I thought I was being rescued, but then another hand grabbed my wrist and began pulling me in the other direction. Oxygen deprivation was taking its toll in my body. I had no time to decide which hand I trusted before I fainted.

***

When I woke next, water was jumping out of my mouth like frogs. Eddie was leaning over me with his hands over my chest ready to administer CPR. He leaned back and helped me sit up. I coughed like an old man facing death. Although, I supposed that wasn't too off.

"Thank God!" Angel yelled running over to hug me. He pulled me away from Eddie into his arms.

"Okay," Loyce said rubbing her hands over her face and into her hair like she was holding back a scream. "Now that crisis is averted, should we start training?"

"Could you give her a minute," Eddie said, standing up. "She almost drowned."

"Sure." Loyce shrugged. "Let's pretend that's she probably not already dead."

"What are you talking about?" I demanded, pulling away from Angel.

Loyce marched toward me. "When we woke up, you were nowhere to be found. We thought you ran away. We spent more than an hour looking for you. Then we wondered if you fell in the water. I first thought maybe you wanted to know your fears. But then I remembered," she leaned in close to my face. "You were gone more than *an hour*. The fact that we found you just before you happened to drown seems unlikely."

"But she didn't drown," Caieta said, pulling Loyce back.

I stared at them and wondered why they had even tried to save. Obviously, they didn't want to. I thought back to what Angel had said the night before. *What if I helped a genocidal maniac? What if I should've let Mathrel kill you?* Loyce was right. They were just pretending now.

"Let's just get started now," Benzi said.

We fell into practice then. For a couple of hours, we did fighting routines and offense training. Loyce was better at everything than everyone else. She made a point to keep me on my toes by punching me in the stomach at random moments. Caieta took an hour to help me practice magic. I was a much faster learner than she anticipated. At around 6:30 I was tired and drenched with sweat. Benzi decided that was the perfect time to try hand-to-hand combat. One against two. Me against Benzi and Loyce. I hardly understood how that was a good idea. But I was kicked in the chest before I could object.

I peeled myself up and glared at Loyce. She shrugged. I rolled my eyes and charged. Loyce threw her fist but I dodged it. Benzi retaliated with a punch to my left cheek. I could feel the bruise forcing its way to the surface. They had circled me twice now. I turned and swung my foot at Benzi and he dipped out of it, but when he leaned back in I struck him in the nose. That left Loyce behind me. She wrapped her arm around my throat. Oxygen seeped out of my lungs like water through a plastic bag. I remembered the feeling of drowning and cursed her for helping me relive the traumatic experience. I threw my head back into her face. She let go and air flooded back into me. Benzi tackled me then. He sat up on my stomach and prepared to punch me. He was a whole lot stronger than I was. One punch would be ridiculously painful. I put my hand in his face. He froze. I pushed him off me and stood up. Loyce gaped at me.

"Magic?" She demanded. "Touché."

I charged at her. She grabbed my hand when I swung at her. Benzi was up. He wrapped his leg around my foot, pulling me to the ground. I hit the dirt with my face. Loyce pulled my hair so my head came off the ground. She hit my face into the ground once. Twice. Three times. Four times.

"Okay!" Angel yelled. "You won!"

"Shut up, Angel!"

"It's over!"

"Sit down." She hit my face again. Blood spilled down my chin.

Angel began over to me, but it wasn't needed. I turned so that I looked up at her. I grabbed her shirt and threw her over my shoulder onto her back. I was glad I could defy gravity because I wasn't nearly strong enough to throw her anywhere. Then I pulled my leg from under Benzi and kicked him in the chest. Then again in the face. When he let go of the other foot I stood up and kicked him again. He was out cold now. Angel stopped under the pavilion and watched. Loyce was up then. She charged at me. I stepped away, so she'd fall. As an alternative, she pulled my arm, so I'd fall instead and she'd gather her balance. But I grabbed her arm and pulled her with me. I fell on my back, she her stomach. I immediately rolled over and stood up. She was just as quick. She charged at me again. But when I stepped away she fell into the steps of the pavilion, breaking through them. I raced up behind her and pulled her away from the stairs. I grabbed the broken board, turned, and swung it at Loyce's face. It shattered on impact. Loyce fell to the ground, out cold.

I collapsed onto my butt with a sigh. I rubbed my hand over my face, wiping off the blood and flinging it to the dirt in front of me. The scars, cuts, and bruises were gone. Angel sat down next to me and sighed.

"What?" I questioned.

"I've made a bad habit of underestimating you."

I laughed to myself. "Thanks." I dropped my head on my knees. We sat there for ten minutes staring at the black pool just beyond Loyce and Benzi. It seemed so dangerous, especially for a small body of water. It was a large bath that haunted everyone, even Angel. Angel. How did he know what he was doing? How could he gather the confidence to think he was doing the right thing? How did he have so much faith? Was he really an angel? I looked up at him. At the magnificent sculpture that was his jawline and cheekbone.

I stood up and walked over to Loyce. I slid my hand over her cheek and lip and did the same to Benzi, watching as the cuts and bruises receded. Loyce sat up about an hour later. She looked around and declared she was hungry. We all filed into the car. We stuffed Benzi into the back seat. We drove back through the woods to the main road, and found a burger place when nightfall began creeping in.

We slept in the parking lot that night. Well I didn't sleep. I stared out the window. Once again, I found myself wondering what I'd be doing if I wasn't Evangeline Welt the Prophecy Child. At almost

9:30, I'd be watching a movie. Something scary no doubt. The moon was hardly visible; a waning crescent. I thought it was so interesting. I studied it until it climbed down and the sun crawled up. I thought about how insane it was that our universe was so perfect. A detailed design that falls perfectly on time. Day after day, year after year.

It was somewhere around eight when Loyce woke. She shook Eddie awake, demanding that he clean his face. Grease from the fries ringed his mouth. Benzi was a mess, too. Ketchup stained his chin. Angel woke up after them, because Loyce's yells of disgust were hard to sleep through. So, we began our short trek to Warren, Vermont.

Only two hours had passed when Angel pulled off to a gas station. Eddie and Benzi went inside to buy some sodas. When Eddie returned he had smile on his face bigger than the Joker's. He came jumping and laughing.

"What you are doing right now?" Loyce demanded.

"I have a great idea!" Eddie laughed.

"What is it?"

"Let's be teenagers."

"…I'm sorry. But I thought that based on your age you were already a teenager."

"No, no. I mean, real teenagers. Human teenagers, who aren't fighting a war. Like Isaiah said. Evangeline turns seventeen tomorrow. The Council and the Leadership will be waiting for a war to end all wars and we'll smack in the middle of it. I'm not saying we let our guard down or anything. I'm just saying maybe we should go to the mall or to a party."

"It's a Thursday," I said. "Teenagers are at school. And Thursday night they're doing homework. No one's throwing any party."

"Really?" He pulled a folded-up flyer from his back pocket. He unfolded it and showed it to us. "Dorothy is." It was a bright purple paper that read in bold letters:

**Dorothy's Spring Party
is tonight at 8!
Be there if you wanna have
a good time!**

An address was below that.

"You guys," Eddie said. "I wanna have a good time. What could it possibly hurt? Other than the high score we've acquired in the game called BOREDOM?"

Angel rolled his eyes. "Then let's go to the mall."

We found ourselves at the Berlin Mall after a 45-minute drive. I realized, then, that I hadn't been to the mall in about three months, and my friends had never gone at all. I didn't want to end up babysitting so the girls and boys went their separate ways. Caieta, Loyce, and I went exploring through clothing stores. As tough as Loyce was, she was still a girl, and she liked to shop. Although, she was surprised by the variety of colors underwear could be.

"Why does it matter what color your underwear is?" She asked continuously.

"Find anything you like?"

She looked up from her handful of colorful undies and frowned. "It seems I have, yes." Then she glared and looked back down.

I huffed. "Let me ask you something."

"Well if I can't stop you…"

I rolled my eyes. "Why do you hate me?"

She looked back up at me and laughed. "I don't hate you, Evangeline. I don't *like* you in any sense of the word and I don't trust you whatsoever. But I don't hate you." She dropped the clothes back on table and planted her hands on her hips. She pursed her lips in a kind of thoughtful way. "But that could change. My brother trusts you. He's probably the only one who does fully. Who knows, things change."

Eddie trusted me. The last person I would've thought, seeing how adamant he was about killing me when we first met. He'd changed so much over this trip. "Is he okay?"

"I don't know." She shrugged. "He's… different. Better. Are you playing with him?"

"What?"

"I don't know what kind of feelings he has for you. I can't tell if it's romantic or if it's just loyalty." She stepped closer to me and planted her finger on my chest. "But you better not break him." I nodded. "I don't know what's going to happen tomorrow. But I swear to whatever is out there that is good and holy, if you break him, I will destroy you." I nodded again. Then she smiled and stepped back.

We went and paid for everything then. I bought a pair of jeans, a leather bracelet, and a Beatles t-shirt. Loyce bought a load of underwear and Caieta bought shoes and a blouse. Little did we realize that we had spent six hours in that mall. We had hardly purchased anything. It was made clear to me then how much I liked Caieta and Loyce. Caieta was really silly and daring, and she had the most contagious laugh. Loyce was unnecessarily mean but she was cool, relaxed, and down to earth.

We met the boys at a shoe store after going to seven other stores. They had hardly anything either. But we still had three hours to kill before Dorothy's party. We decided to go a movie. I changed into my Beatles shirt and jeans in the girls' room before we went.

I also pulled Angel aside. While Eddie and Loyce were going over movie choices I finally gave Angel his present. It was the leather bracelet. I clicked it around his wrist.

"Happy birthday," I said. I watched as he stared at it in disbelief. "Um…I know it's not much, but I wanted to give you something in case I didn't have a chance to later." He said nothing. "If you don't like it –"

"What?" He gawked at me, confused. "Why wouldn't I like it? I just can't even believe you remembered." He pulled me into his chest and wrapped his arms around me. "It's perfect." I laughed. "What's so funny? I'm serious."

"I know." I pushed away from him. "I'm glad you like it."

I walked away from him, fleeing from the emotional significance that moment held. Then we went to the worst movie I'd ever seen. It was a complete waste of money. When it was over, night had fallen. It took us an hour to reach the address on the flyer. And when we got there, we wanted to leave.

"It's a house party," Loyce said. "The cops will be here in no time."

"It's just a high school party," Eddie said.

"How do you know it's a *high school* party?"

"I guessed." She sighed. "Let's just go up to the door and ask."

Loyce rolled her eyes at him. "Fine, let me do the talking."

He nodded but when we reached the guy at the door, Eddie was the first to speak. "This is a high school party, right?"

The guy narrowed his brown eyes at him. "Dude, Lady Dorothy is still in high school. Of course, it's a high school party."

He looked at Loyce and grinned.

The guy rubbed his hand over his chocolate brown face and sighed. "What high school do you go to?"

"Um, the Leadership," Angel said.

"Where is that?"

"California."

"Sorry," he shook his head. "But you're not on the list."

"Like anyone is on that blank piece of paper," Benzi said, "I didn't realize gas station flyers were so exclusive."

Caieta raised her hand to silence him. She walked up to the boy, grabbed his face, leaned in and whispered something his in ear. Then she leaned back and smiled. "Please?"

"Yeah go ahead," the boy said quickly. Caieta seemed flirty and nice, although what she had said was apparently anything but that. The boy looked panicky and frantic. Frightened. Whatever she said had thrown him for a loop.

"What'd you say to him?" I asked.

"Nothing really," she shrugged. "Just that I was going to say please and he was going to say yes. *Or* I could rip his esophagus out with my teeth and use it as a straw to drink his blood."

"…What a nice way to put it," I laughed.

"Exactly," she smiled. She grabbed my hand and pulled me behind her through the crowd. We emerged in the living room, surrounded by dancing teens. "When was the last time you danced?"

"Never," I laughed.

"Well, let me show you." She pulled my arms left and right to mimic the rapid swaying of the people around us. Then Loyce came up behind me and grabbed my hips.

"You're doing it all wrong," she said, and began swinging my waist in a circle.

I felt like a puppet failing to imitate human movement. "You know," I said pulling from them. "I don't think this is my thing." I pointed at the kitchen counter, which had been turned into a bar. "I'm gonna get a soda." I made my way through the sea of people to the polished wooden bar in the kitchen. The bartender looked me over. "Can I get a soda?" The guy nodded and slid the unopened blue can at me. I caught it and popped it open as another guy slid up beside me. I glanced him. There was nothing special about him. He had short brown hair, brown eyes and a regular face. The only strangeness I could find was that he was older than everyone else, and he stared down at me for a long time.

"Hey," he said. "This is boring huh?"

"No," I smiled politely, "I'm having fun."

"Let me show you a really good time." He leaned into me.

"That's okay." I stepped away.

"Come on." He ran his hand over my arm. I pulled away from him. "I can show you something more interesting."

"No thanks." I turned to walk away but he grabbed my arm. I turned back to look at him and suddenly time was racing by. People sped around us, hours zipping forward. I could tell in my panic that I was the one doing it. I pushed him away. Time corrected itself and I was back in reality.

Eddie was there then. He grabbed the guy's shoulder and turned him to face him. "She said no." The guy looked him over. He scoffed and walked off.

Eddie watched as the guy made his way out the back door before turning to me. "I've been looking for you everywhere."

I shrugged. "Well, I've been here. Thanks for that, by the way."

He laughed. "It's my job, isn't it?"

I liked to see him smile. He didn't do it often but I liked it when he did. I remembered when I first saw the voracity of his canine teeth. I thought maybe he'd gotten a jaw transplant from a wolf. But it was different to see them in an expression of joy instead of a threat.

"So," he said, rubbing his hand along the backside of his neck. "Your birthday is in a couple of hours and I figure we weren't celebrating or anything, but I uh…well, just because…I thought…"

I laughed at his nervousness. "Did you get me something?"

"Yeah," he laughed. "I figured it was only fair if I was also accurately represented."

"Also?"

"Angel's necklace."

"Oh yeah!" I grabbed the string of thorns hanging around my neck. I had forgotten that I was wearing it or that Angel had even given it to me.

"Yeah so." Eddie shoved his hand into his pocket and pulled out a ring. "I swear I'm not asking you to marry me." He slid it onto my index finger. "I just wanted you to have this." It was a small sliver stem that wrapped around my finger and bloomed into a crystal rose. It was severely different from the small daggers that hung around my throat.

"It's beautiful," I said, mesmerized by its simple elegance. "Thank you."

He smiled at me again. I bit my lip, unsure of what to make of the moment. *Should I hug him? Should I...? Does it matter?* But I did nothing. Instead, Angel slid into our moment.

"Can I steal her for a minute?" He asked Eddie.

Eddie glanced at me, then stepped back, nodding. I watched him as he made his way over to Loyce who was spinning with the DJ.

But there was still Angel standing in front of me, craving my attention. "Hey," he said.

"Hey you," I laughed. He pulled me in to hug him. He did that a lot. I pulled away from him and laughed again. "What's up?"

"Evangeline, there's something I really want to tell you." I nodded. "You turn seventeen tomorrow, and well, if I'm not there…just I –"

"If you're not there?" I questioned.

"Whatever happens tomorrow, I want you to know that these last two weeks, however stressful, however dangerous, however nerve-wracking, were the best I ever had. I experienced pure joy and legitimate fear and…I wasn't just existing anymore. It's like you…freed me from shackles. I had lived with them my entire life, so I didn't know I wasn't moving 'til I got to walk away." He laughed, then he twisted the leather bracelet around his wrist. "I've spoken to every type of person this planet could birth more than once. But I never met one person like you. So uniquely…magical in every sense of the word." He smiled at me. "I just wanted to tell you that… how much I… I love you. That's all."

I swallowed hard and he hugged me. I hugged him back. The words kept running through my mind on replay. I don't know how such a thing could occur. Angel? Never had I ever guessed that someone would fall in love with me. Especially Angel. I was walking death. He deserved so much more. He deserved someone who felt the same way.

Suddenly, Eddie was tugging both of us out of the building. "Hurry up! What are you doing?" He pulled us through the crowd and out the back door of the house. There we met back up with Caieta, Loyce, and Benzi.

"What took you so long?" Benzi demanded.

"What's going on?" I asked.

"Hunters," Eddie said lightly.

"We need to leave now," Loyce said. We turned to race out of the alleyway to find it was blocked off. Eight men in black cargo pants, black shirts, and black combat boots. They stared at us dauntlessly.

Hunters.

I looked back, debating if going back through the house was a better. I decided risking everyone else's life was not an option. Slowly, we approached the group of men. They stood in a line in front of us. Directly in front of me stood the man from the bar, the one that had tried to get me to leave with him. I should've known.

I glared at him. He was the first to move. The rest of them fell in line behind him. The first man lunged at me. I leaned away from him so that his swing fell behind me. Angel was fighting against two men, so was Eddie. Loyce and Caieta were able to carry their own weight. I came to the conclusion that Huntresses were like ninjas. One moment Caieta was on the guy's back, the next she made good on her on promise to rip someone's throat out.

The guy in front of me just became more and more aggressive. He punched me in the face again and again. I spat out the blood that was flowing from my nose and lips. I managed to punch his gut and then his face. He grabbed my wrist and twisted it so that my arm exposed all my veins. I grabbed his throat and burned his flesh. He jumped back, rubbing his hand over his scorched flesh. Then, he pulled a blade from his boot. It was a long black dagger with a handle you might find in an ancient Egyptian tomb. I jumped to kick it from his hand but somehow, I never made my mark.

Angel had grabbed my arms and spun me around so that I served my kick to the last man Angel was battling. I kicked him in the left side of his face. He fell, and blood spilled out of his mouth to the concrete. He was out cold. My back was still pressed up against Angel's. Suddenly a sharp pain burned into my spine. Blood seeped down my shirt into jeans. I pulled myself away from him and turned back to see what happened. I looked down to find the tip of that black dagger was sticking out of Angel's back into mine. Suddenly it was ripped away. Angel fell to one knee. The man kicked him in the face. He fell on his back. I looked over at the dagger. Angel's blood dripped off it to the ground. I dropped to Angel, attempting to heal his wound before it was too late.

The blade swung down in front of me, hitting Angel again in his chest. My attention and rage turned to the man. He glared at me. I stood up, put my fists together and slammed them into his chest. Hot air rushed out of me, throwing the man to his back. He yelled in agony. He sat up slowly and I kicked him in the chin, throwing him back down. He crawled to his knees, gripping his dagger. I ran and jumped over him grabbing his neck and throwing him over my shoulder. He slammed into ground on his stomach, crushing the concrete. He strained to breathe, coughing and spitting blood. More like vomiting than spitting. I ripped the dagger from his hand and forced it between his shoulder blades.

I turned back to Angel. I raced to him and pressed my hands into his wounds. Nothing happened. He lay perfectly still on the ground. "Angel," I whispered. "Angel?" I shook him. "Angel." He didn't move. "Ang–" I stuttered as the realization that I was too late fell on me. "Angel…" His necklace slowly broke from around my neck and fell in pieces on his chest. Angry tears streaked my face. "Angel. Angel!"

I seemed to be the only one who knew what just happened.

"Whoa!" Eddie yelled. "I feel so alive!" He turned to me and stopped. He looked down at Angel. He walked over slowly. "Wh… Is…" He dropped to his knees. "No. No. Angel. No, Angel." He placed his hands on Angel's chest, a tear dropping down his cheek.

Far away, I could hear sirens. "Let's go," Loyce yelled. "Like now!"

"Evangeline," Eddie said. "We need to go." I didn't move. "We've got to go now." I still didn't move. He stood up slowly and grabbed my arm. "Come on." He tugged me along behind the others. He kept getting faster until eventually he let go and we were running.

We raced through the streets and sidewalks and alleyways. I panted in anxiety and pain. Angel's heartbeat song rang in my ears. *What am I doing?* I thought. *Why is this happening? What am I doing? How did I let this happen?* I stopped suddenly in the street. No one was coming. Anyone in the area was at Dorothy's party. The streetlight loomed over me. Everyone stopped ahead of me and turned back to look at me.

"Why'd you stop?" Benzi questioned.

"What am I doing?" I asked.

"Running for your life, for one," Loyce said.

"What?" I cried. "Why? Why!" Tears poured down my face. "Why is this happening? What am I doing?"

"What are you talking about?" She questioned. "What is she talking about? Where's Angel?"

"He's dead," I coughed. "He's dead!"

"He was stabbed," Eddie clarified staring at the road. "Bled out and died in the alley. But, Evangeline, we need to keep moving." He spoke slowly and clearly, like he was compensating for my current insanity. "Come on."

"You just want to leave his body there?"

"Would you rather drag him through the street?"

"He was our friend. He saved my life. I let him die!"

"Oh, bump this," Benzi began, over my cries. "I'm just going to pick her –"

"Don't you touch her!" Eddie yelled, grabbing his shirt and pulling him off his course. Eddie glared at him through the blue light of the moon. Then he looked back at me. "Evangeline, please. Just come with us."

"Are we in a gang? Cause it feels like it. Like a turf war or something."

"Evangeline?"

I stared at him, then we continued down the empty street. We walked for a while. What would have been a ten-minute run became a thirty-minute walk. Finally, we came upon a hotel. Loyce checked us in, and then we took the long grueling elevator ride up to the third floor. We walked passed the nine rooms to 310. Caieta unlocked the door and we all spilled inside. I walked out to the balcony, closed the door behind me and looked down at the quiet city below. A cold breeze swept around, encasing me in a ball of cold air. My bare arms began to freeze first, then my feet. I realized I was doing this to myself, as the air just kept getting colder. I stood out there for twenty minutes before going back inside. Caieta and Eddie sat on the bed, heavy in conversation. Loyce and Benzi stood on the other side of the room in a conversation of their own. They all turned to me when I walked in.

"Evangeline!" Caieta cried. "Your lips are blue! You must be freezing!" She ran over to me and rubbed her hands on my arms.

"Well," I said robotically. "If you want me to state the obvious, I am a tad bit cold."

"Here. Sit –"

"No." I brushed her away. "I need to go… somewhere."

"Where?" Eddie asked staring.

"I... I don't know."

"Well," Benzi said. "We can't let you leave."

"You can't let me leave," I demanded glaring. "You can't let me leave?" I bit my lip. "You sound just like your father."

"He didn't mean it like that," Eddie said. "He just means it's almost midnight."

"What?" I panicked.

"Four minutes," Loyce clarified looking at her watch.

"No, no, no. I need to go." I charged at the door.

"Evangeline." Eddie stood, suddenly in my way. He took precaution not to touch me. I wondered if he was trying to respect my boundaries or…I don't know. "Stay."

I stared up at him. He stared back. "I can't do this, Eddie."

"Yeah." He nodded glancing down at my hands. "Yes, you can. He died for you." I heaved a heavy sigh and looked down at his shoes. "Evangeline?" Tears trickled out of my eyes to the floor. "Evangeline look at me." I looked up at him. "Angel died. For you. He believed in you. Far beyond reason. Way past insanity. And you know," he smiled. "Angel was always smarter than all of us. You know, he was the stable one too. He always knew what he was going to do next. Yet he was nowhere near predictable. Then, there was me, the reckless and unstable one. The gambler. But this time, Angel took the gamble on you. Don't." A tear spilled down his cheek. "Don't let it be in vain." I pursed my lips to stop crying and nodded at him.

"I mean," Benzi said. "It would be a shame if he died then we had to kill you."

"Shut up, Benzi!"

"You know, Benzi," I said biting into my lip. "You and your dad are two of a kind."

"Excuse me?"

"Your dad knew, didn't he? That I was a Blood? That's why he sent you to watch me. Right?" Benzi didn't say anything. "Moreover, he knew that my prophecies were mixed. That's what he meant by that bloodline comment. Right?" I thought back to his forced smile. "You're here to kill me, aren't you?"

He shook his head.

"Liar," I laughed. "All you do is lie!"

"I'm not! I mean, I was sent to kill you. That's kind of my job. But that's not why I'm here now."

"How did they find us? How did they know where we were? How do they keep finding us?"

"They have your blood. Do you know how easy it is to find a Witch with just her blood? It's even easier to find a Huntress, and you're a half-breed." He shook his head. "I'm not here to kill you right now."

"Why not? Why not just do it?"

"What?" Eddie gaped.

"You're being ridiculous," Caieta snapped.

"If you do it now," I wiped my face, "you won't have to worry about it tomorrow."

"I don't mean to interrupt," Loyce said. "But, five seconds."

"Four," Benzi said.

"Three," Caieta said.

"Two," Eddie peered down at me.

One.

Part 3:
Tears

Seventeen

At the stroke of midnight, everything changed. My body tensed in sheer agony. My eyes as red-hot liquid forced itself from pupils. I rushed into the bathroom and looked in the mirror to see that fire was burning into my irises. I screamed, rubbing my eyes. With another scream, I collapsed onto the floor. My legs gave way as my back snapped in half. Straight up my spinal cord like a Kit-Kat. Like someone just broke it apart. On the floor, I wailed in pain. Eddie's voice pounded in my skull, but I couldn't hear a word.

They pulled me out of the bathroom onto the carpet in the middle of the room. I rolled on my side to get off my back. I lay on my left arm to subdue the pain. Then suddenly, my arm popped. It snapped in half. It did this again and again. My left arm and hand was becoming nothing more than a mess of destroyed bones and weak skin. My right arm was thrown back behind me, and it too demolished itself. Then my right leg and then my left, like someone took a sledgehammer and just beat me in. One by one, destroying each one of my limbs. Before I could even blink next, every bone in my body was shattered. It was like something was fighting to get out. Like crawling through my body to do. Like something, or someone, wanted out.

Eddie, Loyce, Caieta, and Benzi panicked. They decided to roll me on my back, which helped no one. But that wasn't the end of it.

Starting with my stomach, searing pain spread through my organs. My stomach contracted, tearing itself apart. My lungs crawled into my throat and turned themselves inside out. I couldn't scream, I could barely even breathe. One after another, my organs defeated themselves. Blood pooled from my mouth and nose.

And still there was more. One by one, my teeth pried themselves from my mouth. They pushed their way from my gums leaving gaping holes in their wake. All my teeth were gone. I felt like an infant. An extremely miserable and crippled infant.

Hardly anything was left of my heart when it stopped.

***

There were many things I thought I would do before I died. When I was four I thought I would be a princess. I could marry a powerful king and rule a kingdom, wear beautiful gowns, and dance through the night. When I was a six I wanted to be an actress. A gorgeous movie star. I could be in magazines and on posters worldwide.

When I was seven I didn't know anymore. I just wanted to live long enough to be something. When I was fourteen I stopped guessing. I figured I'd find out when the time came. I never once imagined that

I'd be dying a slow and painful death while in my teens. Especially when I was praying I that I could live forever.

***

My brain was pressing against my skull when I woke. I was so cold, but my muscles couldn't work up the nerve to shiver. My gums were bleeding, spilling over my tongue and out of my mouth. My lungs burned as I breathed, and my limbs ached even as I laid still.

I pulled my eyes open to a white light hanging above me. Four fluorescent lights were built into the ceiling, beaming down into my eyes. I looked around once. The room circulated freezing air, getting colder and colder with every loop. I was wrapped up in blue cotton blanket, tightly. I then realized it was a means of restraint. It was subtle but effective. I looked around again. The walls were completely white. A dull, chalky white. To the left of my bed was a row of chairs, one of which held my clothes. My blue jeans, my Beetles shirt, and green sneakers. I prayed I wasn't naked beneath that blanket. Then I realized was in the hospital, in a hospital gown. I turned my head to the right, shifting all the blood in my mouth to spill down my face.

Eddie, Caieta, Loyce, and Benzi stood in a circle whispering. They were panicked, and their words were rushed. They were being too secretive.

"It could be," Loyce said quickly.

"It's not," Caieta retaliated.

"How do you know?"

"Because it's Evangeline! Okay? We know Evangeline."

"Do we?" Benzi questioned.

"Yes!" Eddie exclaimed. "Yes, we do."

"Okay," Loyce rubbed her face. "I know she's your friend but think about it."

"She's right," Benzi said. "I mean, it's Eva. Look at her." I closed my eyes as they turned to look at me. "Her hair is matted and tangled with thorns. Where in the hell did those thorns come from? And her eyes. They're flaming red!"

"And her mouth is full of blood from the teeth that have been replaced with fangs! How can she fix that?"

Eddie nodded. "Okay, okay I get why you –"

"Eddie! My stupid naïve little brother! Stop being stupid and naïve for one minute and face facts! Evangeline…as amazing as she *was*…she's a monster now. And with her being the most powerful Witch to ever exist, we should take advantage of her weakness in this moment. Don't you understand?"

I opened my eyes and strained to speak but instead a thick bloody cough jumped from my throat. They all turned and stared at me. They stood there and gaped at me stunned, wide-eyed, and almost afraid. I coughed again spewing blood all over my blanket. I coughed in frenzy, almost chocking. They still stood there and stared. I sat up, pushing back the blanket as every bone in my body creaked. My neck popped as I turned to look at them. They cringed away. Their eyes were wide, mouths open, and eyebrows furrowed.

They were terrified of me.

I studied them, waiting for them to say something. Anything to know they didn't hate me. But they didn't say a word. I shifted slightly to see their reaction. They jumped. My friends, the only four people that I could trust, were horrified of me.

I couldn't stay here. Not with them. I turned away and jumped out of the bed. I was so glad my gown didn't open in the back. I grabbed my clothes and turned back to them.

"I'm going to change," I said. They nodded.

I slowly skirted around them to the bathroom. They watched me as I flicked on the light and closed the door. I locked it. I put my clothes down on the toilet seat and stared into the mirror.

I almost didn't recognize myself. My curly black hair was twice its original length, hanging at my thighs, tangled with weeds and thorns. But not haphazardly. It was like someone put each twig in, one at a time, by hand. My eyes were not my eyes. The steel blue that I could never get used to, that once filled them was now replaced by a scary crimson red, swirling with a bright flame color. My pupils were dancing like a molting lava. Then, my teeth. No. Not teeth. I didn't even have teeth. Fangs. I had fangs. All those teeth that had pushed themselves out of my skull had replaced themselves with sharp, marble white daggers. They had become stained with red from the blood that still filled my mouth.

I scanned the little room for a brush. I found a comb. I tore it from the sink and began tearing it through my hair. I ripped thorns and twigs out with chunks of my own hair. I pulled and yanked until it seemed as though they were all out. I looked down at the floor at the mess that represented me. When I looked back up at the mirror my hair was once again tangled and ugly. I looked back down at the floor to find there was no mess at all.

"What?" I demanded. "No. Why?"

"Evangeline?" Caieta called. "We want to talk to you."

I stared at the door through the mirror for a moment. Then there was that feeling of something trying to escape. To rip itself out of my body. To free itself. Then, CRACK! The mirror burst into pieces.

My chest began to hurt with anxiety. My heart was pounding radically, and my mind raced like a bullet. *What is happening? What do they want?* I thought. *This is a trap. They're gonna kill me! They think I'm a monster. I...I can't trust them.*

I changed back into my bloody clothes quickly, putting my shoes on the wrong feet. I switched them hurriedly and ripped open the door. I had forgotten that I had locked it, and the frame came off with it. I held the entire door and its fame by the doorknob. My friends jumped away from me, frightened by the severity of my actions.

"Evangeline?" Caieta asked cautiously. "Are you okay?" She searched my face for familiarity but looked away when she couldn't find any.

I gaped at her a moment, wondering if she saw what happened last night. If she hadn't seen me nearly die. *Am I okay? Does it look like I'm okay?* "I'm...fine," I said, trying to seem as calm as I could manage. But my voice came out broken.

"Sit down," Loyce said, gesturing to the bed.

I leaned the door against the wall, skirted around them to the bed, and sat down. They all watched me intently. I realized only then how badly I was shaking. But I wasn't cold. Caieta broke from the crowd first and sat down beside me. "Evangeline," she said again. "Are you okay?"

I looked over at her slowly, making sure not to frighten her. "I'm. Fine."

"You don't seem fine."

"*You* don't seem fine!" I snapped back at her. "You seem afraid."

"Afraid?" She pretended to laugh.

"Don't patronize me!"

"Okay," she nodded. "I'm not afraid of you, of who you are. But what –"

"What I can do?"

"I'm afraid of what…what your ability might have done to your way of thinking."

"What? What! Are you fucking kidding me?"

"Evangeline, you just swore. For no reason. You're agitated and defensive. So, no I'm not kidding. I believe that…your magic…might've taken a toll on your mind."

"Like a poison of something? Well, screw you!"

"I'm saying this as your friend. You're not fine. In my opinion, you're anything but fine."

"And what do you know? I've known you for two weeks! You've barely even scratched the surface, Boo Bear!" Her eyes jumped open. I looked over at Eddie and his expression matched Caieta's. "Oh, you didn't think I heard you gossiping about me! Do you think I'm deaf or just stupid?"

"No," Eddie said. "I thought you were asleep."

I stood up quickly. Just as quickly Caieta was up and staring at me. I marched over to Eddie and stood in his face. "What?"

"What's happening to you? I can hardly recognize you."

"You don't like my new look?"

"Do you like it? Is it an accurate representation of what's inside?"

"What if it is?"

"Then, no. I don't like it."

"What happened to believing in me? You said you believed in me!"

"I'm trying but you're not making it very easy!" He rubbed his face. "Look, I'm trying understand what just happened. Cause you don't look like you anymore. You're not acting like you anymore. Just... what am I supposed to think?"

"And what do you think? That I've changed? That I'm a monster? That all my power has come together and now... I'm Eva?"

"Tell me that you aren't, and I'll believe you."

"Are you really going to give her a chance to manipulate you," Loyce demanded.

"Shut up, Loyce, and sit down."

"Look at her, Eddie."

He turned to her and glared. "Sit down!" She started at him, shocked, then scoffed. He looked back at me. "Tell me that you aren't, and I'll believe you."

I stared at him for a long moment. I wanted to tell him. I did. But I didn't know if it was truth.

"See?" Benzi said. "She can't." He raised his fist as if to hit me. "Might as well –" I raised my hand and he stopped in place, his hand in midair and his mouth open as if to say something. I looked at Caieta. She had also stopped. Loyce and Eddie as well. I ran out into the hall to see if anything else had frozen. It hadn't. Doctors and nurses still raced around us. I went back inside and studied my friends. Eddie's eyes were fierce, and he had turned to stop Benzi. Caieta was stopped halfway between a blink. Loyce frowned, glaring at me, and Benzi was preparing to punch me.

I analyzed them, wondering if it was I who changed in the thirty hours or them. I then made an impulsive decision. I walked over to Benzi, stared at him carefully, and then shoved my hand in his pocket. When I found his keys, I ripped my hand out. I put them in my pocket and raced from the room.

I sprinted through the long corridors of the hospital's white interior. I kept running, straining for breath, until I found an elevator. I went down to the first floor and rushed through the lobby into the parking lot. I didn't realize how big hospital parking lots were until I had to search for a car that looked exactly like every other car there. I sped through the parking lot, clicking the keys, listening for a horn. Finally, I found the van.

I pulled myself into the driver's seat and dropped my head on the steering wheel. I rubbed my hands together aggressively, cutting my hand on the little crystal rose. I looked down quickly, remembering that Eddie's ring was still hugging my finger. Why didn't they take that off? It didn't matter. I ripped it from my finger and stared at it in my hand. Tears trickled down my face into my palm. I sighed, pushing back my anxieties. I pulled on my seat belt, shoved the ring in my pocket, and shifted the van into reverse.

I took an hour to analyze everything that happened since Ben's death.

I had killed the Warlock that cursed my mom.

I met with Mr. Isaiah and gone to the Well of Fears.

I had gone to a party where Angel died.

My friends were plotting my death.

And I had stolen Benzi's car.

I drove without stopping for hours. Not for food. Not for sleep. Not to pee. For eleven hours. Finally, I was in Zanesville. Back home with the only person who truly and unconditionally cared about me.

I pulled into the driveway slowly, turning off my lights before they hit the house. I sat in the car for an hour debating if this was a good idea, if I wanted my mother to see me this way, if I wanted her to know what I'd become. What would she think of me? Eventually, I pried my hands from the steering wheel and sulked to the front door. I pushed it open and slid into the living room. My mom was sitting on the couch, braiding her hair back. The door clicked shut behind me and the sound made her turn.

"Evan– Evangeline?" She asked. Her eyes were suspicious, studying me. I nodded. She walked over to me cautiously and hugged me. "What happened to you?"

"I turned seventeen. I think it killed me a little."

She leaned back and surveyed the blood that stained my T-shirt. Then, she looked up and scanned my eyes. Her attention then shifted to my hair. Disgust flickered across her face briefly. "You're so thin," she said. "How long has it been since you've eaten?"

I thought back. I hadn't eaten on the trip from Vermont and I had been out cold for 30 hours. I hadn't eaten at the party. The last time I had eaten anything was after training, after the Well of Fears. "Four days ago."

"Four days!" She shook her head. "Go upstairs and change and I'll make you something." I nodded and turned towards the stairs. I felt her stare on my back until I went into my room. There, a few pairs of jeans and a couple of shirts were still sitting on my bed from when Benjamin and I had been packing. His face flashed in my mind. I quickly shook it away and pulled out a blue Backstreet Boys shirt and black jeans. I took them with me to the bathroom where I pulled the little ring out of my pocket and got into the shower. Actually, it was more of just sitting under running water than a shower.

Then I pulled myself into my clothes and stumbled down the stairs, into the living room. I crept over to the couch and sat down. I leaned back into the plush cushions. But something was wrong.

***

Suddenly, I jolted up, scanning the room. I had fallen asleep. My mom came in from the kitchen. She put a plate on the coffee table in front of me. Baked chicken, mashed potatoes, and green beans. Looking at the plate made me realize how hungry I wasn't. I looked up at her and back at the plate.

"Thank you," I said.

She nodded, "I'll get you some water." She turned and disappeared back into the kitchen. I sat for a moment staring at the food. It looked so unappealing. But it was a meal I had eaten and enjoyed many times. This time, for some reason, the idea of putting that in my mouth made me sick. The metallic taste of vomit ran across my tongue. Then something caught my attention. The back door had opened. The loud spooky creak only resided in that door. And it was in the kitchen. I stood and walked over to the entrance to the kitchen. I peered in.

My mom had the door propped open and was talking to three men. They were dressed in black.

"You can't come in," my mother said.

"We see that," the first man said, glaring through his brown eyes. His blond hair was messy.

"What did you do?" The second asked. His blue eyes watched her intently and his black hair was gelled back.

"I charmed the house," she said smiling. "Should've done it a long time ago. Only my blood is allowed in."

"Give her to us," the third man said. He was the only one I couldn't see. My mother blocked my view. "And we won't burn down the house."

"Ha! You can't anyway. As long as my bloodline continues, nothing can harm this house. I took very meticulous measures to make sure my daughter has a safe haven."

"Are you sure you understand what you're doing? You're harboring a monster!"

"How dare you?"

"Have you seen her?" The first asked.

"I have," the second said. "Fangs, red eyes. Is that what your daughter looked like?"

"She does now!" My mother snapped.

"Think about it, woman! If Evangeline was fighting for the good of humanity, do you think she'd look like that? Like a demon? She could destroy this world!"

"I don't give a damn if she's fighting for humanity! Or what she destroys! As long as she's safe and pleased with who she is as a person, I'll fight for her."

"Then think of it this way," the third said. "If she destroys this world she will destroy herself in the process! Amena, I know you must hate to hear it, but your daughter is evil. Let us in. We'll take her to Mathrel."

"So, he can kill her?"

"He won't kill her."

"How do I know that?"

"Because I'm telling you! Let us try to help!"

I watched as my mother began to consider it. I wondered if these men who used logic so smoothly came from the same organization that had killed Angel. A boy who they had probably watched grow up. Maybe even trained. I watched as they played my mother like a violin.

"Promise me nothing will happen to her," my mother said quickly.

"I promise you no harm will come to her through me or my colleagues."

She stared at them for a moment. Then she snapped her fingers. They rushed into the house like wolves. They went around my mother, through the kitchen, and in seconds they were standing in front of me. I put my hands up to freeze them but the first grabbed my left hand and snapped a bracelet around my wrist.

"No magic for you," he said. Then he grabbed my arm and the third man grabbed the other arm. I could see his face now. He had a thick scar over his right eye, from an injury that had apparently welded the eye shut. At the bottom of the left side of his face and the corner of his mouth was a scar. It looked like a bear had scratched his face. He smiled at me with the right side of his mouth and they picked me up. They dragged me back through the kitchen and stuffed me into the trunk of their car.

***

Suddenly, I jolted up, scanning the room. I had fallen asleep. My mom came in from the kitchen. She put a plate on the coffee table in front of me. Baked chicken, mashed potatoes, and green beans.

Looking at the plate made me realize how hungry I wasn't. I looked up at her and back at the plate.

"Thank you," I said.

She nodded, "I'll get you some water." She turned and disappeared back into the kitchen. I sat for a moment staring at the food. I had a strong feeling of déjà vu. Then something caught my attention. The back door had opened. The loud spooky creak only resided in that door. And it was in the kitchen. I stood and walked over to the entrance to the kitchen. I peered in.

My mom had the door propped open and was talking to three men dressed in black.

"You can't come in," my mother said.

"We see that," the first man said glaring through his brown eyes. His blonde hair was messy.

I jumped back, a gasp escaping my lungs. I realized this had already happened. I realized the first time it happened, I was asleep. I realized the first time it happened, it was a premonition.

I searched my pockets for my keys. They were upstairs on my bed. I raced to get them, keeping my steps as quiet as humanly possible in my haste. When I came back down my mom was still in the kitchen. I ripped open the front door and ran to Benzi's van. My feet slid in the grass and I fell against the door. I pulled it open and in a matter of minutes, my mom's house was a dot in a review mirror. I scanned my brain for an explanation. *I've had premonitions before.* I thought. *But I couldn't remember them as they happened in reality. How could I have caught it? How could I have changed it? What was different?* Then I realized. *The last premonition I had I was sixteen. Now I'm seventeen. And everything has changed.* I understood what had happened to my mind. But then I was plagued with another thought. *Had my mother betrayed me? Have I, truly, no one?*

That feeling. It was back. Like something to was trying to pry itself from me. This time it brought with it a desire to go back home. To fight. To kill them. For the treachery. For the betrayal. I had to push away this time. It didn't leave on its own. But I couldn't tolerate its presence any longer.

Hours fled by. Night had invaded, and morning rescued the sky just to let the night return. The setting sun was making glares in the dirty windshield. The sun was beginning to prove itself as another enemy. I was in Oklahoma City now.

Anger spread through me as conspiracies began to consume my thoughts. I pressed my foot down on the gas, throwing myself a hundred above the speed limit. But suddenly I began to slow down. My foot didn't lighten, but the car slowed anyway. I pulled my foot off the gas and then slammed it back down. The car shook and rumbled and came to a quick stop.

I beat my fists against the wheel. I shook and wiggled, demanding that the "stupid piece of machinery" did as it was told. It didn't. Finally, I crawled out of the car and pulled open the hood. Hot, thick, grey smoke erupted into my face. I jumped, coughing rapidly. My throat burned like I had swallowed a cigarette. When I was able to expel the smoke from my lungs I glared back at the van, cursing it for failing. *A waste of machinery,* I thought to myself. *A waste. You know what this is? The devil's handiwork! Oh, that little –*

Before I could finish my thought, the engine exploded. The blast threw me to the ground, singeing the front of my shirt. It then read Ba-st Bo-s. I was angry. I really liked that shirt. A car across the street had pulled off. A man had climbed out and was walking toward me.

"Are you alright?" He called to me.

"I'm fine," I said, pulling myself from the ground.

"Are you sure?"

My stare darted to him. "I said 'I'm fine!'" My yelling probably startled him enough, in booming echo out of my mouth, but coupled with my red eyes and fanged mouth, he probably thought I was a demon. Immediately, he turned back to his car and took off down the road. This prying feeling began again. And it wasn't going away.

I stood, for a while, in front of the van. The heat of the fire warmed my skin as I fought the feelings within me. Eventually, a small red car drove up to me. She parked her car across the street and got out. She walked away, down a dirt path just off the road. Moments later she walked over and stood next to me. She stayed completely quiet for quite some time. Her being there slowly made the feeling recede.

"Well," she finally said. "This is boring."

I turned to look at her. She had thick brown hair that fell down over her shoulders. Her caramel skin was pretty in firelight and brown eyes were curious. Her green Kermit the Frog shirt told me she wasn't from the Leadership. Or the Council either, for that matter. "You can leave whenever you're ready," I said to her.

She looked up at me. "Whoa! You look... super freaky cool. What kind of contacts are those?"

"These aren't contacts!" I snapped. "Why don't you just leave me alone?"

"Why are you yelling at me?" She stared at me. "I'm only trying to help."

I rolled my eyes. "Does it look like I need your help?"

"Well, your car is kind of on fire."

"I don't! I don't need your help!"

"Really?"

"Really!"

Her eyes twitched a little. "STOP! YELLING! AT! ME!" She shook her head. "You're the one stuck on an off road with the sun going down. I am the one is who trying to help you. Don't yell at me again."

I sighed, "I'm sorry."

Her smile stretched back. "Is that an 'I'm sorry because I have to say it.' Or an 'I'm sorry because I mean it.' Because they're two different things."

"It's an 'I'm sorry, can you get me off this road?'"

"Sure! I'm Joanna, but if you call me that I'll cut out your tongue." Her smile didn't waver even a little. But it wasn't like Mathrel's creepy smile. No, it was more of an 'I smile too much' quirky kind of smile. A real one. "You can call me, Joanie. I guess I could have lead with that. I know what I'll do next time!" She shrugged. "Let's go." She began toward the little red car.

"Wait. Isn't it a crime to leave this here?" I pointed at the van.

"But that's not even your car, is it?" She laughed. I shook my head. "Yeah, didn't think so. It won't be a big deal no one will know it was you." I stared at her. "Let's go. I don't want to waste any more time on the subject."

"Wh…Where are we going?" I walked away from the burning van.

"I really didn't want to go home this year, but I guess we're going to my dad's."

"Fine by me, as long as his name isn't August, Tannin or Mathrel."

Joanie stopped suddenly and gaped at me. "What did you say? Who are you?" She pulled a gun from her back pocket and pointed it at me. "I said 'Who are you!' How do you know about Tannin and Mathrel? What do you want? Who sent you? Are you a Witch? Huntress?"

I raised my hands above my head. "Both! I'm both!"

"A Blood? Impossible! Who are you?"

Against my own better judgment, I told her my name and a bit of my story, concluding with who Mathrel was in relation to the destroyed car's owner.

Slowly, she lowered the gun. "Oh. You're Evangeline! Damn! Well, why didn't you say so?"

"Because if I tell the wrong person, they blow my head off with the gun they keep in their back pocket."

"Well, can you blame me?" She put the gun away. "As a human living in the world that we do there's not much I can do to protect myself against Hunters and Warlocks. I mean, look at me." She wiggled her arms. "No muscle." I nodded, surprised by her quick transition; "Come on," she said climbing into the passenger's seat. "You're driving by the way." I walked around to the other side to find the keys were still in the ignition.

As we began to drive away, another girl appeared from the dirt, screaming after us. I figured she was yelling for us to come clean up after the van. But I noticed how closely she resembled Joanie. For some reason it seemed strange to me.

"So, how'd you get stuck on Moonlit River Drive? It's on off road, you know. It runs through an unpopular neighborhood that no one lives in. And it's used maybe twice a day."

"Is it abandoned?"

"Oh yeah. There's this story about if you're caught on it after dark you're eaten by the Michaelson family up the street, or you're kidnapped and sent to Mexico."

"Why?"

"I don't know. To help with the labor demand. And the Michaelson family are cannibals."

"N– Why is that the story?"

"I don't know it started a couple decades ago."

"Why would you be on it then?"

"I've always wanted to go to Mexico," she shrugged.

I stared at her. "So, you thought getting kidnapped would be the best way to do that?"

She shrugged again. "Maybe. But you still haven't told me how you ended up here."

I glanced out my window before returning to the road and shrugging. "I don't want to talk about it."

"Okay." She said and took it as an invitation to go on about other folklore she knew about the city. Two hours of endless chatter about vampires and ghosts. Stuff I really wouldn't have believed two weeks ago. At first, I wasn't listening until the topic of a Witch came up. Apparently, seventeen years ago, a Witch and a Hunter ran away together when they found out they were pregnant. They took refuge in Oklahoma for the last couple of weeks of the pregnancy. After the

Witch had given birth, the woman they were staying with never heard from them again. *Were they my parents?* I thought. I quickly shook my head, remembering that my parents didn't know about each other's origins. *But then who was this couple? And who was the lady they were staying with? Or did this couple even exist? It was probably just a story this girl made up.*

"Funny thing," Joanie said. "The woman had the most unusual name. Bibi."

"What?" I exclaimed in utter shock.

"I told you not to yell at me."

"The woman's name was Bibi?"

"Yeah. Funny right?"

Realizing that I was tied to my prophesied destiny in more ways than one, I knew that there was no way to escape my fate. I then conceded to tell Joanie what had gotten me stranded on Moonlit River Drive, starting with the party.

When I was just about finished with my story she was directing me to pull off the highway. She had me get gas, and immediately we were back on the road, driving to her father's.

"So, you left them at the hospital with no way home?" She asked.

"What was I supposed to do?" I demanded. "They were probably gonna kill me."

"Were they? Were they really?"

"They might have." She looked at me quickly, then back to the road. "Okay, what would you have done?"

"I don't know. It just seems to me you were jumping to conclusions."

"Jumping to – You weren't there. You don't know."

She shrugged and pursed her lips. Then she reached over and clicked on the radio. Country music exploded out of the stereo and assaulted my ears. Instantly she began to sing along and for five hours I sat in her car, listening the same guitar chord over and over.

Eighteen

Eventually, we made it to Las Cruces, New Mexico and pulled into a driveway. It was a small adobe home. I shut off the car and jumped out. Joanie bounced over to the front door and before she opened it she turned back to me. She shrugged, "before you go in, you should know that my father is a Sense." Then she pushed open the door and strolled inside.

"Wait. What?" I followed behind her. We walked down an orange hallway into the living room, which was painted brown. A tall man with caramel skin sat on the couch. He was in his early 40's maybe. He was also wearing nothing but a dirty blue t-shirt and boxers.

"Hey!" The man yelled. "What are you doing here?" He stood up quickly and got behind the couch. He seemed to overlook Joanie. Aggression pulsed into the stare he threw at me.

"I'm sorry," I said quickly. "My name is Evangeline Welt. You're a Sense, right?"

I watched as his expression softened. "One moment." He disappeared into one of the bedrooms behind him and reappeared 20 seconds later in a pair of jeans. "Sit down." He gestured to the couch. Joanie and I sat down. He sat down in front of us, across the coffee table. "What brings you here?" He studied me quickly. His eyes hanging on my teeth.

"Her car broke down," Joanie said. "Then exploded."

"Why did you come here?"

"Papa. You know why I brought her here."

"More and more keep finding out about me. This is not good."

"She's not people. She's Evangeline."

"You say you're Evangeline?"

"Look at the girl. Do you really think she's lying?"

He looked me over again. "…I suppose you're not lying."

It was strange to me how Joanie and he behaved. Almost like he wasn't acknowledging her presence. He'd ask me questions to things Joanie had just given him the answer to. Was he ignoring her? Mr. Nickolas, the man, also went on the explain how his gift worked. He could see 30 seconds into the future and everything in the past before that, on any day, anywhere in the world. I'm wasn't sure how that had a thing to do with nose – as he was the sense of smell – or why his nose was perfectly intact. But I didn't ask.

Then I thought, *he can see into the past. He knows who killed my father.* After giving me a word of caution, he told me the story.

"Three men. The first, the one who did most of the work, was Darrell Cottoner. He has become known very well in the Leadership for his cruelty. He is also known for the scar on the left side of his face. Your father gifted him with –"

"A scar over his eye? He can't use it anymore?" I rushed.

"Have you met him?"

"Only in my dreams."

"The second man is also wildly known around the Leadership. Kol Mayor is an expert with his black dagger, which is really more of a sword because of its length." I nodded remembering that dagger and what it had done to Angel. "The third man…Are you sure you want to know?" I nodded again. "Based on his past, he'd be no threat to you in the future."

"Tell me."

"Okay. He's known widely around the Leadership for being the man who killed his twin brother." My heart dropped into my stomach. "Richard Welt." My chest locked and I couldn't breathe. My head spun with a thousand possibilities. But a good excuse never found its way into the options. *This is why he felt so guilty,* I thought. Mr. Nickolas put his hand on my shoulder pulling me back into reality.

"You said you could see the present?" He nodded. "Where is Richard now?"

"He's making a call to your mother."

"Why?"

"To explain. To apologize."

"She won't forgive him. She'll kill him. Won't she?" He shook his head "What is she doing?"

"Biting her nails."

"What about Eddie and Caieta?"

"Eddie's driving. Caieta's in the passenger seat. Loyce and Benzi behind them."

"No new scars?"

"Plenty."

"Tannin?"

"Mourning his son."

I looked down at my lap. "Mr. Nickolas," I said. "I don't know what I'm supposed to do next." I looked up at him. "I don't know what I'm doing."

"I know what you haven't been doing. Using your magic."

"What?"

"For nearly seventeen years, you didn't use your magic or your hunting skills. You used your words. Just remember that."

"Why?"

"I'm gonna send you –"

"Wait." I took a deep breath and tried to stable my thoughts. "Somehow I have human blood mixed around with all the rest of the mess in my veins. How?"

He blinked once. "Both of your grandfathers." I stared at him. I had been thinking it would be farther up my family tree, but it was only one generation away. My mother's father, *and* my father's father. I wondered if they knew. But of course, they knew. My father was raised in the Leadership and my mother in the Counsel. "I'm going to send you to Jeremy," Mr. Nickolas said, breaking through my thoughts.

"Aww. Come on. Really?" Joanie said. I had almost forgotten she was there. I didn't think she could be so quiet. "We're going to Arizona? Really?"

He looked at her briefly. "Be safe." He stood up and led us to the door. Joanie skipped out ahead of me. Mr. Nickolas grabbed my arm. "I may not be able to see the future, but if I look up to see that anything has happened…" He glared me. "I won't be able to warn you."

I nodded. "I understand." I walked away slowly and got in Joanie's car.

A four-hour ride shouldn't be too hard to endure, I thought. I thought wrong. Along with country music, Joanie listened to the absolute most beastly, rotten, lousy audio books a person could ever pretend to like. Four hours of painfully wicked books. I was surprised I didn't break her stereo.

But finally, we arrived at Mariam's Memorial Hospital. I don't know why I decided it would be so much easier to park as far away from the door as possible rather than circle around for a spot up front. But I climbed out of the car. Joanie didn't move.

"Hey, this is your destiny, remember?" She said. "And besides, I really don't feel like punching anyone today."

"Punching…?"

"I just really hate…Never mind," she waved her hand. "You just go. It's room 213. I'll be here when you get back."

I took the long walk up to the hospital entrance, passing empty space after space. *Easier,* I thought. *Pssh.* I took a deep breath and got onto the elevator. Then once again I was in a hospital feeling completely unwanted and uncomfortable. I walked down the empty hall to room 213. I stood at the pale green door, debating if entering was the best idea. I was going to go back out to Joanie and tell her some story about the guy being heavily medicated and how he was of little help. But just as I was about to turn back and walk away, the door swung open. Suddenly a tall boy, probably no older than nineteen, was standing before me. He wore blue jeans, a gray t-shirt, black sneakers, and a black leather jacket. He had thick, long brown hair that he had slicked back like he was in the movie *Grease*. He glared at me through his dark eyes.

"Who are you?" I demanded.

"I could ask you the same question," he said, looking me over.

"I *did* ask you that same question," I said, frowning.

"I don't have to answer to you."

"Neither do I."

"Fine," he looked me over again. "*What* are you? Are you going to a costume party? You look like a vampire reject."

"Who the – You have no idea who you're dealing with."

"If you told me, I would."

"Not a chance."

"Then I guess I'll *never* have a clue who I'm *dealing with*."

"Do you think I'm joking?"

"Well, you do look like one big joke."

I glared at him, wondering if this was the punch that Joanie was talking about. After a few seconds, I decided it was. I reached up and grabbed his throat. Before I could blink, my fingers were locked around his neck. In my mind I had the upper hand. I could make this guy do anything I wanted now. But, again before I could blink, his hands were tangled around my throat. I then remembered how awful it was not being able to breathe. Suddenly we pulled away from each other with a mutual, unspoken agreement not to do that again.

"Who are you?" I coughed.

"Devon," he grunted. "Your turn."

"…Evelynn," I lied "Now if you'd excuse me, *Devon*, if that's even your real name, I have business to attend to."

"Not here you don't."

"Enough!" A bloodcurdling yell erupted from the hospital room. We both turned to look at the man lying in the bed. "Come here!" Neither of us moved. "You two, come here. Now." Devon and I walked in and went around to either side of the bed. I went around to the man's right, Devon his left. The man looked over at me. "How old are you?" He asked.

"I just turned seventeen," I confessed.

He looked to Devon. "How old are you?"

"You know how old I am," Devon scoffed.

"Excuse me, that's not a number."

Devon sighed, "Almost eighteen."

The man frowned at us. "Almost young adults, behaving like nine-year-old children. What is wrong with the two of you?"

"We don't know who this woman is!" Devon protested. "For all I know she could be here to assassinate you."

"Assassinate? Really?" I questioned.

"Well, it's not like you have the friendliest appearance."

"Well," I huffed. "You looked you were dragged straight from *Grease: The Sing-A-Along.* Hey, John Travolta called, he wants his hair back."

"Enough." The man cut in. "She's not going to assassinate me."

"She choked me!"

"You choked me!" I yelled.

The man rolled his eyes. "Stop. Stop. I know this girl."

"You know her?" Devon questioned. "This girl, here? Evelynn?"

"Evelynn? Let us all get acquainted, then, huh? I'm Jeremy Salander." Devon shook his head. "This is my younger brother, Damon." Devon, actually Damon, slammed his palm to his forehead. "Damon, this is Evangeline Welt."

"Damon?" I demanded. "You said your name was *Devon.*"

"You said your name was Evelynn," he protested. Then suddenly any aggression or anger in his face melted away. "When in reality it's Evangeline Welt. The girl born with two destinies."

I rolled my eyes. "Dang it! Why does news travel so fast?"

"The curse of being famous," Jeremy said.

"Famous? Is that what I am?"

"In this world, or war, you are. Let's not waste any more time. I'm the Sense of Touch." I then took the time to look him over. I realized he hadn't moved a single muscle in his body but his mouth and eyes. Not even his neck had shifted in the three minutes I had stood before him. His body was tucked snugly beneath a white blanket. His hands sat on top of that blanket. On his right forearm, tattooed in in deep blue ink, was "Great power brings even greater sadness." Then it occurred to me that I didn't see or hear that phrase at Mr. Nickolas' house.

Jeremy's head was held up by two cotton pillows. His light brown hair was stuck firmly to his forehead with sweat. I didn't see a real resemblance between the two boys until I saw his eyes. They both had those dark, scary brown eyes. They had a layer of intimidation but behind that I thought I saw a layer of fear. "Yes," he continued. "I am paralyzed. And even though I'm not going anywhere, I don't like to waste my time."

"A habit he acquired when he was mobile," Damon explained.

"I'm not gonna beat around the bush or send you anywhere or have you do things without knowing the outcome. I'm going to do what Isaiah does best and lay out the facts. I'm sending you to Washington, DC. On the way there you'll encounter your old friends. You forgive them, okay? They did nothing but follow the instinct imprinted on them as Hunters. When you get to Washington you'll go to a forest, there the Council and the Leadership have already begun fighting. Soon it'll bleed out into the rest of the world. This feud revolves three key elements. Humanity, Witches, and Hunters. And you are a creation of all three. Witches, Hunters, Vampires, Sense, Demons they were all human before they were this. All of them.

The thing is, the Leadership and the Council hate each so much because they think the other will bring them to an end, so they much do it first. And they lump humanity in with other. The Leadership blames human for being a distraction so they must be disposed of. The Council blames them for siding with the Hunters for protection all those years ago. This war is just about self-preservation, survival.

They're expecting you arrive and pick a side, finally helping one of them survive. You will need to go and make them aware that you only purpose is to *end* the war. One way or another. Even if it may not be in either way that they wish. This all started with a false accusation in a court room and it should end with the truth among the same jury. But it didn't so now you are jury and judge. Every decision you make from here on out will be final. The only reason I breathe right now is because you let me. It's over now and the only blood that needed to spill was your own." He stopped and gritted his teeth. "My only flaw is, I don't know how that meeting ends. But I haven't felt the world's end so…"

"That's good," I said, hopeful. "For once I know what I'm going to find and how to prepare myself emotionally and mentally. I finally know how this going to end, that it is going to end."

"That's just it, Evangeline. It is going to end. But for you…"

I glared at him. "What do you mean? You just said I'm jury and judge."

"You may think you have your mind made up in regard to whom you call Eva, but if there is a sliver of doubt, the two of you will split each fighting for your own cause. The world will be decimated regardless of who wins. But staying united will bring you no fortune. You have two very different destinies living within you that cannot coexist and you're mortal. Merging them will end you." I didn't say anything for a while. Jeremy stared at me. "Do you understand what I'm saying?"

That feeling. Like something was trying to leave my body. It was Eva, trying split. Tring to escape. "So… I will…die?"

"I'm only telling you facts and –"

"fact is that I'm going to die! Yes?" He nodded. "…Damnit!" I stared at my feet a while, running my hands through my tangled hair. I wrapped them around my own neck and then pushed them down my chest. They ultimately dropped, in fists, against my sides. "I should probably leave now."

"Of course. Damon, you go with her."

"What?" Damon demanded, glaring.

"Just escort her down to her car." Damon rolled his eyes but walked around to my side of the bed and grabbed my arm.

He began tugging me along when I asked, "What if I don't go?"

"Well, blood will flood streets and fire will consume cities." He smirked. "But, you know, it really doesn't matter what you decide to do. The war will come to you."

I thought for a moment. "...Damnit." Damon resumed tugging me down the hallway. My mind spun with the new information I had just acquired. *How could this be?* I thought. *How could I have a destiny so great just to die? Was my sole purpose on this planet for nothing more than to be a pawn in someone else's game? Why not? Angel was. Bibi and Isaiah are. Jeremy, he most certainly is. Would I be living beyond my purpose? Is that it?*

I ripped away from Damon's grip, turned and punched him in the gut. He doubled over in pain and I fell to my knees. I buried my face in my hands. "I killed people!" I screamed. "People got killed! Because of me! For my survival and I'm just gonna die!" My body shook as I sobbed into my palms. I felt Damon's presence over me. He didn't move. He didn't say anything. He just watched me cry. When I had finished, I came to the conclusion that this was my fate. It was already written in the stars. I could go down with my head held high or I could fall with my eyes closed. I wiped my face, stared at Damon a moment, and continued to the parking lot.

We walked outside to the edge of the lot. I could see Joanie on her phone leaning against the car. I stood there next to Damon. We didn't say anything, just silent understanding.

"Damon," I finally said. "That tattoo on Jeremy's arm, it just appeared, right?" He nodded. "How long has he been paralyzed?"

"Three months."

I nodded and looked over at Damon. His eyes met mine. I smiled at him and began walking out to Joanie.

"Evangeline," he called. I turned back to him. "Just for the record. If you were a vampire, I think you'd be a pretty cool one."

I laughed. "I hope you're cast in *Grease* someday," I said. "You make a great Danny Zuko"

"Yeah, I know…Hey, about earlier. I'm not just saying it because…you might die. Really. I think I misjudged you."

I laughed, "maybe you didn't." He watched me as I stared at him awkwardly. "Hey, let me ask you a question." He nodded. "What happened to Jeremy? I mean, he didn't just wake up…what paralyzed him?"

He glared at me for a moment. "His fate, I guess. He was standing at the altar when he collapsed. They wanted to keep it small, so only her close family was there. Our parents died years ago. When his fiancée found out he'd probably never move again, she stopped visiting. It wasn't long after that he started getting these feelings, that he couldn't feel but knew were real. Then that tattoo appeared. I started doing research, mainly folklore because none of this could be explained with science.

"I was sure he was a Sense when he started screaming about the pain in his legs, one day. For hours he screamed. 'They were missing,' he said and he demanded to know where they went. Two days I had gotten lost in the halls. I found myself on the floor above where I meant to be. Moments later a woman was rushed into the hospital missing then bottom half of her legs. And she said everything Jeremy said *word for word.* For hours." He shook the tears from his face. "I don't know why it had to be Jeremy, or why it had to be this way. But I do know that it happened instantly after the last Sense died. And that he will spend the rest of his life this way."

I bit my lip. "I'm sorry."

"Sorry?" He laughed. "You're sorry? Don't be. You know what 'sorry' is? It's an emotional barrier that you put up to make yourself feel better. 'Sorry' won't get my brother out of that bed but it will waste my time." I stared at him for a moment.

Then I turned back and continued to Joanie. I thought the last three weeks had been the worst my life could come to. Little did I know that some people don't even get to live. Even still, I had to deal with the fact that these three weeks would be the last I'd ever get to experience. I got to walk back to my friend knowing the reason for my birth, and that I only lived to die.

Nineteen

I sat in the driver's seat of Joanie's car with my hands gripping the wheel tighter than necessary. Silence passed between Joanie and me. I debated my worth to this world as we sped down the highway. Three hours had passed. I fumbled with my fingers. I was feeling for something. Slowly I ran my hands over each other. I gasped when I realized it wasn't there.

"What?" Joanie asked looking over at me. Once again, she had been so quiet I nearly forgot that she was there. She was so…content with the quiet, yet she was so talkative at random times.

"I left my ring," I said expecting that to enough of an explanation. "We have to go home. Then we'll go D.C."

"Home? D.C.? Whoa. I could tell Jeremy told you some big things but D.C. big? Whoa."

"I have to go get it." I took a turn and began towards Zanesville.

I realized then that I hadn't told her what Jeremy had told me. Or anything besides the hospital incident and how I got stranded. I took the next seven hours to do that.

Finally, after the sun being set for more than four hours already, Joanie decided it was about time we stopped for the night. We had just made it to Amarillo, Texas. That was merely a fraction in our 29-hour trek across the country. But that's 29 hours if we didn't stop to sleep, for food or even to pee. It occurred to me I hadn't used the restroom in a while. Which is really weird.

Joanie convinced me to pull off the highway and we drove around for a while until we could find a hotel. We checked in, went up the three flights of stairs, went down the hallway and into our room.

We each climbed into our separate beds but sleep never came for me. I lay awake all night waiting for Joanie to get up, so we come continue our journey. When she woke I was already pulling on my shoes. We went down stairs and checked out, then climbed back into the car.

Joanie had this way of knowing just when not to speak. Long stretches of time would go by where she wouldn't say a single word. All that surrounded me was the still quietness echoing off the road that made me feel like I was driving alone.

Some while went by before she spoke again.

"Oh," she said. "We're now in Rolla, Missouri. Let's stop."

"I'm hungry. Just because you've decided to fast doesn't that I'm not going to chow down."

I gaped at her for a minute. "Alright, but we can't waste a lot of time."

"Why? We're making good time. Besides why do you want to rush to –"

"My death?"

"I was gonna say 'a boring meeting.' But that works too."

"Because the sooner I get this over with the sooner other people stop dying."

"Evangeline," she said we pulled into a Jane in the Bowl parking lot. "You're a very morbid person." Then, she pushed open the door and went inside.

She left me in the car with the keys. Probably thought she'd be in and out so quickly, it'd be tedious to make me come with her. I contemplated taking the car and saving her the trouble of driving with me to my ultimate demise. But with my luck she'd probably hitchhike to D.C. and kick me in the shin for stealing her car. Before I could make a real decision of what I wanted to do, she was back. She put her seat belt on while stuffing her mouth with a handful of curly fries.

"Really," she said through her mouthful, as I turned on the car. "You're just so… saddening." She stared at me a moment chewing furiously. "You know what? Go back to the main road and turn left."

"Left? The highway –"

"Just follow my directions."

She guided me to another hotel and had me park in the back lot. Then she pulled the keys from the ignition and jumped out of the car. When I stayed seated she turned back to me. "Well, are you coming?" I stared at her a minute wondering why we were wasting the time. "Evangeline. You are *sick*. Mentally and emotionally, you are very ill."

"I'm fine!" she pursed her lips and looked away from me. I sighed, remembering that I shouldn't yell. "I'm fine, okay? Can we just leave?"

"Get out of the car."

I sucked in a deep breath and exhaled slowly. I climbed out of the vehicle and walked up to her. She locked the car and glanced up at me. Then she started walking to the back of the hotel. I followed. She walked out the edge of the back parking and stared out at the distance. I rubbed my temples trying to decipher her insanity.

"Look," she said, her mouth full again.

I looked out at whatever it was she was staring at and saw nothing but grass and rocks and trees. I shrugged.

"Look."

I looked again and this time I could see some blue in the mix of greens. It was maybe four miles away. "It's a river. I hope you have a good pair of shoes on." I looked down at my blue high tops. Then she began out into the brush while forcing a burger into her mouth. I watched her, wondering where she developed all this energy. Quickly I ran up behind her.

It took us nearly an hour to reach the river. Bright blue water rushed by us, sweeping nearby debris along with it. It was so blue and so clean. It was like thousands of tiny diamonds were the substance of this river. Suddenly I found myself creeping towards it.

"Pretty, right?" Joanie asked, ripping me from my trance. "Now, take off your shoes and roll up your pants." She spoke the command as she did it herself. Then she slowly waddled down to the water. I copied and trailed behind her. When we were both in the water rose up to our shins, she slowly turned to look at me. "What's wrong with you?" I stared at her. "I mean you're depressing. You're sad. You're hollow. You have everything going for you and –"

"I have death coming for me."

"If you choose to look at it that way."

"Choose? That's the only way to look at it."

"Or? Perhaps you start living now. Taste life while you're still alive. Jeremy didn't say when you had to go to DC, he just said you had to go. After all, you're no longer racing against the clock, your birthday has passed."

"So, what? I'm supposed to wait until I'm eighteen? Or nineteen? Thirty-five? I have a responsibility!"

"No one says you're neglecting your responsibilities by being a teenage girl!"

"Being a teenage girl got Angel killed."

"… You can't blame yourself for that. His fate was sealed. What was meant to happen was decided before he even met you." I looked down at my feet. "You have the power to destroy worlds. You have the sun, the moon, and all of the stars on your side." My chest became tight. "Look at me." I looked up at her. "And you have the whole earth to do your biding. But somehow, you've developed the idea that you have nothing. You have people who love you, you have everything. And anything you don't have, snap your fingers and it's yours."

"I didn't ask for that."

Suddenly the wind picked up. "But you have it! It's all yours. You get to do whatever you want with it. But you choose to be miserable? Really? I'm just girl. But you are so much more."

I gaped at her. "You don't get it." Dark clouds rolled in overhead. "I burn the world or save it. That's always what I was meant to do. And if I don't save it... what does that mean? It means that I'm Eva. And she will rip herself free a burn the world." The wind started blowing harder and could feel her clawing at my spin. "And I've got to die to stop her!" Joanie didn't say anything else. "But I don't want to die!" It started raining. "Eva can do whatever she wants, and she doesn't die, does she? I can do what I want too!" I could feel her pushing me to let her out. My eyes begin to glow as the storm grew bigger around us. "I can do whatever I want!" Tears began to spill down my face. "And I don't want to die! And Eva doesn't die! I want to be Eva! I want to live, and I have to do it let her out, let her become me and I live! And no one will stop me!" My fangs had grown to poke lips. I froze. I looked around at how large the storm had grown. I could hardly see it ended. Lightning cracked, striking the ground in numerous places around us. Thunder burped from the in repeated roars. *I did this,* I thought. *No. They wouldn't stop me. They'd be too afraid too.* "Look what I can do!"

Lightning electrified the sky. Screaming sparks of red ripped through the clouds. Fire was burning at the edge of the atmosphere. *I could end this all right now.* A dark cardinal color spread overhead. Lightning stroke around the river. I could feel the glowing in my pupils and the blood streaming from my eyes. I was the master of my own destiny. I threw my hands into the air and screamed, fire shooting out of my palms into the clouds. Instantly lightning shot back down into the river. The energy electrocuted my legs in water.

I fell backwards, my butt hitting the rocks. I looked down at the smoking water. I sighed. "But I don't want to be this." Instantly the storm dissipated, and Eva sank back inside of me. "I don't want be a monster. I don't want to die but I don't want to be her even more." I leaned back so that I was completely submerged in water. I thought about maybe staying under. Drowning myself. But I did have a job to do. When I sat back up I was spitting out rocks. No, teeth. I felt in my mouth to find that my fangs were gone and had been replaced with teeth. And it was painless. I leaned forward and sucked in water. I swished it around my mouth and spit it out. My hair fell over shoulders into my face. It wasn't tangled, and it wasn't black. It was white. It was bone-straight and white.

I looked up at Joanie. "I don't want to be her. I never want to be her."

The walk back to the car dried me off. We climbed in and got back on the interstate. I stared at my newly foreign reflection in the mirror, surprised at how much better I liked this one than the one I grew up with.

Nine hours melted away and we finally passed the sign:

You're Now Entering

Zanesville, Ohio

A couple minutes later we were pulling into my mom's driveway. Morning was creeping into view. Joanie turned to me and sighed.

"Well," she said. "This is gonna be intense."

I looked at her and nodded. Then turned to look out the window. Parked directly beside us was a black BMW. I threw myself out of the car and raced to the house. I pushed open the door to find Eddie, Loyce, Caieta, and Benzi sitting with my mother. They all stood up when I entered.

"What did you do to your hair?" Eddie asked, gawking.

"What are you doing here?" I demanded.

"We were looking for you?" Caieta said.

Behind me Joanie run up and fell into me. She pulled herself up when she saw the group in my living room. "Wow! I didn't know you were having a party." She let go of me and walked over to Benzi. She put her hand out. "Hello there. The name's Thomas. Joanna Thomas." Benzi didn't even look at her. She laughed. "Ok, I'll stand back here." She walked back to me with an awkward smile.

I ran my tongue over my teeth. "I don't – who said you could come to my house?"

"We were looking for you," Caieta repeated.

"Why? So, you could take me to Tannin so he could hang me? Or maybe to Mathrel so he could drug me up?"

"To help you," Eddie said.

"Why do I find that so hard to believe?"

"Oh, I know!" Joanie laughed. "Because of the events at the hospital."

"Yea, you betrayed me back there."

"We – You stole my dad's van!" Benzi yelled.

"And destroyed it," Joanie laughed.

I nodded. "It went up in a ball of flame."

"What? No, no, no! Tell me you didn't!" He stepped around the coffee table and began towards me. I stepped around him and went up the stairs. My bathroom had remained the same since the last time I was here. I grabbed the ring off the sink and stared at it a moment. A reminder that someone used to care about me, and possibly still did. I shoved it on my finger and marched down the stairs and hugged my mom. Then I went and stood before my friends again. Joanie had already gone outside.

"I want to hate you. You!" I said pointing at Eddie. He bit his lip. "For being mean to me. For being nice to me. For being afraid of me. I want to hate you, but I can't bring myself to do it. Not really. Because I know you have a right to feel any way you do. But I have to leave you."

"Please don't."

"Get out of my house. If you ever set foot on this property again, it will be the last step you ever take."

I understand why you are so angry," Eddie cut in. "I can't say that I wouldn't be either." He grabbed my hand. "But I do care about you."

I believed him. I really did. "You can't come with me." So, he couldn't watch me die. I pulled my hand from his. "My warning stands. Don't come back to this house ever again." Then I turned to leave. I was half way out of front door when Eddie grabbed my arm. I turned to push him away when he grabbed my other arm. He didn't say anything. He didn't do anything. He just stared me. He pleaded with me in the silence. Eddie, who had made so many leaps and bounds in our time together. Eddie, who was so perfect who he was. Eddie, the ferocious and caring being. If Eddie went with me, he would die with me.

"I'm sorry," he said. "I'm sorry."

I thought back to what Damon had said. "If 'I'm sorry' helped anyone, no one would be dead." I turned away from him and got into the car with Joanie. They'd think I was angry at them. For the rest of their lives they'd think I died angry with them. But they couldn't have come with me. I had to spare them that. I had to spare the vision of my death.

The trip to Washington really shouldn't have taken a long time. A six-hour drive was all it was. Compared to some of our other drives it was hardly anything. But somehow time seemed to slow to a crawl. Joanie and I hardly spoke but I was getting used to her lingering silences.

Six hours. No conversation. I'd spent more time than that without talking to someone, but it felt different with her being there and not speaking. Almost like she wasn't really there. I frequently had to look at her to ensure that she hadn't thrown herself out of the window while I wasn't looking. Which of course, she didn't. It was just strange to me how she'd be so present in some moments and distant in others. Like she was slipping in and out of my conscious and subconscious and was only relevant in my conscious.

We didn't speak until we were parked in front of City Hall. There I realized that I don't know where to look for this epic battle. Then I remembered the whole extraordinary powers thing. So, I took a deep breath and projected sight as far as it could go in every direction. *Where are they hiding?* Then I found them. The smell of copper burn in my throat twelve miles to the east.

I pierced my lips and sighed, turning to Joanie. "Thanks for coming. I'm sure you had more…other places you'd need to be"

She shook her head. "I'm exactly where I'm supposed to be. Besides," she pointed behind her. "I'm not the only one who came."

I looked around her just as Loyce was climbing out of the BMW. I marched over to her while Eddie, Caieta, and Benzi fell in behind her.

"You shouldn't be here," I barked.

"I know you don't want us here –" Caieta began.

"No, you *shouldn't* be here. You don't know what's going on."

"Look," Eddie said stepping around Loyce. "We're sorry. I know you don't want to hear it. But I mean it. And I'm not going anywhere."

I pursed my lips. "It's not about that. What's about to happen …I don't really know Joanie." He furrowed his eyebrows. "It won't hurt her, what she sees." He shook his head, confused. "I don't want you to see what's about to happen." I smiled at them. I could finally see the injuries that plagued them. They were now faded and barely visible, but they seemed so apparent to me. Benzi had a bruise on his left cheek that stretched across his mouth. Caieta had a new scar over her right eyebrow to replace the one Ben had given her a week ago. Beside her left eye was a big purple bruise that reached back to her ear and her bottom lip was busted. Loyce had three deep scratches in her right cheek and a fourth one over her left eye, though, she could still blink freely. Eddie had the worst of it. His left eye was blackened, the right side of his top lip was swollen and the other side making home to a deep cut that was turning into a scar. He had a bruise on the right side of his jaw working its way up to his cheekbone, and his neck was stained red in the shape of a hand. These were only the remnants of injuries on them that I could see.

I looked back at Joanie. But she gone. Of course. She had no obligation to me. She left before got ugly and that's fine. I turned back to my friends. "Thank you," I said. "For risking your lives for me when no one asked you to. You are good people." Tears swelled in my eyes. But I was really growing tired of crying. "I have only had seven friends in my lifetime. One died at my own hand and he will always consume my thoughts. Another has died at the hand that plagued my mother. But I have the five of you and I am grateful for that. Live long and blessed lives." I grabbed Caieta's hand and kissed her forehead. All of the injuries that stained her face washed away. I went to Loyce and did the same thing. Then Benzi and ended with Eddie.

I hugged him, but he didn't let me go. His hair had grown out and was soft against my face. I knew he hadn't showered in a while, but he smelled good. His embrace was warm. His arms wrapped around me like a blanket. I felt safe. I felt protected. I didn't want him to let go. I didn't want him to leave.

But it was just a hug.

"What are you doing?" Eddie asked in my ear. "What's about to happen?"

I ignored his question. "I love you," I said and pulled away from him. "If you guys see Joanie –"

"Ok," Benzi said, rubbing his temple. "Who is Joanie?"

"I don't know where she went but she was with me when I went to my mother's house."

"There was no one with you," Loyce said, shaking her head.

"What…" I thought back to how Benzi had completely ignored Joanie. I just thought he was a jerk. But her father, also. hardly even acknowledged her. And the girl yelling after us as we drove away from the fire. And the fact that she had me drive. I thought back to when she ate Jane in the Bowl. Where did her trash go? Those long stretches of silence when I'd forget she was there.

"You've been doing this thing, where you talk to no one and it's freaking weird."

"She was…wasn't real," I gasped. She a manifestation of my mind. To keep me sane. "She was…she convinced me…I convinced me…" I shook my head. "She was me."

"Joanie?" Eddie questioned.

"She got me here." I nodded. "She convinced me that I wouldn't mess this up. That I wasn't defined by a legend. But it was me. I got me here." I turned and began my march towards the woods.

"We're coming with you," Caieta said.

"I can't tell you not to. But I don't want you to."

Then I turned from them and continued. Hours had elapsed. Sun was beginning to set but I could hear them through the brush now. The fighting the screaming. The smell of blood burned my throat. Just a few feet and we'd be in the middle of it.

Just then, Eddie grabbed me arm. "One more thing," he said. "Benjamin and Brad. I think they were two different people." I turned back to him. "I was thinking about how he died and how quickly he turned at the beach. It didn't make sense to me. But I thought, what if Benjamin was only developed after meeting you. Like he developed a split personality to accommodate to you and to be your friend. Ben was always your best friend, but Brad. Brad used Ben death as a last stab at you. To know that you killed your best friend along with him. I could be –"

"A split personality," I nodded. "That makes sense. It all makes sense."

Then I turned, I pushed through the brush, and I waltzed out onto the battle. People were flying through the air. Along with detached limbs, blood, and screams. My entrance did little to interrupt it. The two sides were very clearly laid out. To the left, the group was dressed in all black and carried a range of weapons from guns to swords. To the right, they all wore thick cloaks and the few pieces of revealed skin were tainted with ancient markings. I could Tannin and Mathrel in the far back of their respective sides, watching their comrades fight to the death. I walked down the middle of the rift avoiding fireballs and spears. Richard was there too, behind the

Leadership, but he wore all white and was not fighting. When I passed him, pain stretched through my chest. I continued walking until I was standing between Mathrel and Tannin on either side of field. I looked around the field. So many people had already died and still many more were fighting. The grass was stained a crimson color. I wasn't sure I how deep it went.

    I turned to face neither of them. I looked up at the trees that surrounded the battle field and I saw him. I blinked once. When my eyes jumped back open I was no longer wearing anything I had ever dressed myself in before. I wore a blood red leather bodice with gold buttons down the sides to keep it closed. I had black jeans woven shut by black shoelaces along the outsides of my legs. Thin, white pieces of leather tangled themselves around my neck to look like vines holding up the bodice and boots that folded over at the ankles. And a thorn necklace strapped to my wrist as a reminder. I felt like an Elfish warrior princess from a fantasy movie. Then I stopped my foot. The ground shook and everyone rose from their feet and fell.

    I had everyone's attention now. Benzi, Caieta, Eddie and Loyce stood at the entrance of the field where the two crowds spilt. I looked around at the glares and fists and snarls. The group looked more like a pack of animals than an angry mob. I didn't say anything as my eyes danced around every person out there. Then my stare settled on Tannin and Mathrel, my eyes bouncing back and forth between the men. They were the only two whose gaze wasn't plastered on me. Instead, they were glaring at each other, stabbing one another with their stares.

    "Look at me," I spoke softly. I let my words reach out and do my biding. The essence of my voice wrapped itself around their thoughts and diverted them from each other. Instantly, their scowls darted to me. They fought the urge to look at me, but ultimately their eyes were mine. Slowly they began out from their hiding positions to stand in front of me. "Listen carefully," my voice booming out across the field. "Because I won't repeat myself."

"Why?" A voice called out. "Why should we?" It was from the Leadership's side.

"Yeah," another said. "Why does anything you say matter?"

"Good questions," I said. "But an even better question is…why are you two still breathing?" My gaze never shifted from Tannin and Mathrel, but I knew exactly which two men had spoken. Suddenly, the two men began coughing and panting for oxygen. They strained to breathe against my control. Air flooded into their lungs just before they collapsed. "Let me ask you all a question." My inspection ripped from Tannin and Mathrel to the two men and then to sweep around the rest of them. "Have you ever experienced the force of a tornado or a hurricane? The actual, physical force that a Tornado has? Not any of you, I doubt. But imagine it. And multiply it by a million, maybe two, or three. Now imagine all of that might combined and contained in a single vessel. Are you imagining it? Good. Understand that my soul is that vessel. That my wrath and power have the ability to consume you all in a blink of an eye. It's taken me three weeks to understand how much power resides in me and what I have described for you now was probably not even a fraction." Anxious glances were exchanged throughout the crowd.

"Why are you telling us this?" A woman asked from the Council's side. I glanced over to her. Half of her face was cover in blood and her cloak was torn to reveal the pealing flesh underneath.

"Because obviously the sound of my voice isn't enough to frighten you all yet. Very soon just the thought of my name will leave you quivering." Suddenly I felt pain register in my chest and burn its way up to my throat. Magic. Quickly I suppressed the pain and found the culprit. It was a small woman hiding beneath her cloak as she edged her way out into the woods. "How dare you?" She froze in place. Slowly she turned to look at me, stunned to find that I was still breathing.

"Ho– how did you," she stammered. "… It's not possible. You should be dead! As of seven seconds ago your heart should've burst from your chest!"

"Are you not paying attention?" I screeched at her. Her hood blew back, blowing her hair out of her face.

"You are –" Before she could finish her sentence she screamed, her eyes rolling back in her head as she fell. Everyone scurried away from her lifeless body.

"So, are you listening?" I asked. Nods spread through the crowds. "I will only say this once. You will stop. This *war* will end now."

"End?" A Huntress asked. "So, they can wreak havoc on the world? Why would we let that happen?"

"What's happening? In the last century, how many humans have died at the hand of a Warlock? The Leadership has killed more of humanity trying to keep their bloodline pure than the Council has! Just because Warlocks were known to kill humans for fun hundreds of years ago doesn't mean that's how it remains. And if it is, then I will handle it.

"But you're half Witch," a Hunter said. "How do we know you're not lying to the Leadership?"

"I'm also half Hunter. Does that mean I'm lying to the Council? This is the 21st century and magic is not as terrifying as it used to be. Let them walk among humanity. Let them be freed of persecution. Warlocks have killed Hunters, but Hunters have killed hundreds of Warlocks as well. And you sometimes even kill your comrades!" My gaze darted to Richard.

"So, we're supposed to stop? The one thing we've been doing for generations, is supposed to cease?"

"Yes! You're killing each other! Family! Friends! They're dying around you! Do you not understand that? Children you have raised! People you have grown up with! They're dropping as easily as flies! Do mean to tell me that your wife yesterday could be alive and tomorrow she could be dead, and you could continue on like she never existed?"

"King Tannin did," a Warlock called. "When his wife died, he remarried three days after."

"What was I to do?" Tannin said, his gaze still trapped on me. "My youngest son was two when I was given the choice of him or his mother."

"Shut your mouth!" Kytra screamed. My gaze darted to her. Her golden dress was untouched, but her arms and hands were stained red. She gasped at the loss of her tongue and covered her mouth.

"Don't act like people don't already know!" Tannin continued. "You killed my wife for a chance to be queen and used my son to do it. And guess what? He's dead anyway. Both of my sons are dead!" His fists shook in agony. "Dying for this cause! If I don't win now, what was it for?" He bared his teeth. His whole body shook as he tried hard to fight back his anger. The Council seemed surprised to find out the story of the first queen's death. Many of them removed their hoods.

"Then there's Mathrel," Benzi said. "When his wife died in labor, he blamed his son."

"Shut up!" Mathrel barked.

"He turned his attention to perfecting the purity, disguise, and force of the Leadership and punishing his son for a sin he didn't commit." Mathrel had a frown so fierce glued to his face it almost looked like it was carved in. "He never moved on. He just covered it up with power. The more he got away with the better he felt and did it all in the name of the *Leadership*. He has his son, he just pretends he doesn't."

"I'm going to kill you boy."

Benzi looked down, shaking his head. "Maybe I never really wasn't ever your son."

I could feel Eva then. Fighting to get out. To plunder the field. Blood began to drip from the corner of my mouth. I looked around again. The crowds seemed to have dissolved into one. I spoke softly. "This feud was something for your ancestors. It should've died with them. But instead it will die with me. Here."

"What'll happen to you?" Eddie asked.

"It doesn't matter what happens to me! You're not doing it for me. You're doing it for your sons!" I looked at Tannin "You're doing it for your brothers!" I looked at Eddie. "For those you've failed to love!" I looked at Mathrel. "I know very little about your feud. For as much as I've tried to learn, I still don't understand it. But I know that I hadn't see so much pain and blood and felt so much aguish and loss in my entire life as I have in these last three weeks." I shook my head. "This war has been futile." Blood trickled off my chin. "The blood of your family and friends has polluted everything you know! You've lost reason for this! It's been over 300 years! You can't honestly believe that you're still fighting for the same cause! Can't you see everyone is dying? No one is going to win!" A cough exploded from my lungs. "Those Senses were wrong. Fire will not pollute these streets because I will not be supporting one side or the other. I was never supposed to come in and slaughter one of you. I was just the one to end this war. I am just a face to represent it. I will take in the death, the blood, the pain into my own body. And with me, it's over." I coughed again. Blood splattered to the grass. "We will store this event in our shared history and call it The Tears. Not only in remembrance for how it brought upon this difficult peace," I looked at Eddie and Tannin, "but also for those we've shed tears for." I looked around one more time. "It ends with me." I struggled to breathe.

"We should kill her!" A warlock called. "Look! She's weak!"

"Weak?" I screamed. I casted out my hands and striking them all with a bright light, a vision. That of their death. "Do not dare to mistake me for someone in your past!" Shocked and scared faces filled the crowd. I squatted and shoved my hands into the earth. My blood shot across the ground, they all jump back. The grass turned red before back to green as the blood receded into the soil. "I will everywhere. And in my death, I will see everything. Anyone who dares to defy my words, let my grave torment your mind and your soul be plagued with the fires of hell!" Eva had stopped fighting but she was ripping a whole in my soul. My breathing became shallow, but I let my voice ring out into the trees. "I will crawl from my grave and my corpse will crucify you. I say this not as a warning, but as a threat." My heart rate slowed. "Each and every one of are witness to this moment. Let my name strike fear in anyone who dares to revive this feud. Let it stretch across the earth and the world know it as the ender of wars and the punisher of fighters. You will not receive this warning again." Then I stopped. Eva was furious with me as to let us die. But it was only she who would leave.

My skin shed, and soul erupted from my body with a fire. A beautiful demon, a wicked angel, before them in ghastly allure. I was no longer Evangeline Welt, the Blood, confined to flesh. No. I was more than that. I dispersed, and then, I was everywhere.

The End

Epilogue

She imagined her death a thousand different ways. And she knew most little girls dreamt about their weddings or the beautiful castles they'd one day have. But she dreamt about her death. I guess she was always funny that way. Though, when she thought about it, she had always thought there would be a fight. That she would be wounded in battle. Or that her time would just tick away.

But neither of those things happened. When I came to collect her, instead, I saw something else. Something I hadn't seen since His death.

They never see me until just before the end. Always seconds away from closing their eyes. But she saw me long before that. She looked me in my face and recognized me. She knew who I was. She held my gaze. And when it came time to go, she didn't leave. To make sure I knew her soul wasn't mine she ascended into a goddess. She went heaven. She spoke to Him. She went to hell. She went to every earth.

Even born as a mortal, she was a being even beyond my reach. Evangeline Welt was the hand chosen by Him to do so much more than end a war. What that was, was yet to be discovered.

The crowd stared at Evangeline's former body. Just a shell now. Mystified by what they'd seen, no one dared to move. Only Mathrel. He made his way up to look upon the girl. What he saw was an enchantress.

The fat man ran a hand through his grey hair. "I believe that she is dead."

"Not dead," Tannin said. "She is far from dead, my friend." Slowly, he made his way up to her. "What we're looking at here is an empty vessel. But the driver is very much alive. She is the Tears."

"The Tears? Yes. So, *friend,* what do we do now?"

"You do what you were told," Edmund called from the back. He made his way through the crowd and up to face everyone. "You now know the consequences of your disobedience. Just go out and live. Not by anyone's standards or rules. Not in hiding or in fear." He laughed. "Just don't make a mess." The crowd mumbled amongst themselves for a while before Edmund grew impatient. "Go!" And one by one the crowd disappeared. The only people who remained were Benzi, Caieta, Edmund, Loyce, Mathrel, and Tannin.

"She should have a memorial and a statue build over her grave," said Tannin.

"Wrong," Mathrel shook his head. "She should be cremated and sent among stars."

"Of course, you want to burn a witch."

"I want to honor a Huntress."

"Then honor her with glory and memory."

"I will decide –"

"No!" Edmund cut into their bickering. "I will decide what happens. You two will not decide another thing outside of your respective households."

"Excuse –"

"You're dismissed. See your own way back." Mathrel stared at the boy for a while. Edmund's face was stern and emotionless. He stared at the woods in front of him, his mind barely present. "Did I stutter?" Then Mathrel and Tannin left the field.

When the men were gone, Edmund's defenses fell. He dropped to his knees in front of Evangeline's body. His breathing became short and rapid. Agony stretched across his face. Pain ripped through his body. Unlike the pain he felt on Evangeline's birthday because from this he knew she would never come back. He bit into his knuckle to keep from wailing. But it didn't keep back the tears.

"Eddie," Loyce called to him. "Eddie, are you okay?" Loyce didn't know her brother very well but she didn't want to see him like this. In so much pain.

"Loyce," Caieta grabbed her arm. "Maybe we should give him a minute."

Loyce nodded and let herself be pulled back out into the brush. But even alone, Eddie couldn't pull himself to touch her.

"I know this was your destiny," he said. "This was what you were supposed to do. But I was supposed to protect you. To care about you. And I feel like I did those things too late. I don't know what I'm supposed to do now. Where I'm supposed to go." He stopped only to grit his teeth. "I hate this feeling that I have. I feel broken and vulnerable. And I guess I've always felt that way. And it was you that made me strong. Cause I wanted to be that for you. And I know that you are so much better than this world, but can I ask you to come back?" He beat his fist against his chest. "I know that's selfish. But I – I need you back."

But then something even I don't understand happened.

She woke up.

She sat panting and coughing. She clawed at her chest as if trying to escape her skin but instead just ripped open her bodice. Edmund sat in disbelief. A silence stretched on between them as she strained to breathe.

"You were dead," he finally said. She nodded, not looking at him. "How…?"

"They needed a martyr." Her throat was dry, and her voice was rough. "A visual representation of the war ending. One final blow I guess."

"But how?"

She looked up at him and made a decision. She would never tell him what actually happened. All that she'd done after her ascension. Where she'd gone. What she'd seen. Instead she said, "A simple magic trick."

He stared at her a moment, before grabbing her and kissing her like he wished he had a long time ago. He took her face in his hands and said, "Don't ever do that again." He stared at her a moment. "I can't lose you."

She frowned at him. "I wish you were lying."

"What?"

Evangeline pulled away from him and stood up. "I'm supposed to be dead. No one is supposed to know I'm alive."

Edmund jumped to his feet. "Then I won't tell anyone."

"I know. I just..." She pierced her lips a moment. "I have to go. And you know that I'm alive and I just... I want you to be able to move on."

He gapped at her. "Are thinking about erasing my memory?"

"Just this one. You won't even know I woke up." He shook his head. "You have people to go back to."

"Who? My family?"

"Your sister. You just got her back."

"And she did and will do fine without me."

"Someone has to tear down the Leadership and if I'm not here, you're the –"

He stepped toward her, cutting into her train of thought with his approach. "I don't care." He was standing ridiculously close to her. Inches from her face. "You could give me excuses and reasons that are all probably legitimate, but I don't care." He wrapped his hand around the back of her neck and pulled her in to kiss her again. Then he pressed his forehead to hers. "You see thing is... I don't think I'll know how to survive without you."

Made in the USA
Middletown, DE
02 April 2018